Amigas and School Scandals

Amigas and School Scandals

DIANA RODRIGUEZ WALLACH

KENSINGTON BOOKS
http://www.kensingtonbooks.com

KENSINGTON BOOKS are published by

Kensington Publishing Corp.
850 Third Avenue
New York, NY 10022

All Kensington titles, imprints, and distributed lines are available at special quantity discounts for bulk purchases for sales promotion, premiums, fund-raising, educational, or institutional use.

Special book excerpts or customized printings can also be created to fit specific needs. For details, write or phone the office of the Kensington Special Sales Manager: Attn. Special Sales Department. Kensington Publishing Corp., 850 Third Avenue, New York, NY 10022. Phone: 1-800-221-2647.

Kensington and the K logo Reg. U.S. Pat. & TM Off.

ISBN-13: 978-0-7582-2555-9
ISBN-10: 0-7582-2555-5

First Printing: November 2008
10 9 8 7 6 5 4 3 2

Printed in the United States of America

For Jordan,
for always believing in me

Acknowledgments

I'd like to thank my agent, Jenoyne Adams, for the support she leant to this novel. Her advice was invaluable as this series unfolded, and I truly appreciate the work she did to champion the development of this book. I'd also like to thank her team of amazing editors, specifically Kelsey Adelson, Candice Smith, and Kerry Evans. Their time and advice are greatly appreciated.

I'd also like to thank my editor, Kate Duffy, for making this series a reality and for always answering my many publishing questions. In addition, many thanks to Kate's assistant, Megan Records, for her immense patience as I navigated the copy editing process.

The Cornell scenes in this novel would not have been written if it were not for the friendship of my husband's fraternity brothers. While I only made it to a few parties and Victory Clubs during my visits, your wealth of hilarious stories helped to add humor to many scenes.

It should also be noted that during a time when I struggled with the direction of this novel, the advice in Stephen King's *On Writing* truly helped me to cross a major hurdle. And I will always remember sitting in the Philadelphia Book Festival when I was finally struck with the ending for the novel. So I'd like to thank all involved with sparking my inspiration.

There are also many people who generously offered their time, and their rolodexes, as I began the promotional side of my career. I'd like to thank Gail Bower for her advice while planning my book launch and for offering me her generous connections within the Philadelphia community. I'd also like to thank my brother, Lou, for promoting my novels to countless influential Philadelphians. Who knew that engineers were so good at dealing with people? I truly appreciate all your efforts.

I'd also like to thank the Wallachs for showing so much enthusiasm for my novels. And I'd especially like to thank Paula for offering her very useful assistance during the copy editing process. Additionally, my sister Natalie has always believed in me and offered me endless motivation. More importantly, I'd like to thank my parents for their encouragement throughout my life. It always makes me happy to hear that you've passed my novel onto another friend or acquaintance. Your support and love means so much to me.

Finally, I'd like to thank my husband, Jordan. I could not have written this novel had he not encouraged me to pursue my passion full time. His collaboration—from colorful college antidotes to copy edits to photocopying—is immensely valued. I wouldn't be where I am in my life (both professionally and spiritually) if it weren't for his love and support.

Chapter 1

"Are you sure you wanna do this?" I asked as I piled clothes into my jumbo-sized suitcase.

It was officially my last night in Utuado, the tiny mountain village in Puerto Rico where I had spent the summer. I was going back to Spring Mills.

"Of course," Lilly answered as she scanned my tenth grade schedule.

My mom had snatched it from the mail before she hopped on the plane to the island, and I was incredibly grateful that she did. Not that I didn't already know which classes I'd be taking, but it was nice to see the schedule in its official form. Now I knew which teachers I had, which electives I got, and how my day would be laid out. I loved the predictable, comfortable order of home.

"Wow, that's a lot of classes," Lilly muttered.

"It's the normal course load. You get used to it."

I tossed my bathing suits into my luggage. I wouldn't be breaking them out again for quite a while. There was something sad about packing up a swimsuit for the season, as if it signified the end of fun.

"So, how are your parents dealing?" I asked.

"Eh, they've mellowed a bit. I know they want what's best for me, and to be honest, I've been thinking about it ever since you and Vince got here. . . ."

"Switching schools is a big deal."

"I know." She nodded. "I just see your dad and . . . I want more than this."

She waved her hands around my bedroom. I guess it wasn't really my bedroom anymore, if it ever really was. I glanced one more time at the rock-hard mattress on my twin bed, the powder blue walls, the cement floor, and the stained white window shade. I was going to miss it. I was going to miss all of this.

Alex stood before me, his eyes smiling. He kissed me every time my parents weren't looking. They probably looked away on purpose, so they could deny any evidence of my emerging love life. Though I doubted one semi-boyfriend really counted as a love life.

His lips pressed against mine. I wanted to lock the feeling into my brain, soak it in one last time, but before I could, my father subtly blew the car horn. Alex pulled away. His brown eyes looked dull, and his eyelids drooped slightly. A lump pulsed in my throat.

"So, you gonna meet some other American tourist tomorrow? Take her salsa dancing?" I asked with a nervous laugh.

"Absolutely. I've already got one lined up. Only she's Canadian," Alex replied with a grin.

"Canadian, eh?" I mocked, tossing in the one bit of slang I knew from our neighbors to the north. "Well, be careful. They might look like us Americans, but they're a whole different breed. Bad weather, hockey, bacon . . ."

"I like bacon."

He smiled and hugged me tight. I let my head fall on his shoulder. His shampoo smelled like oranges.

"Mariana, it's time to go," my father said, exiting the car.

I paused and stared at my great aunt and great uncle's mountain house one last time. The blue concrete facade I had dreaded with a passion two months ago now seemed like home. Uncle Miguel, Aunt Carmen, my cousin Alonzo and his "friend" José—who were gathered on the bright green grass watching our family load up the car—now felt like family. In some odd parallel universe, I could almost see my life fitting in here, but instead, my brother and I were headed back to our normal lives.

Well, almost.

Lilly pushed the porch door open and propped it with her newly purchased—courtesy of my father—travel bag. Her auburn hair was pulled back in a high ponytail, and two duffle bags hung from her shoulders—she looked a lot like I did when I first arrived. She paused to wipe the sweat from her freckled brow, and I could tell she was trying to mentally block the Spanish mumblings of her parents. They were chasing after her, rambling on, with their faces tightly twisted in worry. Lilly had spent the past few days reassuring them, in every way possible from conversation to pantomime, that this was *exactly* what she wanted.

She was moving to the States.

Once my dad realized how advanced Lilly's bilingual skills were and how dedicated she was to her education (she got straight A's at her English-speaking school), he couldn't help but offer her a chance to learn in Spring Mills. He wanted to give her the opportunity his parents gave him, and Lilly jumped at the offer. The girl had been riding on a bus for more than two hours each day just to get to and from school. (Meanwhile, Vince and I complained when there was no parking in our school's private lot and we had to walk an extra ten feet.)

"Will somebody please tell my parents that I'm doing the right thing, because I don't think they can actually hear the words coming out of my mouth. They're acting like the universe is going to explode if I step foot off this island!" Lilly exploded as she yanked her suitcase from her father and hauled it across the lawn.

My dad immediately darted toward Lilly's parents. They knew she was in good hands. She was going to be with family (even if we were distant cousins who were totally unaware of each other's existence until a few weeks ago). Plus, my dad had covered every detail of his plans with them numerous times. Within three days, he managed to enroll Lilly in Spring Mills High School (conveniently, the dean went to our church and played golf with my dad on weekends), have the housekeeping staff prepare one of our spacious guest bedrooms, and book all of my cousin's last-minute travel arrangements. He then kindly traded in Vince and my first class tickets for three coach seats. (He and my mom still planned to take advantage of the plane's luxury accommodations without us.)

Lilly's parents were thrilled at my father's generous offer, and they knew it was a life-changing opportunity for her. They had agreed to the move days ago, but still, Lilly was their only child. She was fifteen and had never traveled farther than San Juan. Now she was moving to Pennsylvania where she would attend an American school, and meet new friends and boyfriends, and live in a world completely separate from theirs. A world full of posh amenities they'd never even contemplated.

She was moving to Philadelphia's Main Line—a far stretch from the mountain town where she was raised. There would be no tropical rain forests, exotic birds, wild chickens in the back-yard, or laundry duty at her grandfather's run-down hotel. Soon her biggest worry would be which marble bathroom to shower in and which gourmet meal to order from takeout.

"So, you really ready for this?" Alex asked as my cousin trudged over.

"Are you kidding? A chance to be rescued from the island? I think I've been waiting for this since birth," she joked as she dragged her luggage to the back of the car.

Alex hurled it into the already packed, shiny new SUV, which stood out drastically on the mountain road.

"Ya gonna miss me, Alex?" Lilly asked with a big grin.

"Funny, I was wondering the same thing." I smirked.

"Oh, really. Well, I'm sure he'll miss you more, even though

I've known him my entire life. Apparently years of friendship pale in comparison to a few weeks of smoochy, smoochy."

"Hey!" I screeched, my cheeks burning.

"I will miss you both," he replied, squeezing my waist a few times.

I giggled and squirmed as he pulled me tighter.

"See! You two are disgusting! Vince, can you see this?" Lilly asked my brother.

He had been sitting in the car and ready to hit the road for more than a half hour. His escape to Cornell was merely days away, and he couldn't wait to detach himself from our parents.

"I prefer to believe my sister is asexual," he said flatly, leaning out the window of the car. "Mom, are we *ever* gonna get out of here?"

My mother was seated patiently in the passenger's side. I could tell the week-long trip had been a whirlwind for her. Not only could she not speak Spanish (and thus not understand a word anyone was saying around her), she was forced to drink rum (I had never seen her sip any alcohol other than a crisp white wine), shower in moldy accommodations, and succumb to the humidity-induced frizz in her blond hair. Her locks were currently tied in a sloppy ponytail akin to my own. It made me realize just how similar we were.

"We're gonna leave in a second. Let your father smooth things over with the Sanchezes. Lilly, why don't you go over there and help?" my mom suggested.

Lilly groaned.

"It *is* the last time you'll see them for a while," I reminded her.

"I know, I know. I guess I need to pretend that upsets me."

"Lilly, you are going to miss your parents," Alex stated plainly. "I don't think you realize how different Spring Mills is going to be."

"Are you kidding me? I know all about Spring Mills. She hasn't stopped talking about it since she got here. 'Back in Spring Mills, back in Spring Mills.'" Lilly nudged my shoulder as she headed off toward her parents.

They were engrossed in conversation with my father. But I knew he'd have the final say; he always did.

A few hours later, we boarded the plane headed back home. I was squished between Vince and Lilly. Since Lilly was technically our "guest" (even though we were still on a plane and not yet on American soil), I felt compelled to offer her the window seat. Vince's extra inches of leg won him the aisle, leaving me stuck in the middle for four straight hours.

I sipped my tiny bottle of water and fought my brother for the armrest. The elbow war was the only thing distracting me from my impending Madison and Emily drama. I knew they wouldn't let my MIA status this summer drop easily. They hadn't returned any of my e-mails from the past week, and they still had no idea I was bringing a five-foot-four, redheaded souvenir back from the island. But they were my best friends, my only friends before Lilly. They couldn't hate me forever.

"Hey, you thinking about Alex?" Lilly asked, looking up from the gossip magazine she'd purchased at the San Juan airport.

She wanted to brush up on Hollywood celebrities before she landed, which I agreed was a virtual necessity. If she didn't know Tom and Katie's latest relationship woes, there would be no way she'd fit into Madison's world.

"Nah. We'll keep in touch. Or at least I know you guys will, so he can't exactly drop off the face of the Earth—"

"Are you kidding?" Lilly interrupted. "Trust me, you have a better chance of hearing from him than I do. I wouldn't be surprised if he goes to college in the States next year just to be near you."

"Oh, please! Like that would ever happen! I wish I had that much influence over boys."

"You do. . . ."

"Whatever," I scoffed, readjusting the hairband holding back my stringy red mop. I flicked my eyes toward her. "You scared about moving?"

"A little," she said with a sad smile. "I'm excited, scared, sad, and happy all at the same time."

"I still can't believe you're really doing it. There's no way I'd be able to up and move. I mean, you've got your whole life back in Utuado. . . ."

"Yeah, and if I didn't do something now, my life would always *be* Utuado. My parents have never left the island. Ever. I don't wanna be like that."

"Still, it's a pretty big leap from traveling to moving." I pumped my eyebrows.

"I figure I'll give it a year and, if it doesn't work out, then I'll just go home. What's the worst that could happen?"

I stared at my hands. "You could be away for so long that your whole life evaporates. You could come back to a world that's completely different. . . ." I said softly.

"I have a feeling you're not talking about me," Lilly said with heavy emphasis. "Lemme guess, the infamous Madison and Emily?"

I shrugged with a knowing nod.

"You think they'll hate me?" she asked.

"Well, right now they hate *me*," I mumbled.

"If they're half as good of friends as you say they are, they'll get over it. And if not, you've got me, *chica*."

Just then Vince turned toward us and unplugged his earphones. We had only been on the plane for an hour, but already his dark brown locks were disheveled from the headrest.

"Hey, I just remembered that when we were on the plane to Puerto Rico, and you were sulking like a baby, I bet you that you'd be crying when we left. And that you'd have fun this summer. I *so* won that bet."

"Too bad we didn't put money on it," I snipped. "Besides, I'm not crying."

"I think I saw you shed a tear. 'Oh, Alex, I'm gonna miss you *so* much.' Mwah, mwah, mwah," he teased, planting exaggerated noisy kisses on the back of his hand.

"I don't sound like that!"

"Sure you do," he mocked with a crooked grin.

"I wasn't talking to you anyway."

"No, but I heard you. You're acting like Madison and Emily will never speak to you again. I thought they were your *best friends*," he whined, wiggling his fingers.

Then he plugged his earbuds in and turned his attention back to his iPod.

"They'll speak to me again," I muttered under my breath.

At least I hoped they would.

Chapter 2

It was good to be home and even better to witness Lilly's reaction. It was the first time I had ever seen the Main Line from an outsider's perspective. The enormous stone houses, sweeping green lawns, and oak-lined streets were rather impressive, especially compared to the unair-conditioned mountain village where I had spent the summer.

"*¡Caray!*" she squeaked, expressing her surprise as she gawked out of the window. One behemoth house after another passed by, each enclosed by thick stone and iron gates. "*One* family lives there?"

I nodded. In fact, I knew exactly which families lived in most of them. Many had kids who went to my school.

"They're bigger than my grandfather's hotel!"

"Well, your uncle's hotel was kinda small. . . ."

"It had a restaurant."

"Trust me, your family's restaurant could probably fit into the pantries of their kitchens."

"What, do they have, like, twenty kids?" she mumbled, shaking her head.

"Actually, I doubt they have more than two. The rest is just . . . space."

"It's a little different from Utuado," my father offered, glancing at her through his rearview mirror.

"Uh, yeah."

"But it's home," he added.

"*Your* home," I cheered, grabbing her arm.

While my welcome to Utuado had been boisterous—featuring a couple dozen distant relatives, a banquet of food, and a makeshift dance floor in the living room—Lilly was only greeted by a giant poodle and a busy maid. (Josephine was frantically completing a last-minute dust of our crisply-clean, lemon-scented home.)

My mom said she'd order Chinese food, unless Lilly wanted something else; my cousin silently nodded in agreement. I showed her the guest room she'd call home for the foreseeable future and left her alone to adjust. I remembered that all I wanted when I arrived in Puerto Rico was time by myself. So I gave her the luxury that I didn't receive and hurried into my bedroom. Everything looked different.

After two months of sharing a cement shoebox with my brother, in side-by-side twin beds, my shabby chic, four-poster pillowtop queen looked like a cloud-covered paradise. Dozens of decorative pillows were perfectly positioned in front of the headrest. Two fresh gardenia candles sat on the bedside table. The sun beamed through the skylight in twinkling streaks.

I tossed my suitcase on top of my hope chest. My luggage was completely packed with dirty clothes. I should have just deposited it in the laundry room, only I couldn't wait to be alone in my own space. I hadn't realized how much I missed the solitude. Back in Puerto Rico, the house was so small and crammed with relatives that it was hard to get the bathroom to myself. Now I had a private marble bath adjacent to my bedroom, and no one to walk in while I showered.

I could hear Lilly sifting through the drawers in her room next to mine as I slowly plopped onto my bed and sprawled out. I stared at the cordless phone on my nightstand. I knew I should call Emily or Madison, but the thought made my shoulders stiffen. I didn't want to fight, or even worse pretend that everything was fine when we all knew that it wasn't. But I knew the more I avoided the phone call, the more my insides would knot, so I picked up the receiver and dialed the memorized digits.

"Hey Mad. It's Mariana. I'm home."

We sat in my bedroom staring at each other. No one was speaking. I picked at a loose thread in my comforter and tried to act normal (though I had no idea what that looked like anymore). The silence made me nervous—a sensation I tried to hide behind a weak, forced smile. I swallowed a solid lump.

"Look, I'm sorry I missed your party. It sounds like it was awesome," I choked softly, my finger still pecking at the thread.

"It was. I mean, please, Orlando Bloom was there. It doesn't get any better." Madison shook her pale blond hair.

"I know. I can't believe I missed the party of the year. That totally sucks."

"Well, you should have seen Jody Marsh's Sweet Sixteen. It was so lame. Her DJ actually played the Electric Slide, and she served mini hot dogs. How tacky is that?" Madison scoffed.

"They're called 'pigs in a blanket,' and they weren't that bad," Emily corrected from her seat at my desk.

"Whatever. They were gross."

"Still, I wish I could have gone to yours. I can't believe I was stuck in Puerto Rico."

I had weighed the situation upside down and backwards. I didn't have many options. Madison and Emily were my best friends. I wasn't going to lose them over some forced vacation, and I had a hunch that anything positive I said about my trip would only tick them off more. Madison had made that very clear when I had called earlier. She subtly opened our conversation with, "Oh, great. The *chica's* back from Puerto Rico. Wait, you still speak English, right?"

Not to mention, I had yet to drop the big bombshell: that I was now living with a distant Puerto Rican cousin who would be attending our school. Oh, wait, I forgot to mention that I wanted her to be our new best friend. I was sure that would go over like candy in kindergarten (yeah, right). Thankfully, when they got here, Lilly was off on the other side of the house getting the "grand tour" by my mother. My friends were still blissfully unaware of her existence.

I figured that the only way I could prove to Madison and Emily that I hadn't turned into some body-snatched impersonation of the girl they once knew was to pretend that I hated my trip and that I missed them nonstop. That's what they expected when they left me at the Philadelphia International Airport and that's what I was going to give them.

"Well, aside from Madison's party, did I miss anything else?" I asked, glancing at Emily.

She rolled her eyes and ignored my question, flipping the page of the magazine she was scanning—the same one Lilly had read on the plane. I flinched slightly.

I had expected Madison to be annoyed with me, but I had thought that I could count on Emily to be the rational one. Madison was the drama queen, not Emily. Only now she wasn't just sporting a new attitude, she was sporting a whole new look. Her dark brown tresses, which used to fall to her waist, were now chopped to her shoulders. It was the shortest I'd seen her hair since grade school, yet she never even mentioned the new do. I had no idea when she cut it, but from the way she casually tugged at her ends, it looked as if she were long used to the style.

"So, what ever happened with you and Bobby?" I asked, hoping to spin the conversation.

It was the first real date any of us had ever been on—well, if you didn't count me and Alex. And since they barely knew he and I had a relationship, he pretty much didn't count. At least not to them.

"It was nothing. We went to a movie with a bunch of people. Then, he left for Dublin."

"Is he back yet?" I asked.

"I think so, but it doesn't matter. I'm not his girlfriend."

"Oh, please! He likes you! You know he does. Why would he have asked you out if he didn't?" Madison's tan legs spread out before her on the carpet. Her freshly polished, "cherries in snow" toes peeked out of her nude sandals. "Stop being all 'bah humbug.'"

Emily shrugged and shook her head.

"I can talk to him, if you want," I offered. "We're locker buddies. I'll see him almost every day, once school starts."

"No, don't! That would be awful. Just drop it." Emily's green eyes stretched wide.

"Em, if you don't make a move, then nothing's gonna happen," Madison said.

"Whatever. I'm sure he has plenty of things to think about other than me. Plus, he probably met some hot redhead in Ireland and fell madly in love."

"Never underestimate the power of a redhead," I joked.

Just then, a crash erupted from the guest room next to us. It sounded like boxes tumbling onto the floor.

"*Ay, mierda!*" Lilly shouted as Tootsie barked at the commotion from downstairs.

"Your maid speaks Spanish? I didn't know that." Madison's blue eyes squinted.

"Um, no. That wasn't Josephine," I stated quickly.

"Mariana! Will you help me? All this crap just fell out of the closet. It looks like a bunch of old photo albums. I think they're yours," Lilly yelled through the walls, her Spanish accent squeaking through.

"Who the hell is that?" Madison asked.

"Oh, well, um, I was going to tell you. But I was waiting for the right moment. You see, when I was in Puerto Rico . . ."

Before I could finish, Lilly popped in the doorway, her auburn hair piled loosely atop her head, her freckled face gleaming with sweat, and her lips curled in a grin almost identical to mine.

"Whoa," Madison mumbled.

Emily dropped her magazine.

I stood up and rushed toward Lilly, my dark eyes full of warning. The hair from my ponytail was falling into my face, and I realized that we must have looked like carbon copies.

"I didn't realize you had company," she muttered as she yanked at her too-tight tank top. About three inches of cleavage was showing—our one striking difference.

"Yeah, no biggie," I said, nodding at her before facing my friends. "Um, guys, this is my cousin, Lilly. Who I told you about, remember? Um, well, she's going to be staying with us for a while . . . to go to school . . . at Spring Mills."

Madison and Emily froze, their eyes almost popping from their skulls.

"What?" Madison screeched.

It wasn't exactly the warmest welcome.

"I've moved in," Lilly cheered. "I'm gonna see if I can follow in Mr. Ruíz's footsteps."

Madison blinked at her as if she were a ghostly vision that would eventually go away. When that didn't happen, she slowly grabbed the car keys from her purse. (Her parents bought her an Audi for her sixteenth birthday.)

"Ya know, I gotta get going," she said softly. "Em, you coming?"

She looked at her friend, who was already standing, shoving her feet back into her sandals. They peeled out within seconds, not uttering another word to Lilly. They barely said goodbye to me.

There wasn't much I could defend about their behavior.

"So, your friends totally hate me," Lilly said as we trudged towards Vince's room, still reeling in their wake.

I had offered to help him pack for Cornell, and I figured he'd be much friendlier company at the moment. He was obligated by blood to be nice to us.

"That's not true," I lied as I stuck my head into Vince's room.

His stereo was blaring an indecipherable screaming rock band as he taped a cardboard box closed. He was leaving in less than a week, and he had to find time to shove the entire contents of his room into boxes while still having a "raging send-off" with his high school buds. It didn't help that my mom had inconveniently planned a family barbeque in a few days to welcome Lilly into our home and to wish Vince luck in college. He hadn't stopped complaining about the impending get-together since we had landed.

"Thank God!" he cried when he saw us. "Can you label these boxes?"

"What's in them?" I asked as I sifted through a collection of soap, underwear, CDs, and bedsheets all lumped together in a carton.

"Everything," he grumbled. "Just label."

He tossed me a marker. Lilly collapsed onto his bed amidst a heaping pile of towels and sweaters.

"Vince, Mariana's friends hate me," she whined.

"Don't take it personally," he grunted, not looking up from his T-shirt-packed suitcase. "They hate everyone but themselves. I've never seen three people so obsessed with each other."

"Shut up, Vince!" I yelped, chucking a balled sock at him. "We're friends. Maybe some day you'll know what that's like."

"I have friends. Lots of them. More than two." He sat on the suitcase and tried to yank the zipper closed. There was about six inches between the seams.

I scrunched my nose at him, then peered at Lilly. "If *I* like you, they'll like you. Trust me. It'll work out."

Of course I really wasn't so sure. Madison and Emily had gawked at Lilly as if she were a three-headed elephant. They didn't even give me a chance to explain what she was doing here, and how my father had invited her, and how she'd get a better education in Spring Mills. They just bolted out, and at this point, I didn't know if they'd ever warm up to *me* again, let alone my newly imported cousin.

"Can you believe Mom's hosting a stupid barbeque?" Vince choked as he tossed a couple of T-shirts out of the suitcase and tried to force the zipper closed once more.

"Oh, give her a break. She's trying to be nice," I stated as I continued scribing an itemized list of contents on the outside of a box.

"Nice to who? She's totally ruining my last week here!"

"By throwing you a party? Gee, how selfish of *her*," I moaned.

"Ya wanna wish me well? Send me a card . . . with some money in it," he joked.

"Well, I wanna meet your family," Lilly stately plainly.

"See, Vince? It's not all about *you*," I noted. "Plus, Mom loves stuff like this. . . ."

Our mother was our very own Martha Stewart, only she didn't do any of the work herself. She delegated her "party ideas" to a staff of experienced helpers. This "End of Summer BBQ" had been arranged while we were still in Puerto Rico. My mom had been planning it for weeks, only it was originally intended simply to welcome me back from vacation and to wish Vince luck at Cornell. Now she had Lilly to add to the festivities, and I figured she might as well throw in the fourth cause for celebration: the new addition to our family. After all, my uncles still didn't know about our run-in with Teresa, and I was sure they would be thrilled to find out we had all bonded with their illegitimate half sister—the one who had caused the whole family to flee Puerto Rico when they were teenagers and never look back. I was sure they were just dying to relive those memories.

"Hey, you think Dad's gonna tell Uncle Roberto and Uncle Diego about Teresa?" I asked.

"Well, he has to. Doesn't he?" Lilly asked as she watched us pack.

"You clearly don't know our family," Vince said, still aggressively pushing the suitcase closed. "Here in the Ruíz household, we don't talk about uncomfortable family dramas. In fact, we pretend they don't exist."

"What are you talking about?"

Vince peered at Lilly.

"Well, for instance, I got arrested a couple of years ago for underage drinking. It was no big deal, but my dad totally blew it out of proportion. He freaked out and grounded me for, like, eternity. But every time my neighbors or my uncles asked why I wasn't out on a Saturday night, my dad would say 'Oh, he's just studying. Gotta keep those grades up for the Ivy Leagues.' " Vince rolled his eyes as he finally wrenched the suitcase zipper closed.

He pumped his fist triumphantly. I chuckled, then turned toward Lilly.

"And before our grandfather died, our parents totally downplayed his illness," I said. "They acted like he was going to get better any day. So when he didn't, it was a complete shock."

"Why would they do that?" Lilly's forehead crumpled.

"We have no idea; that's the point. Our family's weird. And our uncles are the same way. They would have never told us about their bastard sister. . . ."

"Vince!" I interrupted. "Don't call her that."

He shrugged.

"Well, it's not like you guys can act like nothing happened this summer," Lilly said. "I mean, just because your parents act that way doesn't mean you have to."

Vince and I exchanged a look. We didn't say anything. It was as if the thought had never occurred to us.

Chapter 3

After two days of nonstop planning, the day of the big cookout had finally arrived. Our house was packed with catering staff clad in black pants and white aprons serving hors d'oeuvres table-to-table. Grill stations were being lit throughout the backyard preparing to serve everything from chicken to burgers to veggie kabobs. The sun shined in the pure blue sky as the scent of charcoal wafted in waves. It would have been the perfect end to summer, if only my guests had been able to tolerate one another.

I had spent the past forty-eight hours trying to reassure Madison and Emily that Lilly was a completely normal person worthy of their friendship, while simultaneously trying to convince Lilly that she would love my friends once she got to know them. But I could tell that no one was really buying it. We now sat on my patio—surrounded by extended family and packs of Vince's friends—listening to an endless loop of stories from Madison's "super cool Sweet Sixteen." Even *my* eyes were glazing over.

"So, you should have seen the dress that Tracy Beckett wore to my party. First off, it was lime green. I mean, the girl has bright red hair. Uh, 'HELL-O!' Clash much? And secondly, it was barely long enough to cover her butt, and you know how big that butt is," Madison said as she plopped her two-pound Chihuahua on the ground and filled a tiny bowl of water.

"I heard it was really expensive," Emily mumbled.

"The dress? God, I hope not. But I guess money can't buy taste." Madison glanced at me. "Where's Tootsie?"

"Oh, the poodle's inside. My mom's worried about people's allergies."

"Ah, Tweetie doesn't cause allergies. Do you Tweetie?" she cooed at the tiny pooch.

Lilly shot me a look, then turned her focus toward my brother who was setting up a serve. He had put up a volleyball net that afternoon. He figured that if he had to invite his friends to a family party, with no alcohol, he'd have to provide some means of entertainment or none of his boys would stay for longer than five minutes. So, for the past hour, they'd been killing each other with serves and spikes that looked more like assaults than friendly competition.

"And did I tell you that Luke hooked up with Mandy on the dance floor? You should have seen Carly's face. I thought her head was gonna spin in circles. You know she's still obsessed with him," Madison continued.

"So do *you* have boyfriend?" Lilly asked, her head cocked.

"Um, no. Why?" Madison said, slightly deflated. She grabbed her dog off the grass and placed him protectively in her lap.

"Oh, I don't know. I'm just surprised. You seem to be *so* popular." Lilly's lips curled in a grin.

"I didn't say that."

"Really? I guess it's just the way you've been talking. It sounds like everyone must love you. You did hang out with Orlando Bloom."

"Wait, I didn't tell you that." Madison's eyes narrowed.

"No, I heard it on the *radio*."

Lilly shifted away from Madison to end the conversation, and my friend instantly spun toward me. Of course, she knew I had listened to her "Life as a Hollywood Extra" interview on Philly's number one morning show. Her and Emily being cast as walk-ons in Orlando's action flick was the most monumental thing to hit Spring Mills in decades, if you don't count the certain Hollywood heartthrob who made an appearance at her Sweet Sixteen (even if it was only because he happened to be staying in the hotel, and Madison's high-powered event planner called in a favor from her old college roommate—Orlando's publicist). I had sent her an e-mail from Utuado raving about how fabulous it all was. But she had no idea that I had shared all the details with my cousin. And it was clear from Lilly's tone that she didn't find Madison's party, or her radio debut, nearly as impressive as Madison did.

"I talked about you guys so much that I wanted Lilly to hear you on the radio and get to know you," I explained quickly, jabbing Lilly with my elbow.

"Oh, yeah. She talked about you constantly. 'Back in Spring Mills, back in Spring Mills,' " Lilly droned.

"What? You don't like it here?" Madison crossed her arms against her chest.

"I didn't say that. I haven't even been here a week. . . ."

"Exactly. So maybe you shouldn't be so quick with the opinions."

Madison and Lilly glared at each other. I held my breath.

"Mariana told us all about your party too," Emily offered, placing her palm on Madison's forearm.

"Oh yeah, the 'quince-crap-era' . . ." Madison said with a snarl.

"*Quinceañera*," Lilly corrected.

"Oh, my bad."

I rose to my feet.

"All right, I think I'm ready for some food," I stated carefully. "Lil, you wanna see if my mom needs help in the kitchen?"

"Fine," she huffed.

She stood up and adjusted the tiny pink T-shirt stretched against her bulging chest. I straightened the seams of my—rather short—khaki skirt, and looked up in time to catch Madison rolling her eyes behind Lilly's back.

"Guys, we'll be back in a minute," I stated, glaring at Madison who smirked in response.

"By the way, nice skirt Mariana. Funny, I don't remember you wearing things that short before you left."

I paused, then grabbed Lilly's arm and strolled toward the sliding glass doors. I was not about to antagonize her further.

I closed the door behind us, but not before I heard Madison whisper. "So, how long do we have to put up with this *chica*?"

Lilly didn't seem to catch it.

I glanced at my mom. She was rearranging the crab-stuffed mushroom caps on the wait staff's trays. Her hands moved frantically as she muttered incoherently. (Either she was talking to herself or to imaginary caterers, because there was no one else around.)

"Mom, you need help?" I asked as Lilly and I walked to the granite-topped island.

"It just doesn't make sense. If they're butlering the hors d'oeuvres on round trays, then obviously they should present them in a circular pattern. I just don't get it. . . ."

She carefully adjusted the circumference of her mushroom formation. I could see three trays beside her with the morsels arranged in straight lines. I grabbed a tray, handed another to Lilly, and began mimicking her circular prototype.

"Thank you, Mariana," she said, smiling at me.

"So, where are your uncles? I haven't met them yet." Lilly asked as she followed my lead.

"Oh, they should be here any minute. They're always late." My mom stayed focused.

Her eyes were so wide that, for a second, I thought she was going to bust out a ruler to make sure her design was perfectly symmetrical.

"So, what are you gonna tell them?" Lilly asked.

"About what?" my mom mumbled.

"About Teresa?"

My mom coughed slightly. "Excuse me?"

"Well, I assumed it would come up." Lilly stopped arranging the mushrooms and peered at my mom.

"I'll let Lorenzo handle that."

"Oh, okay. I'm just saying that they'd probably want to know."

"Lilly, drop it. You don't know them," I warned, shooting her a look.

"Fine, it's just . . ."

"I'm sure my dad will tell them. Right, Mom?"

My mom paused and fixed a pleasant smile across her face. Then, without a word, she swiftly lifted her tray and took it to a nearby waiter.

"Real subtle," I mumbled.

"What? I'm a guest. I thought I could get away with it."

"Yeah, I wouldn't test that theory too much, especially not with my dad."

Before my mom could return to work on her next tray, I heard the front door swing open. I didn't have to see who it was. My Uncle Roberto's deep belly laugh traveled halfway across the house. They were here.

The burgers were burnt, though it wasn't the caterer's fault. My mom was paranoid about a recent E. coli outbreak and insisted that the red meat be served well-done. As a result, my aunts and uncles (who arrived more than an hour late) were whining about the "tasteless gray stones" doused in ketchup and fancy mustard.

I introduced Lilly, then left her with Vince so I could spend time alone with Madison and Emily. I had to believe that I could fix our fractured friendship. While I'd fought with them before, usually it blew over after a brief confrontation and a sincere apology. But I had tried that already. Now after ten minutes of sitting across a picnic table with barely a spoken word between us, I was doubting whether Lilly was the only root to our problems.

"Sorry my aunt made you put Tweetie inside," I grumbled, mustard dripping onto my chin. I wiped at my face with a white linen napkin and placed my burger back on my plate.

"Please, like a dog that small can really cause allergies . . . *outside*," Madison griped. "But, whatever. I'm sure Tootsie's keeping her company."

I smiled, nodding as I chewed.

"Ya know, these burgers kinda suck. I wouldn't hire these caterers for *your* party," she added as she picked at her uneaten meal.

"What party?"

"Your Sweet Sixteen! You *are* having one, right?"

My birthday was in less than two months and, aside from a less-than-serious conversation with Lilly and Alex in Puerto Rico, I hadn't really considered a party. It's not like I wanted to compete with Madison's bash. Regardless of the Orlando Bloom sighting, Madison excelled at details. Her party had everything from flowers to match her highlights to a designer gown for her Chihuahua. Anything I concocted would look lame in comparison. But I also didn't want to overlook the day entirely.

"Oh, I don't know. I guess I'll have something. If anything, it'll be pretty low-key."

"Gee, sounds like a blast." Madison rolled her eyes at Emily, who nodded in agreement.

I had been dodging snotty looks from them all day. In all the years we'd been friends, I'd never known either of them to act this spiteful.

"Look, guys, I'm sorry I lost touch this summer. Seriously. But how long are you gonna treat me like a leper?"

Madison blew out a frustrated sigh. "Mariana, since you've come back, everything's been about 'Lilly this' and 'Lilly that.' It's annoying."

That was almost funny considering I hadn't heard her utter more than a sentence that didn't revolve back to her Sweet Sixteen. But I was sure she didn't notice; she was too busy making me feel guilty for being shipped off to Puerto Rico against my will and making the best of the situation while there. Like somehow it was a crime for which I needed to beg forgiveness.

"Well, maybe I thought you guys would *want* to hear what I did this summer. Would it kill you to take an interest in *my* life?"

"Well, maybe we would be interested, if you didn't bring back Chiquita Banana over there."

"Don't call her that," I said, my eyebrows raised.

"Why? 'Cause she's your best friend now?" Madison bobbed her head. "You spent two months with this *chica*, and now you're ready to replace us?"

"Call me crazy, but I thought maybe we could all be friends."

"We can," Emily offered, finally speaking up.

"Oh really?" Madison spat, glaring at her weakened ally.

Emily ran her hand through her trimmed maple locks and stared at the checkered tablecloth.

"Mad, it's done. She lives here now. And Mariana's our best friend. . . ."

"Well, I don't see why you just get to dictate who our friends are," Madison interrupted, waving her hands at me. "Just because she's *your* relative doesn't mean she has to be *my* new best friend. Are we ever going to hang out with you again alone, without her?"

"You guys don't have to be BFF. I just want you to try to get along. Is that too much to . . ."

Before I could finish the thought, a crash of broken porcelain resounded from Lilly and Vince's table. I swiveled to catch Lilly staring doe-eyed at my Uncle Diego, who was looming in front of her, eyes fiery and a plate of food splattered onto his pants.

Chapter 4

It was a heck of a first impression. When asked how she was related to us, Lilly explained that my Uncle Diego's uncle (my Great Uncle Miguel, whom I had spent the summer living with) was her grandfather. She could have left it at that. But she didn't. She went on to add that she had also invited my Uncle Diego's sister, Teresa, to her *Quinceañera*. That's when he dropped his plate.

I rushed over seconds after my father.

"What happened?" My dad asked, though by the look in his dark eyes I could tell that he already knew the answer.

"I was about to ask you the same thing. When exactly were you going to tell me that you met with that tramp and her daughter?" my uncle asked, a vein in his forehead pulsing in a manner very similar to my dad's.

My father took a deep breath, closed his eyes, and stroked his ebony mustache. When he pried his eyelids open, he looked almost defeated. It was an expression I had never seen on his face before.

"Yes, I spoke to Teresa, but not to her mother," he explained.

"I can't *believe* you." My Uncle Diego scanned the crowd for his other brother, clutching a butter knife tightly in his hand. If it were sharper I would have feared for my father's life. "Roberto, did you know about this?"

My Uncle Roberto looked as startled as the thirty-five party guests surrounding him. He shook his head.

"This wasn't planned," my father continued. "Vince and Mariana were there this summer. They met her. There was nothing I could do."

"Did you talk to her?"

"Yes."

"Great," Uncle Diego hissed. His knuckles whitened as he continued to grip the shiny steel knife. Then he thrust the blunt weapon at my father like a pointer. "Well, did you tell her how her horrible excuse for a mother ran us out of town? How she ruined our family? How *our mother* was never the same again, because of *her*?"

"No, it wasn't like that. . . ."

"Then, there was a lot you could have done, Lorenzo. You chose not to. And you know what? I'm choosing to get the hell out of here." He slammed the knife on the table, his eyes large and black.

"Diego!" my aunt yelled.

"Don't!" he screamed at his wife through clenched teeth.

Then he snatched his keys from the picnic table and charged toward the back door of our house, my aunt and cousins chasing after him.

"Dad!" I yelled, my eyes pleading. "Do something!"

But my dad just stood there, motionless, watching his brother storm away.

"What in the world were you thinking?" I asked Lilly, plopping down on the picnic bench beside her.

The guests around us were starting to disperse. The spectacle was over and apparently enough to trigger the end of the festivities.

"I don't know. I didn't think he'd react like that. . . ."

"Lilly, I get that maybe your family back home tells each other everything. But I told you that's not how it works here." I shook my head at her, my red hair flopping into my eyes.

"I know, I just thought that maybe you guys could benefit from a little honesty. Maybe if I got the ball rolling . . ."

"Ya got the ball rolling all right!" Vince exclaimed with a cocky smile. "No need to ease into it or anything."

"Um, Mariana, what's going on?" Emily asked softly as she strolled up behind me with Madison on her heels.

"It's a long story," I mumbled, stroking my forehead. I could feel a headache forming behind my eyes in throbbing waves.

I looked at Madison and Emily, and for the first time since I got off the plane from Puerto Rico, they looked like my old friends. Madison's face was soft and concerned. I squished over on the picnic bench and made room for them beside me.

"It all started at Lilly's *Quinceañera*. . . ." I explained, launching into the story.

I relayed every detail, from my insulting a stranger's screaming child at church to finding out that that stranger was my illegitimate aunt. I watched as Madison and Emily's jaws sunk towards the freshly mowed grass below.

We were the only ones left at the now defunct barbeque. My Uncle Roberto and his family left immediately after my Uncle Diego, not saying a word. Almost all my parents' friends and neighbors slowly skulked away, pretending not to notice that anything uncomfortable had happened. Vince's friends quickly followed their lead, mumbling something about wanting to test their fake IDs before heading off to college.

"I had no idea any of that happened," Emily mumbled.

"Well, it isn't exactly something you put in an e-mail." I tossed my head back and stared at the branches of the oak tree stretched above us.

I used to climb those knotty branches when I was little. My dad would scream at me to get down, certain that I would hurt myself. I never did. It seemed funny now to think of the things that my parents chose to protect me from, while ignoring the things that really scarred.

"Well, this chick's in Puerto Rico, right? It's not like you're ever gonna see her again," Madison pointed out. "Can't you just forget about her?"

Lilly groaned.

"What?" Madison shrugged.

"The woman is her *aunt* and her father's *sister.* She's not just 'some chick.' She's family."

"Family they were happily living without until a few weeks ago."

"Still, it's different now," Lilly insisted, tapping her chewed nails against each other with the knack of an experienced fidget.

"Why?"

"Because I know her now," I answered, rubbing my temples. "And she's nice."

"I'm sorry, but your uncles have every right not to like her. And, seriously, why do you care?" Madison tossed her manicured fingers in the air.

On some level, I knew she was right. I couldn't judge my uncles for how they chose to deal with a horrible situation that happened years before I was born, but still I couldn't stop feeling as if what they were doing was just plain wrong.

"She has a point," Vince said, raising a chin towards Madison. "We should stay out of it."

"We're already in it!" I shouted. "*We* started all this."

"Like it's *your* fault?" Lilly rallied.

"It's Grandpop people should be pissed at."

"Vince, don't go there right now."

"It's true," Madison added.

"What do you know?" Lilly challenged.

"I know that you should stay out of other people's family business!" Madison said, looking powerful.

"Mariana, if you like this woman, there's no reason you can't stay in touch with her," Emily urged politely. "But Madison's right. You can't force your uncles to do anything."

A lull fell over the conversation. I could hear a bird chirp in the distance, and it reminded me of Puerto Rico. I couldn't believe I was there just last week. It already felt like so long ago.

"It's crazy that your family's suddenly got all this movie-of-the-week drama. I thought you guys were boring," Madison joked.

"Yeah, so did I," Vince and I said almost in unison.

The sun was starting to dim, and I saw the glint of a firefly in the lawn. School would start in a few days, and Vince would be gone for good. Everything was changing. And I couldn't control it.

Chapter 5

Vince's suitcases were piled in the foyer along with his mountain of cardboard boxes. By the time he finished packing, he had taken everything from a bathing suit (even though Cornell was nestled in frigid upstate New York) to his MVP baseball trophy. Seeing his empty room made me even happier that Lilly was staying with us. Not that I would ever admit that I might miss my older brother, but he would leave a noticeable void in our five-thousand-square-foot house.

"Mom! Let's get out of here!" Vince hollered up the stairs.

"What? You afraid Cornell's going somewhere?" I asked, my arms folded.

"When it's your turn to leave for college, trust me you'll understand."

He tossed a black duffle bag onto his shoulder and gave Tootsie a final pat on his curly black head. Vince's nails were chewed nearly to the cuticle.

"Doesn't that hurt?" I asked, staring at his mangled fingers.

"Doesn't it hurt when you wax your eyebrows?"

"Good point."

Our mother finally bounded down the steps dressed more for a Sunday brunch than a four-hour drive. Her sharp pink suit would have made Jackie O. proud. My father, who was strolling behind her in a blue button-down shirt and pressed gray slacks, appeared equally out of place.

"You guys realize that we're going to be sitting in our cars half the day, right?" Vince asked, his eyes perplexed.

"Well, we're not going to have time to change before dinner tonight," my mom explained, smoothing the lines of her skirt.

"We're going to dinner?"

"Of course. Dr. Cohen said that all the parents go to the John Thomas Steakhouse. It's supposed to be fabulous." Her lips formed an elegant smile as if she had been practicing it.

"You've got to be kidding me. I thought you guys were just gonna help bring my stuff, then leave tomorrow."

I could almost see his dreams of a wild first night fade from his muddy eyes. Instead of burgers and hot freshmen girls, he'd be chilling with filet mignon and doctors' wives. I covered my lips with my hand to hide my amusement.

"Mom!" he whined.

"Vincent, we'll leave you on your own tomorrow. Is it really too much to ask?"

My father peered directly into my brother's eyes. Vince blinked first.

The packed SUV pulled away more than an hour later with Vince's similarly packed BMW trailing behind it. When you have two men who can't agree on anything, let alone how to organize two cars to fit more luggage than they have interior space, it can slow down the departure process.

Lilly and I were finally settled onto the couch with a bag of popcorn laced with M&Ms and a deeply tragic "E! True Holly-wood Story" to entertain us.

"So, you nervous about starting school?" I asked during a commercial, shoving a handful of chocolate-covered kernels into my mouth.

"A little. I'm more nervous that people won't like me."

"Are you kidding? People'll love you. They always do. You had, like, a bazillion friends back home."

"Yeah, in Utuado. But I've kinda gotten the impression that things are a little different here. . . ."

"Eh, not so much. Plus, you got me. What more do you need?"

"Yeah, and your friends just love me," she grumbled, diving her hand into the snack bowl.

"You were a bit of a shock. Just give 'em time," I stated as the doorbell rang.

Tootsie dashed in from the kitchen, barking with excitement, as Lilly and I swiveled toward the door.

"You expecting someone?" Lilly asked.

I shook my head.

"Well, might as well make myself useful." Lilly stumbled to her feet and trotted to the door. She pushed back the sheer curtain on an adjacent window pane.

"It's like they heard us," she muttered, holding back my giant poodle.

As soon as she unlocked the dead bolt, the door swung open, and in barreled Madison and Emily.

"What up, girl?" Madison greeted, as she patted Tootsie's head.

"What are you guys doing here?" I squinted at them.

"What do you think? Your brother's gone, your parents are gone, and you're racked with guilt over some family drama. We're here to cheer you up!" Madison exclaimed as she pulled a pint of gourmet ice cream out of her pink leather bag.

The two girls walked briskly into the kitchen to fetch the spoons. They knew where they were, and they didn't need permission. For more than a dozen years, we'd invaded each other's homes unquestioned.

I followed them in. Lilly followed me.

"Ya know, I don't need cheering up," I said as I pulled out a stainless steel stool from under the island. "I'm totally fine."

"Oh, so you're totally cool with the whole bastard aunt thing?" Madison asked, eyebrows pushed high.

"Why does everyone keep calling her that?"

"'Cause it's true. I mean, it's not her fault or anything. But it's true."

I snatched the pint of ice cream from Madison and dug in. "I don't know. My dad's acting like nothing happened in Puerto Rico. And no one's talking about my uncle's hissy fit at the barbeque."

"Well, what'd you expect?" Emily asked as she rested her elbows on the black granite.

She and Madison were standing on one side of the island; Lilly and I were seated on the other. It felt like the great divide.

"That we'd all just get along . . ."

"Yeah, welcome back to Spring Mills," Madison said with a forced chuckle.

"Seriously. Since when do our families discuss anything important?" Emily added.

Her face faded, but when she realized that I'd noticed her shift in mood, her eyes quickly livened. I brushed it off.

"I may not know Teresa, but I know your family," said Madison. "And trust me, the Ruízes are gonna ignore her until she goes away."

She stared straight at Lilly as she spoke, her lips curled in a sneer.

"Hey, I'm gonna go check my e-mail. See if my mom contacted me," Lilly remarked, hopping off her stool.

"Yeah, *adios chica*," Madison said with a hollow laugh.

I smiled and pretended like she was kidding. Lilly didn't look amused.

Ten minutes later, Madison, Emily, and I were deeply involved in a conversation over what to wear on the first day of classes. We only had a couple of days before sophomore year kicked off, and, while I wasn't a fashion victim, my style sense couldn't compare to Madison's expertise. The girl could teach a collegiate course contrasting this year's fall colors to those of previous seasons, and she always made sure we benefited from her wisdom. Each fall, without fail, she'd help Emily and me put together the most fashionable outfits possible so we'd start the year off fresh. It was a mini-bonding experience I looked forward to every Labor Day.

She was in the midst of dissecting why brown was the new black, when Lilly cried out from my dad's study.

"¡Ay Díos mío! Mariana!"

"What? What's going on?" I rushed toward her.

The study was located just off the kitchen, accented by a giant bay window framing the lush backyard. It was my father's home within a home; he spent more hours there than he did in his bedroom. I halted in the doorway and registered Lilly's wide-eyed focus on the flat screen computer. Madison and Emily stopped behind me.

"It's Teresa! You are *not* gonna believe this."

My breath caught in my throat.

"She's moving."

"So?" I asked.

"To the States."

The blood squished from my brain to my toes.

"She met a guy on the Internet. She's moving to Jersey. Like, in two weeks."

My stunned, wounded gaze drifted to a family portrait my father had nuzzled on a nearby bookshelf. It was taken years ago by a renowned Philadelphia photographer. We were all grinning wide in front of a cloudy gray background with my grandparents standing proudly at our sides. I locked on my grandfather's face. He looked so foreign to me now. The man who lived his life ensconced in secrets seemed so different from the man who rested his weathered hand on my shoulder that day. We all looked different—less innocent.

Chapter 6

I didn't tell my parents about Teresa, at least not yet. When they got back from Cornell, they looked so happy—full of pride for their Ivy League son. They raved about the campus, the restaurants, and the quaint collegiate location. I didn't want to strip them of that poignant, parental, "just-dropped-my-firstborn-off-at-college" moment by informing them that the remainder of their family was about to implode when the next flight landed from San Juan.

I convinced Lilly to stay quiet until I determined the right moment to drop the news. She easily agreed. She had bigger things to occupy her brain waves, namely her debut at Spring Mills High School.

She spent thirty minutes straight talking to her mother about "expectations" and how she needed to appear *"muy inteligente."* Lilly was already intelligent, and I didn't expect her to have to work very hard to prove that to her new teachers. But her parents were understandably nervous—Lilly's academic performance had to justify their losing their daughter for a good chunk of her teen years.

"Last chance to change your mind. You sure you're ready?" I asked as I opened my custom-made jewelry box and pulled out the diamond stud earrings that my parents had given me for my confirmation.

Lilly was carefully selecting her "first day of school" outfit from my closet. She insisted that I show her what "everyone else would be wearing," but I doubted that I was the best judge. I tended to lean more towards the casual, comfy attire rather than the sleek, trendy looks Madison (and most of the female student body) preferred. I did, however, have a closet full of skirts and dresses from family occasions gone by, and after ten years in the district I knew that dressy attire was a safe choice on day one.

"It just seems a little formal for school," Lilly said, glaring at the array of skirts flowing in my walk-in closet.

"Look, I could tell you to mimick an outfit from the celebrity pages of last week's *People,* but I think it's a little late for that. Trust me, a lot of girls will be wearing skirts."

"Skirts with ruffles?" she asked, flicking a pale pink frock.

"Those are box pleats, and yes, girls will be wearing stuff like that."

I had already selected my outfit. I was planning to wear the dress I wore to Vince's graduation. No one outside the ceremony had seen me in it, and I thought it was safe to say that even those who had would have forgotten after three months of summer vacation. "It seems kinda boring," Lilly said as she held a black skirt to her waist.

"Well, our school's kinda weird about clothes. We don't have a dress code, but there's a 'code of conduct' that eliminates any item that could be worthy of MTV."

I clipped the price tags from my new leather school bag and filled it with pencils and pens from my desk. My mom had bought Lilly and I a complete set of new notebooks, binders, folders, rulers, and calculators. I love school supplies.

"So, Madison's picking us up tomorrow at 7:15," I stated.

"Oh, great," she grumbled.

I stared at Lilly, my head tilted. "Give her a chance. You haven't seen the real her yet."

"Well, maybe I won't need to," she said as she arranged a navy skirt and ivory top on my bed.

"What's that supposed to mean?"

"I don't know. I guess I just need to figure this Spring Mills thing out, you know?" She collected the outfit in her arms, along with a matching pair of navy sandals from my shoe rack, and headed toward the door.

"You will. And I'll help you."

"Hey, I'm a big girl. I can tie my own shoes."

"That's the beauty of Spring Mills. You don't have to tie your own shoes. You can hire people to do that for you," I joked.

Lilly shook her head and left the room. She seemed impeccably calm for a girl about to enter a world that was utterly unfamiliar. I think I was more nervous for the start of school than she was.

Madison's red Audi smelled amazing. I wish they could bottle that new car smell, because I would drench my entire house in it. I slumped my head onto the black leather headrest and inhaled deeply.

"So, Lilly, how you feelin'?" Emily asked from her permanent seat in shotgun.

Since Lilly and I shared a residence, and therefore always had to be picked up together, we were designated backseat passengers. Not that I minded, but I knew that if Lilly wasn't around, then Emily and I would at least rotate positions in the front.

"I'm okay. I'm mostly worried that I'll be behind in my classes."

"Aren't you at all freaked out that you're going to a school that speaks a foreign language?" Madison asked, looking at Lilly through the rearview mirror.

"Like my English sucks?" Lilly rolled her eyes. "Besides, considering my school back in Puerto Rico was almost entirely Americans, I don't think it'll be too strange. How different could it be?"

Madison pulled into the driveway that led to Spring Mills

High School. The lawn was speckled with students clad in designer clothes and toting leather backpacks. A couple of guys kicked a soccer ball back and forth; a group of elite senior girls were cuddled on the laps of their football stud boyfriends; a few familiar sophomores goofed off on the steps; and the remaining kids chatted in small groups with headphones or cell phones attached to their ears.

The flower beds, which were everywhere, were so freshly fertilized that the earthen scent floated into the car even with the windows sealed and the air conditioner blasting. The stone building shone with recently painted windowsills and new red doors at the column-flanked entrance.

"Wow," Lilly mumbled under her breath.

She tugged at her borrowed blouse (only two inches of cleavage showed, which I considered a vast improvement).

"It's nice, isn't it?" Emily grinned as she twisted to look at Lilly between the leather seats.

"You should see how crappy the schools outside the Main Line are. When we play them in sports, I feel like we're rolling into a prison," Madison boasted.

"Mad, you're a ballerina. Since when do you play sports?" I asked.

"We've gone to some of the football games," she said, her blue eyes twinkling.

"Once."

Madison pulled into the student parking lot and eased into a spot near the fence that led to the tennis courts. I grabbed my new messenger bag and climbed out of the car. My chocolate wrap dress hung below the wide belt cinched at my waist. I tugged at the hemline.

"First day of school, gotta love it," Emily stated as she flung her plaid tote bag onto her shoulder and adjusted her black skirt.

Madison checked her hair in the car window and yanked at the waist of her designer jeans. She was wearing an exact replica of an outfit Cameron Diaz was photographed wearing on Rodeo Drive last week, down to the red ballet flats.

"So what does your school look like in *Puerrrto Riccco*," Madison purred in a fake Spanish accent.

"Not like this," Lilly mumbled.

A few minutes later, I walked Lilly to the front office. Since my dad had registered her via cell phone while the dean was on a par three, she hadn't received a printed schedule in the mail.

We stopped in front of the glass doors. Three secretaries hurried behind a large wooden counter handing out rosters that students had lost over the summer, checking doctors' notes, and reviewing homeroom discrepancies. The office always buzzed with chaos in the mornings.

I reached for the door handle, but Lilly grabbed my arm.

"What?"

"I want to go in alone."

"Are you nuts? Why?"

"Because I want to."

"Lilly, I know all of the secretaries. I can help you out."

"I wanna do it on my own." She stared through the glass into the bustling office.

"So, what, you just want me to leave you here and go to class?"

"Yes," she said firmly.

"Lilly, you don't know where anything is. At least let me look at your schedule and show you where your classes are. You still have to find your locker," I said, foolishly assuming my tenure in the district would make me rather useful.

"You've done enough already. Trust me. I can do this by myself. I can't be 'Mariana's cousin' forever."

"It's the first day of school! Where are you getting 'forever' from?"

Lilly angled her head and peered at me.

"Mariana, I have no friends here besides you. And I can't just assume that your friends will be my friends. We live together; we eat dinner together; we go to school together. If I keep following you around, we're both gonna lose it."

If I had been in Lilly's position, actually *when* I was in Lilly's position this summer, I had no desire to branch off on my own.

Lilly's life was my life. Aside from the occasional trip to the Internet café, we did everything together. I needed her in Puerto Rico, at least until I met Alex. But I even met him through her. I wasn't good at meeting new people. Madison, Emily, and I had been glued to each other for so long that I had forgotten how we had become friends. I couldn't imagine that Lilly didn't need me in the same way.

"Okay, go for it. But if anything happens, you have my cell."

"Mariana, *I* don't have a cell."

"Oh. We should make sure my dad gets you one."

Lilly turned toward the door, took a breath, clutched the metal handle, and pushed it open. I watched for a moment until she attracted the secretary's attention, but once they were involved in conversation, I took my cue to leave.

Chapter 7

My locker looked exactly the same. Students kept the same metal storage unit with the same combination throughout the duration of high school. So with each passing graduation, the hierarchy of the class wings rotated. The senior wing from last school year now housed freshmen, and my hall of lockers went from being the "freshmen wing" to the "sophomore wing." It was odd to see freshmen roaming the hall that my brother had occupied with his senior buddies last year, but that was the cycle of Spring Mills.

"Hey, Locker Buddy! You're back!" I cheered as Bobby McNabb approached the locker adjacent to mine. "How was bloody ole Dublin?"

"I think that's a British accent you're attempting there, 'cause the Irish definitely don't sound like that." He swung open his locker door, his blond curls flopping onto his forehead.

"Oh, so you're an expert now?"

"I am, brutha," he smirked, peeking at my butt. "Hawareya? Nice arse."

"Okay, I'm gonna pretend you did not just look at my butt," I said, a shocked smile across my face. Bobby's cheeks flushed.

I hung my messenger bag on the hook in my locker and pulled my small red purse from inside.

"So, did you do the whole film thing?"

"Yeah. It was cool. Ireland's awesome. We traveled all around. I filmed the whole thing. You'll have to see it." He cleared his throat. "Anyway, I heard you went away. To Puerto Rico?"

"Yeah. It was kind of a last minute thing. Didn't really have much of a say in the matter thanks to my brother."

"He at Cornell now?"

"Yup, left last week. He was beyond excited to get out of here."

"I bet. So, whatcha do in Puerto Rico?"

"Well, I brought back a five-foot-four replica of myself." I grinned as I slammed my locker door closed. "My cousin Lilly moved back with me. You'll see her. She's a freshman, looks just like me."

"Seriously?"

I nodded, tossing my purse on my shoulder.

"Well, she must be pretty hot then."

My head jerked back slightly, but before I could react Bobby shut his locker and headed down the hallway. I watched him walk away.

By lunchtime, I had started to sense that a major shift had occurred in the world of Spring Mills High. I had been approached by more than a dozen students, each one commenting on how "cool" and "awesome" my new cousin was. In the ten years I had been in this school district, I couldn't remember a single classmate ever calling me cool. But in less than a few hours, Lilly had not only met the elite of our student body, she had won them over.

"Okay, so how many people brought up my party to you this morning?" Madison asked as we sat at our "usual table" in the cafeteria.

"Like, everyone," Emily stated, shooting me a pointed stare.

"Oh, yeah. Me too," I added quickly. "They all said Orlando was so hot in person."

I fidgeted with the dangling starfish on my silver necklace. Between Teresa's impending arrival, which I still hadn't mentioned to my parents (it just didn't seem like breakfast conversation), and Lilly's insistence on being utterly independent of my presence, I was starting to feel consumed with drama. I needed solutions. So, I decided that I would tell my parents about Teresa at dinner tonight (how I would do that, I didn't know). But I still hadn't determined how I would check in on my cousin. Since Lilly was a freshman, a year below me, we didn't share any classes. I hadn't passed her in the hall once all day. I had no idea how she was reacting to the new environment, though the peer reviews did give me reason to suspect that she was doing just fine.

"Have people mentioned Lilly to you at all?" I asked, dropping the charm to grab another low-cal potato chip to go with my rubber no-meat hot dog. It was better than the bottled water and carrot sticks Madison called a meal.

"No, why would they? She hasn't even been here a day." Madison straightened the collar of her designer shirt.

"It's just, a bunch of people have come up to me today. Like, people who don't normally talk to us."

"Like who?" Emily asked as she bit into a cookie.

"Like Sarah Weaver and Chad Murray."

"You know those guys?" Emily grumbled through a mouthful of chocolate chip cookie.

"No. That's just it. I didn't even think they knew I existed. But all day I've had jocks and cheerleaders talking to me about my cousin. Like Lilly's already one of them."

"Mariana, that's impossible. No one becomes instantly popular. Not in Spring Mills." Madison swished her shiny blond hair over her shoulder, brushing off the conversation.

"Hey, Mariana! I met your cousin. Dude, she's awesome!" yelled Derek Jansorn, captain of the JV lacrosse team.

He was standing in the snack line with a group of lacrosse buddies, who were tall, built, and arguably the best-looking guys in our grade. I hadn't held a conversation with any of them since elementary school.

"See!" I squealed, nodding to the boys.

"Okay, that was weird," Emily muttered.

"I know, and it's been happening all day."

I flicked a small wave at the guys and grinned awkwardly. I wasn't sure what the proper response was to their comment. It wasn't like I could thank them or take credit for Lilly's "awesomeness." Actually, it amazed me that someone who practically shared my skin could even be deemed "awesome," given that our shared appearance hadn't done much for me in the popularity department over the past fifteen years. Of course, I was noticeably missing her double D's.

"Maybe something happened this morning we don't know about," Madison suggested, frowning.

I nodded, though I didn't agree. I saw Lilly in Puerto Rico; I saw how many male friends she had and how guys reacted to her presence. There was something about her they were drawn to, and I was guessing that whatever that "something" was, it followed her across the ocean.

Chapter 8

I walked into the classroom—sophomore chemistry. It was one of the most dreaded courses at Spring Mills. It required all students to memorize the periodic table. This might be useful if we all pursued careers in chemical engineering, but considering most adults (including our parents) admit to not knowing the molecular formula for any compound other than water, it was hard to convince the student body that we would need this information "in real life."

Science, however, had always come naturally to me, so I refused to believe the doom and gloom rumors about the course could be true. I made it through biology last year, and that course wasn't exactly known as a "no-brainer."

It was my last period of the day. Mr. Berk was quietly seated behind his teacher's desk scanning the attendance chart. Almost all courses—gym, English, chemistry, whatever—followed a virtually identical formula on the first day. Students received assigned seats. Then, teachers reviewed objectives for the course and expressed their expectations. Finally, we'd have a lame discussion about some current events topic that vaguely connected the subject matter to the outside world.

In gym, we sat on the basketball bleachers and discussed the chances of an Eagles playoff run and whether the QB's ability to throw outside the pocket could lead them all the way to the Superbowl. In English, we discussed recent plagiarism scandals, the importance of citing sources, and how cheating of any kind would get us expelled from school. In geometry, we analyzed the angles of Citizens Bank Park and discussed how the Phillies could improve their game by using geometric formulas while batting. Now it was Mr. Berk's turn to convince us that the periodic elements impacted the daily life of a teenager.

"Mariana! Hey, Mariana!"

I spun around and saw Boddy McNabb seated at a lab table equipped with a stainless steel sink, a few Bunsen burners, and several glass beakers. The stool next to him was vacant.

"Hey, Locker Buddy! I can't believe we actually have a class together this year." I plopped onto the cold metal stool beside him.

"Yup. I guess we'll be more than locker buddies now." He adjusted the black-framed glasses that sat on his slender nose.

He was the only boy I knew who could pull off the look. Somehow the thick plastic frames weren't dorky on him. They were funky and cool and matched his intentionally messy hair and his button-downs layered over "emo" band T-shirts.

I peered around the classroom. It was the usual suspects. Spring Mills believed in tracking students by their academic ability. So since the eighth grade, I had been in Level 1, which placed me with the top ten percent of our grade. It made it easier to participate, since none of us was winning any popularity awards, and therefore we had no need for dumb acts or class clown routines.

Madison and Emily, however, were in Level 2, which housed approximately sixty percent of our grade and ninety percent of our school drama. That's why Madison felt comfortable inviting half the student body to her birthday party—she did actually spend time with them (even if they were merely a source of entertaining gossip). She spent most of her classes whispering to Emily rather than listening to her teachers. Not that it mattered much.

Madison's dad was an alumnus of Duke University, and so were her mother and her brother, and her sister was currently a Duke sophomore. Madison knew where she was going to college, and her father knew how to get her in. She was a legacy, and she just needed to maintain the solid academic record to back up his influence. Emily had a similar set up. Her mother was a poetry professor at Swarthmore, an elite liberal arts college not far from where we lived. Every time we went to her house, Mrs. Montgomery spat poetry and harped on the importance of a solid liberal arts background to achieve a well-rounded life. Emily was destined to be an English major on the school's quaint campus, whether she wanted to or not.

Unfortunately, I did not share in their family connections. My dad put himself through night school to get his degree. He made no hefty alumni contributions, nor did he have any deep connections with high-level administrators. Vince and I had to be accepted to college the old-fashioned way—by earning it. I already knew I was competing for spots in the Ivies with every other member of my Spring Mills advanced classes, let alone every other school in the country, so I couldn't afford to fall behind.

"All right, everyone!" hollered Mr. Berk as he stood up from his teacher's desk. "Look to the student beside you. That's your new lab partner. Now, let's get started."

I turned to Bobby. When I'd sat down I hadn't realized I was handing him control over so much of my grade. I knew he was smart, but if given a choice of a lab partner, I would have gone with Sarah Fliesher. She was first in our class and had won a county engineering competition last year.

"Don't worry. I'm not a slacker," Bobby whispered, as if reading my expression.

"I, um, I didn't say anything," I stuttered, turning my gaze toward my three-ring binder.

"You didn't have to. But that's cool. You know, I can do more than just shoot movies."

"You're right. I've seen you open a mean locker," I teased.

"You too. You're pretty quick with that dial."

"Well, I practice at home. I have a simulated locker set up in my bedroom, so I can increase my locker-opening speed and maximize my time between classes." I offered a smile.

"Oh, well, that explains it," he chuckled, his gleaming white teeth peeking through his grin. "You know, Mariana, this could be the beginning of a beautiful friendship."

"Spoken like a true film geek."

I opened up my binder just in time to hear Mr. Berk start his lecture on how various chemical properties affect everything from our morning makeup applications to our weekly dry cleaning bills. It went on for ninety minutes.

After class, I headed straight to Madison's locker and waited for Lilly. She was late.

"Are you sure she knows where to meet us?" Madison asked.

"Yes, I'm positive. I told her." I scanned the hallway.

"Her locker is pretty far away," Emily noted.

Since Lilly was a freshman, her locker was located on one of the upper wings—actually not far from where Vince's locker used to be.

I peered down the hall once more and finally spotted my cousin turning the corner. Her auburn locks flowed as her borrowed clothes swished in a way that they never did on me. Three guys, whose names I didn't know, but whose faces were popular on local sports pages, were tailing her. Their tongues practically left trails of saliva on the floor as they panted. Beside Lilly was Betsy Sumner, Spring Mills' very own Olympic-bound tennis star.

"Hi, guys. Sorry I'm late, but it turns out I'm not gonna need a ride home today," Lilly announced as she approached. "Betsy invited me to watch her tennis match. I'm thinking of joining the team, if it's not too late."

She smiled at her perky blond friend.

"Oh, don't worry. I can totally get you on. Mrs. Silver will do anything I say." Betsy's orthodontia-perfected grin nearly lit up the hallway.

"Well, you *are* the star," said one of the guys, gleaming at Betsy.

"Maybe Lilly will become your secret weapon," another guy stated dreamily, his green eyes oozing devotion toward my cousin's cleavage.

"Well, I've never played before, so I doubt it." Lilly flipped a glance toward him, and a wave of pink fluttered across his face.

Back in Utuado, guys reacted like this to Lilly all the time, but I had assumed their feelings were based on long-standing relationships. This spectacle, with these guys, in my hometown, was grounded merely in a first impression. She had an instant impact on my classmates. She was accepted. My chest clamped as I swallowed hard.

"Well, whatever. We gotta go," Madison stated through clenched teeth.

"Yeah, see you at home," I added, shaking my head to knock the puzzled expression from my face.

Emily clutched my shoulder and pulled me away.

After an hour of "Oprah" and an endless conversation about how Lilly's Spring Mills debut seemed oddly fitting for the social pages of the *Main Line Times*, Madison abruptly shifted the conversation toward a new topic—my birthday plans. And while I realized turning sixteen was a monumental moment in Madison's life from which all else circled, I just wasn't feeling the same enthusiasm (though I had a hard time getting this point across to my friends, no matter how bluntly I put it).

Realistically, I didn't have the largest social circle, and inviting the entire sophomore class, all 276 of us, didn't seem appealing (nor a financial undertaking I could reasonably talk my father into). So, if I were to go through with the dreaded celebration, I would have to resort to inviting either my honor society classmates or a bunch of relative strangers whom I passed in the hallowed halls of Spring Mills, but to whom I rarely uttered a syllable. Sure, Madison had no problem doing this when it came to her party. She shared classes with jocks and cheerleaders and class clowns, while I was not a blip on their radar. And even if I were (due to the superstar Latina down the hall), I wasn't sure I wanted to spend my birthday celebrating with them. They weren't my friends, nor did I wish them to be.

"You could have a theme party," Madison suggested as she grabbed a catalog off my desk. "Make everyone wear white. Or throw a Parisian bash with mini Eiffel Tower favors. Or hire a fortune teller . . ."

"Or you could throw the whole thing at that cool new bowling alley in the city, or rent out a club and have live music," Emily offered as she leaned against a bed post.

"Guys, I'm sorry, but I just don't know if I'm into it. It's not like I've got much time to plan. My birthday's in a month."

I was sprawled lazily on my bed, staring at my giant poodle cuddled in a ball at the foot of the mattress. His subtle snoring was more interesting than this conversation.

"Mariana, it's your Sweet Sixteen. You *have* to have a party," Madison ordered as she flipped through the designer lingerie catalog.

My mother was on a mailing list for every clothing and home goods store in the Western world. We received at least two color spreads per day, along with at least one mail-ordered product.

"You could just rent out a restaurant or something," Emily suggested.

"Yeah, and bore us all to death?"

"So? If that's what she wants . . ."

My mind drifted from the conversation. I couldn't stop thinking about Lilly. She had found new friends in a single day. I suddenly felt embarrassed for latching onto her so tightly in Puerto Rico. She must have thought I was a loser. Why couldn't I adapt to Utuado like she was adapting to Spring Mills? And why wasn't she happy with just being friends with my friends? I was sure Madison and Emily would warm up to her eventually.

"Mariana! Are your friends staying for dinner?" my mother called from downstairs.

I looked to Emily and Madison, who both shook their heads.

"No!" I screamed toward the kitchen.

"Hey, did you tell your dad about that woman moving here?" Madison asked, looking up from her catalog.

I groaned, standing up from the bed and shoving my polished toes into a pair of flip-flops. Tootsie's curly head popped up; he was annoyed that I had disturbed him. I rubbed his belly. "No, not yet. I'm thinking of bringing up Teresa over dinner. God, I can't tell you how much I hate this. I just want my family to be normal again."

"Like it ever was?" Madison joked.

"Seriously, there's nothing you can do," Emily said, her expression hardening as she pulled a hair elastic from her wrist. "At least it's your aunts and uncles who are fighting, not your parents."

She gathered her dark brown hair atop her head, her short locks creating more of a bunny tail than a ponytail. It looked nothing like the long sweeping mane I remembered.

"I know, but my dad . . ."

"Your dad, what? Spic, you can't change the fact that he has some bastard sister," Madison snipped candidly.

"Okay, there are so many things wrong with that statement that I'm not even gonna go there." My shoulders tensed.

"What? Why are you getting all defensive?"

I cocked my head at Madison and didn't respond. There was no point in explaining it. She didn't want to understand.

Chapter 9

Lilly came home not long after my friends left. She was buzzing about her newly forged tennis career and asking to borrow my old racquet. I had lasted one summer's worth of private lessons in sixth grade before realizing that ballet was my only true talent. Of course, this realization came only seconds after the fuzzy green ball was served directly into my nose. There's still a bump.

"Betsy is *so* nice!" Lilly glowed. "I can't believe she got the coach to put me on the team. I mean, I'm only on JV, but still. They've already been practicing for a month now. Did you know that teams start practicing in the summer before school starts?"

"Uh, yeah, Lil. I do live here, remember?"

"Oh, right. And Chad gave us a ride a home. He was really impressed with your house, by the way. He said he'd never been down this street before. Have you ever been to Chestnut Grove? That's where he lives. He said it's near some lake."

"I know where Chestnut Grove is," I moaned, dismissing her praise.

"Oh, I keep forgetting. It's all so new to me."

"I know," I muttered, before trudging out of my bedroom and down the hardwood stairs toward the kitchen.

I could smell the sauerkraut simmering, and frankly the scent of Lilly's borrowed Chanel perfume ("Betsy carries it everywhere!") was beginning to make me nauseated.

"Good, I was just about to call you," my mother stated as I entered the kitchen.

She held out a thin white plate, which I grabbed before lifting the lid off a sizzling pan of kielbasa and pierogies. It was one of my favorite dishes and one of the few Polish meals my mom learned to make before my grandmother passed away.

"Make sure you take some sauerkraut and salad," my mom insisted, gesturing toward a brimming bowl of lettuce. "Lilly, do you know what all this is? Pierogies are like dumplings, but they have different fillings—meat, cheese, potato. You can put sour cream on them."

"And I dip the kielbasa in mustard. It makes it kinda like a hotdog."

Lilly sniffed the pan cautiously, her nose wrinkled.

"My family's Polish," my mom explained. "This is what I ate growing up."

Like my father, my mom grew up in low-income housing. That's how my parents met—they went to the same Catholic school in Camden. My mom's father was a factory worker, and my grandmother raised the kids. I still vaguely remember their house in Jersey—a beat up row home with tomatoes growing in the tiny fenced-in yard and a porch with thick chunks of paint peeling from the wooden posts. My grandpop died when I was seven, and my grandmother had passed away last year. After her funeral, my mom started cooking more Polish meals.

"I'm sure Lilly's a better eater than Mariana," my dad nagged from his seat at the kitchen table.

"Dad!" I whined.

"What? Like it's a big secret. We practically had to force feed you growing up."

"You should have seen her in Puerto Rico," Lilly chimed. "She barely ate rice."

"I can imagine," my dad chuckled, peering over his newspaper.

"Gee, just gang up on me why don'tcha?" I griped as I filled my plate in defiance.

"Hey, if everyone ate like you, the world would be a thinner place," Lilly exclaimed as she breathed in the sauerkraut's pugent odor.

She winced slightly. Then she lifted a slice of kielbasa to her mouth, her eyes mildly confused, and quickly brushed her tongue on the meat. I smiled.

"You'll like it," I whispered. "It's kind of spicy."

I strutted back to the table and plopped down in time for my mom to catch my dad scanning the business section.

"Lorenzo, don't you think you're setting a bad example for our guest?" she asked, her blue eyes round and bulging.

"She's not really a guest, Mom. She lives here," I said as I bit into my kielbasa.

My father folded the paper in his lap.

"So how was the first day of school?"

"Fine," I grumbled.

His eyes swung toward Lilly.

"Great," she chirped as she walked toward the table with her tiny portions of food. "Everyone was really nice. I met this girl named Betsy, who is an all-star tennis pro, and she managed to get me on the team. Mariana said I could borrow her racquet. Practice starts tomorrow. And I met a bunch of really cool guys. This boy, Chad, drove us home. He was super nice, and he knows Vince. I think they played baseball together. He even tried to speak Spanish to me, which I thought was funny and kind of cute. . . ."

My father stared at Lilly, his face altered with shock. She could have been speaking Spanish, English, or Swahili for all it mattered, because he was fundamentally unable to understand "girl." That's why I never told my parents any personal information. Sure, I kept them updated on my grades, extracurricular activities, and ballet schedules, but that was about it. Madison, Emily, and I made sure to keep our conversations to a minimum when around any of our parental figures—so did almost every teenager I knew. It was basic survival. Lilly, however, was from an alternate dimension where families were close and her mother was her confidante.

My mom's eyes sparked to life while my dad's gaze turned back to his stock reports.

"That's great, Lilly! So, tell me all about this boy, Chad. Mariana do you know him? Did *you* make any new friends today?" asked my mother, dripping with excitement.

My dinner quickly lost its flavor.

"Mom, I've been going to Spring Mills for ten years. Do you really think there's anyone there I don't know?" I stared at my plate and shoved another mound of pierogi into my mouth.

"Well, possibly. Lilly's new, and she made new friends. Maybe Chad has a few friends you would like. . . ."

"Mom!"

"What?"

"I have friends. I don't need any more."

"Everyone could use more friends." She sighed as she fixed my father's plate.

I shot Lilly a look and kicked her lightly under the table.

"*Sorry,*" she mouthed.

"Maybe if you just gave people a chance . . ." my mom continued, her blond hair sweeping into her eyes as she spooned the food.

"Speaking of giving people a chance," I interrupted, hoping to shift the focus off me. I knew the mention of Teresa should do it. "Dad, I have to tell you something."

I spun toward him. "Dad."

He didn't look up.

"Dad!"

He flinched and put down his newspaper.

"What?" he asked firmly, his dark eyes tired.

"Lilly got an e-mail from Teresa while you guys were at Cornell."

He sat up straighter.

"She met some guy on the Internet. And she's moving to be with him."

I paused a moment and looked at Lilly.

"Dad, he lives in the States. In Jersey."

My mother dropped her serving spoon, and my father cleared his throat.

"I thought you should know."

My father said nothing.

"I mean, the way Uncle Diego reacted . . ."

"Mariana, I'll handle this," he said matter-of-factly, rising from his chair.

"Wait, did you know about this?"

My father exhaled loudly. "She said it was a possibility while we were in Utuado." He was clearly fighting back his irritation at having to explain himself.

"Wow. That's just great. I don't know why I'm surprised. Our family's just a mountain of secrets lately." I wiped my mouth with my cotton napkin and stood up.

"Mariana," my mother warned, not moving from her spot behind the stove.

"What? Let's face it, Mom. Every time I turn around, I find out something else you've been keeping from me. Why didn't you just tell us in Puerto Rico? Why the hush-hush?"

"Because I didn't know if she would go through with it. And, really, it has nothing to do with you."

"Oh, of course not. She's just my *aunt*. I'm just the one who happened to uncover her existence this summer."

My father's lips tightened. "Oh, stop being so dramatic. There are a lot of other people involved here. Not just you."

My body surged with grisly defensiveness as my face flooded with heat.

Before this summer, my father and I had never fought. Vince was his sparring partner. But ever since I was shoved on that plane, I had harbored a lot of unsettled resentment toward my parents.

Frankly, I was sick of my father acting like the family's self-proclaimed dictator.

"You're right Dad. Why should I care about what happens in this family? Maybe I should just wait for you to tell me how I feel."

I spun around and headed for the stairs.

"Mariana!" my father shouted.

It was too late. I was already halfway to my room.

Lilly knocked on my door a few minutes later. I rolled over on my rumpled bed and turned up the radio. Tootsie was the only company I could tolerate right now, and I was thankful Lilly took the hint and retreated to her bedroom. A few minutes later, I heard her hop on the phone with her mother, which only further justified what I was feeling.

Lilly might be family, but she couldn't possibly understand the complexity that was my father, anymore than I could understand her parental upbringing. Actually, there was only one other person in the world who had as much experience dealing with my dad as I did. I picked up my cordless phone.

"Hey, Vince's room . . . hehehe," giggled a sultry female voice.

"Vince, stop!" she cooed, still giddy. "Oh, yeah. Mmmmmm . . . "

My stomach turned in nauseating loops.

"Um, hello," I hissed.

Heavy breathing filled the line.

"*Hell-O*! Sister here! On the phone! Get off my brother, skank!" I shouted.

"Oh, hey, Mariana. Wassup," Vince panted as he grabbed the receiver.

"You are so disgusting. Do I even want to know?" I clenched my eyes shut, trying to block out the mental image of what might be occurring on the other end of the line.

"Vince, baby, where you going?" whined the pouty female voice.

"I think I'm gonna puke," I groaned, clutching my abdomen.

"Dude, sorry." He cleared his throat.

I could hear his footsteps and guessed he was walking out of his dorm room. Loud voices filled the background.

"Okay, if you've got some nasty chick in your room, why the heck are you answering the phone?" I asked, still cringing.

"Dude, Mariana, did she say what her name was? Because I seriously can't remember," Vince muttered.

"How am I related to you?" I gasped. "It is some freakish biological screwup!"

Vince chuckled on the other end. "These chicks are so easy that it's not even funny. It's like they're begging me to . . ."

"Nahahahahahah!" I shouted into the phone, holding the receiver away from my ear. "I don't wanna hear it! Not listening, not listening!"

I could hear Vince bellow with laughter. "All right, all right!" he said between breaths.

I slowly placed the phone back on my ear.

"Anyway," I huffed, hoping to shake off the last thirty seconds. "How's college, aside from Professor McSkanky?"

"It's awesome. Parties every night, people are totally cool. Classes suck, though. They doled out mega assignments on the first day."

"What, no lectures on the practical applications of high school chemistry?"

"I wish. One professor gave us seventy-five pages to read. Seriously, like I don't have any other classes?"

Actually, right now, college courses and dorm rooms sounded like absolute heaven. I closed my eyes and tried to picture what it was like where he was. I could almost see the stone buildings, the grassy quads, the kids in jeans and baseball caps. I could feel leather-bound books against my skin and smell the stale beer. I wished I was there. Part of me wanted to dive in a car and drive up to visit him right now—only I'd need a driver's license first.

"So, why you callin'? Boy trouble? Ballet catastrophe?" he asked.

"No, I wish," I grumbled.

"Don't tell me, you finally realized our parents suck, and you've run away from home," he joked.

"Well, close . . . Teresa's moving here. Like soon. She met some guy on the Internet . . . from Jersey."

"Seriously? That was quick."

"I know, right? But get this. Dad already knew about it. She told him this summer when we were in Utuado."

"And let me guess, he didn't tell you?"

"Of course not. Teresa e-mailed Lilly."

"Man, Dad's gotten shady." Vince chuckled.

"It's not funny. You saw Uncle Diego at the barbeque. He totally spazzed."

"Yeah, but what are you gonna do? Grandpop had another kid. End of story."

"But it's not just that. It's *Dad*," I hissed in a burst of frustration. "You should have heard him tonight. 'Mariana this has nothing to do with you. You're so *dramatic*.' Like I don't exist. Like I don't have a right to have an opinion on my own family."

Vince's voice swelled with amusement. "Well, finally! Welcome to my world. You've been some sort of Daddy's girl your whole life. It's about time you got a taste of the real him."

"Oh, please. He made himself very clear when he shipped me off to Puerto Rico."

"But, still. You didn't believe me all those years I fought with him. You thought *I* was the jerk. Trust me, it goes both ways."

I closed my eyes and sighed. I didn't want to fight with my dad the way Vince did, but I also couldn't stop the hostility that was slowly poisoning our relationship.

"Mariana, you're almost sixteen. You've got two more years before you go off to college. My advice: figure out a way to live with Mom and Dad 'til then."

"So, this Teresa thing? What, I should just let it go?"

"Yup," Vince answered assertively. "You are not gonna change Dad's mind. I learned that the hard way. Just find a way to deal."

"Easier said than done."

"Hey, you can come visit me and get away from it all. I promise, a half-case of beer, and you'll forget all about Dad."

It didn't sound like a bad idea. Any place was better than here at the moment.

Chapter 10

By Friday, I had found new reasons to be annoyed with my parents. Along with lying (by omission) about the impending arrival of my illegitimate half aunt, my mother was beginning to act as if she liked Lilly more than she liked me. In the past forty-eight hours, my mom had not only suggested that I be more like my cousin ("Mariana, you should hang out with some of Lilly's friends." "Mariana, maybe you should try tennis again."), she was also insisting I encourage Lilly's newfound fame.

Over breakfast this morning, she not-so-subtly recommended that I stop by Lilly's tennis practice to "offer support," which was interesting because in fifteen years, I couldn't remember anyone swinging by a ballet rehearsal on my behalf. But I didn't say that. And of course, my mother knew I'd do what she asked. I always did.

The trick was getting my friends to do it too.

"I don't see why we're being dragged into this," Madison protested as she slammed her locker shut.

"To make my mom happy."

"Why do *I* need to make your mom happy?" She cocked her head.

"You don't, but I do. And you're my ride to ballet practice."

In an hour, I'd be putting on my ballet shoes for the first time since I got back from Puerto Rico. I didn't want to think about the pain I'd feel tomorrow. Two months and I was already out of shape.

"You're lucky I'm such a good friend," Madison grumbled as we strolled toward the tennis courts.

"You're right. I am."

I nodded politely at her before discreetly rolling my eyes at Emily. She smiled.

"So how long has Little Miss Puertorriqueña been playing tennis?" Madison asked.

"A week."

"Are you serious?" she shouted. "This is ridiculous."

"Hey, we'll pop in, watch her hit a few balls, and go. My mom thinks I've been ditching her all week."

"Whatever! She's the one who's up Betsy Sumner's butt," Madison corrected nastily.

"I know, but try telling my mom that."

"Uh, guys, what the heck is that?" Emily stopped and pointed toward the bleachers.

A crowd of freshmen boys sat behind Lilly's court, hooting and hollering at the action. I watched, motionless, as Lilly dove for balls, her chest heaving as she swung violently at the fuzzy green targets. Each ball she rocketed into the parking lot only made her legion of fans cheer louder. My mouth hung open. I had never seen anyone make a lack of talent appear so endearing.

"Oh. My. God," Madison choked. We watched as Lilly bent to pick up a tennis ball and delight the crowd of spectators. "I don't get it."

"She has a fan club," Emily stated.

"It's not even a real match. It's just practice," I noted.

"How? Why?" Madison asked in a muffled voice, clearly dumbfounded.

I silently grappled with the spectacle, my insecurities surfacing with unprecedented force. I didn't draw this much attention from my own parents, let alone a pack of teenage boys. I couldn't imagine what that felt like.

Finally, Emily swung toward us.

"She's the new girl. That's it. We go through this every year, especially with exchange students. Don't you remember that French chick from last year?"

"Oh, Micheline. You have a point," I said softly, as I watched my cousin wave to her fans. "Vince had a shrine to her."

"I think every boy had a shrine to Micheline. The football team practically erected a statue in her honor," Emily added.

"They erected a lot more than that." I giggled.

"Still, it's different. She's your *cousin*." Madison tossed her hand towards Lilly, who was preparing for a serve. "She looks just like you."

"So? What's that supposed to mean?"

"Nothing. It's just, I don't see why everyone's going all gaga over Version 2.0, when they have the real thing right here," Madison covered, smiling innocently at me.

I watched Lilly bat two serves out of bounds. The boys in the crowd applauded her effort with a standing ovation. She pretended to remain focused. She pretended not to notice their reactions. But I knew she was loving the attention. How could she not be?

"You know, I really don't think Lilly needs your support right now," Emily stated as my cousin tossed a tennis ball into the stands and a half-dozen guys dove for it.

"Yeah, I think the Spring Mills Kournikova has enough of a cheering section," Madison spat as she grabbed her car keys from her bag. "Let's go."

I didn't fight her. Actually, I agreed. I had seen enough.

We marched to Madison's car and piled in. Emily immediately settled into shotgun. She didn't even pause a moment before clutching the handle. Like it didn't occur to her that I might want to sit up front.

"You know, it makes sense," I said as I slammed the car door closed. "You should have seen the guys in Puerto Rico. They tripped over themselves to get near her. All of them . . . Well, except for Alex."

"Alex is the guy you made out with, right?" Emily asked.

"Well, yeah. But it was more than that," I mumbled.

"Have you heard from him?"

"We e-mail each other—"

"Whatever," Madison abruptly interrupted, changing the subject. "I'm sick of talking about your cousin and anyone associated with her. Let's move on."

I glared at the back of Madison's head. Though my cousin had just created a bit of a scene, I knew Madison's reaction had nothing to do with her. She hated hearing any nugget about my trip that generated even a speck of happiness in my voice, including any mention of Alex. For weeks, I'd been pretending not to notice, but lately I was getting a little sick of trying so hard to be friends with my own best friends.

"So, it sucks you missed ballet camp," Emily stated, easing the tension in the car. "Madame Colbert is gonna be thrilled to see you back."

"Yeah, camp was awesome," Madison said as she pulled out of the parking lot. "You should have seen Emily's solo."

"And Madison was in the best company. Their performance got a standing ovation."

I could tell from Emily's tone that Madison had danced a very small part (like always), and that she was trying to make her feel better by complimenting the company. It amazed me that Madison didn't quit ballet and find something she was more suited for. But Madison kept on dancing, even if she was always overlooked.

It felt good to have my practice clothes on again. I missed the ballet slippers and tights, the taut buns and burning blisters. I missed feeling like a ballerina, feeling tall and strong, like I excelled at something.

More than a dozen girls were sprawled on the hardwood floor intensely stretching their legs, backs, and feet. But as soon as Madame Colbert floated in, we hustled to the barre, found our centers, aligned our feet, and waited for the music. Gracefully, we bent our knees in first position and raised our arms in a demi-plié. Our instructor never said a word, yet we were in perfect unison. We had been doing this for years.

The class continued as usual, moving from the barre to center floor work. My muscles flamed from holding positions they'd forgotten about during two months of salsa dancing and plantain eating. Emily looked amazing, however. I could tell she had learned a lot in Manhattan this summer. She'd always had bad feet—low arches and thin, tapered toes that forced all her weight onto her big toe (she got killer ingrown nails and often hated wearing flip-flops). But her turnout was flawless and her back flexibility had gone from beautiful to unbelievable.

Madison, however, didn't have a dancer's body. She was thin as a rail, but also cursed with short legs and a short neck. No matter how much she practiced, she could never move like a dancer. Her posture looked off, though, technically, she was doing nothing wrong. She just hadn't been born with the physical attributes of a ballerina. I had. And sometimes I felt guilty for not appreciating my frame enough, especially when I watched Madison struggle to extend her leg behind her in an arabesque. Her movements would never soar as high as the rest of the class, and most of us were barely trying.

When class ended, our faces were flushed and sticky, and our hairlines were drenched in sweat.

"Hey, your jumps were pretty good for being out of practice," Emily said, as we changed into our street clothes.

"Omigod! You were incredible! I can't believe I missed camp. You look like you got a lot out of it." I smiled at Emily as I dabbed my forehead with a towel. Madison sat silently behind her, changing her shoes. "You too, Mad. Your flexibility looks good."

I didn't look her in the eye; neither did Emily.

"Yeah, sure," she mumbled.

A lull fell over the conversation. I stood up and slid my feet into my sandals.

"You know, my dad can probably get us tickets to *Firebird* next week," Madison stated, breaking the silence. "His boss has season tickets to the Academy, and he's not using them."

"No way," I stated, perking up.

"Yeah, he mentioned it last night."

"That's awesome. Count me in," Emily cheered.

"All right, three tickets to the ballet." Madison peered intently at me as she spoke.

I knew she was subtly excluding Lilly, but I doubted my cousin would mind. It's not as if she had any interest in ballet. Plus, she already had her own friends (with some fan club members to boot). Still, it would have been nice to extend the invitation and to expose her to my dance world, since I had spent most of the summer engrossed in hers.

But that really wasn't the reason I wanted her included. Right now, she was the only person who truly understood what I was going through on a daily basis—with my friends, with my parents, with Teresa. It was like I finally had a sister who would always be on my side, no questions asked. (Not that I didn't appreciate my brother, but let's face it, a sister would have been nice.)

"Miss Ruíz, nice to see you back," said Madame Colbert as she popped her classical CD from the stereo. "Work on your feet. And Miss Montgomery, I see real improvement. Keep at it."

Our instructor grabbed her purse and left without a glance in Madison's direction. It was like she didn't even see her standing next to us. I smiled sympathetically, but Madison simply clutched her duffle bag and walked out. Emily and I followed her lead.

Chapter 11

When I got home from ballet, Lilly was in the shower. September is a rather warm month in Philadelphia, and if I were this sweaty after an indoor, air-conditioned dance class, I could only imagine what a few hours of aggressive tennis could do.

I turned on the glistening faucet in my sunken tub and lit some candles. Just another raging Friday night comprised of a warm bath and a rental movie. I was exhausted, and I knew I'd see Emily and Madison tomorrow at Suburban Square for our weekend shopping ritual. That was enough for me.

I collapsed into my ocean-scented bubbles and closed my eyes. No sooner did my muscles loosen than a knock pounded on the door. Before I could answer, the door opened.

"Hey!" I yelped, covering myself with a layer of soapy foam.

"Sorry, sorry!" Lilly shrieked, her hand blocking her eyes. "I know you hate it when people come into the bathroom."

"Uh, maybe because I'm naked!"

"Whatever. I'm not looking," she replied, her eyes scrunched tight.

Lilly's family didn't believe in personal boundaries. They'd use the toilet while you cleaned yourself in the shower. It was a disgusting habit that I never got used to in Puerto Rico. And they all thought my reaction was hysterical.

"Couldn't this wait until, I don't know, maybe I had some clothes on?" I scolded, plucking a fluffy white washcloth from the side of the tub to cover my nonexistent chest. It was sad that I didn't need more fabric than a washcloth to cover my A cups.

"Sorry, it's just that I'm leaving soon, and I wanted to see if you'd like to come."

Lilly's eyes were closed, her head was tilted away from me, and her palms were covering her face. At least she was attempting to respect my modesty.

"Well, where are you going?"

"Betsy invited me to this football bonfire. She said half the school would be there. It's, like, a pep rally or something."

"I know about the bonfire, Lilly," I said, shaking my head. It was annoying that my cousin continuously thought she knew more about Spring Mills than I did.

"So, are you going?" Lilly asked, popping her eyes open before remembering I was naked in the tub. "Sorry, sorry."

She tightly clenched her eyes again.

"No, I'm not going. I never go," I mumbled.

"Why? It sounds like fun."

"Because it's just a bunch of jocks."

"No, it's not. Betsy's friends will be there. Plus, you'll know people from your classes. Come on, it's a *fiesta*."

I stared at my feet. I could see fresh blisters already forming. My back was sore, and my shoulders were throbbing. But the thought of attending the Football Bonfire was a bit intriguing. Madison, Emily, and I had always felt uninvited to sports events. We thought we'd be intruding upon someone else's ritual, like if the football players suddenly dropped in on a ballet performance. We wouldn't exactly welcome their attendance. Actually, it would be pretty annoying.

"I'll think about it. Who are you going with?" I asked.

"Great, I knew you'd come! Chad's picking us up in twenty minutes. Hurry up and get dressed."

Lilly rushed out of the bathroom without waiting for a reply, which was probably smart, because I would have rejected the entire plan. Only she didn't give me a chance. I grabbed the shampoo and lathered my hair. There wasn't much time to get ready.

A football player was being burned at the stake. Not a real person. It was just a uniform from the opposing team stuffed like a scarecrow and tied to a pole. The kindling below hadn't yet been lit, but the couple hundred kids in attendance were waiting with anxious savagery.

Chad, a fellow sophomore classmate whom I had never spoken to before in my life, had picked us up right on time. I was barely able to dry my hair before the car was honking in the driveway. I threw on a pair of Vince's old jeans, a fitted navy T-shirt, and matching flip-flops before heading out the door. Unlike me, Lilly wore a face full of makeup, a tight skirt, three inches of cleavage, and enough hair product to keep the people at Paul Mitchell in business for quite a long time.

We followed Betsy, Chad, and their friends through the crowd, slinking our way toward the front. Lilly's drooling freshmen fan club kept its distance after receiving only a brief wave at our arrival. I think she may have had enough of their antics during practice. The poor boys looked devastated.

While I recognized almost everyone around us, I didn't see a single student from my classes. We honors kids supported the mathletes more than the athletes. Lilly was my only real friend in attendance.

"Wow, this is super cool," Lilly whispered staring at the crowd of teens gathered on the field. "In Puerto Rico, sometimes we used to hang out on the beach at night. I guess this is kinda like your version of a beach party."

"Sure, just without the sand, the ocean, or the tropical scenery." I smirked.

Lilly elbowed me with a snarky look. "You know what I mean. Anyway, are they really gonna light that thing on fire?"

"Looks like it, though I'd think it'd be a pretty serious fire hazard. I'm surprised the school lets us do it."

"There's a fire truck waiting out back," said a voice from behind us.

I turned and saw Bobby McNabb, video camera in hand.

"What are you doing here?" An involuntary smile slid across my face.

"Filming it. I feel it's my responsibility to document the rituals of upper middle class teenage America."

"Is that your thesis statement?" I asked, an eyebrow raised.

"Only if it makes it to the Philadelphia Film Festival."

"Good luck with that."

Lilly cleared her throat beside me.

"Oh, Bobby, this is my cousin Lilly. She just moved here from Puerto Rico."

"Yeah, I've heard," Bobby replied, nodding to her.

Lilly's eyes flicked back and forth between us.

"You know, I'm gonna go catch up with Betsy. Why don't you look for me later." She grinned and started to walk away.

"Wait!" I yelled. "I'm coming with you."

I turned to Bobby.

"Have fun filming."

"Oh, um, yeah. You too. I mean, have fun tonight," he stammered as he fiddled with a button on his camera.

I grabbed Lilly's forearm and followed her into the crowd.

"Okay, what was that?" she whispered so loudly we caught stares from the students around us.

"What was what?"

"He was totally into you. Why didn't you stay with him?"

"Bobby? What-ev," I said, rejecting the implication. "We're just locker buddies."

"Well, it looked like more than that to me."

"We're lab partners. But that's all. He asked out Emily this summer."

"*And?*"

"*And,* they went out on a date."

"One date?"

I nodded.

"I see," Lilly hummed.

"What?"

"Well, maybe he's moved on."

"I would never, ever date anyone that Emily is even remotely interested in."

"So if Orlando Bloom asked you out, you'd say no?" Lilly curled her mouth.

"That's different."

"See there's always an exception."

Betsy, Chad, and a crew of about fifteen students stood huddled a few feet from the stuffed football player. It was almost time to burn the poor soul in effigy, a rather sick tradition really. In any other circumstance, burning a life-sized replica of another human being would be considered a murderous threat or at least a kooky act of voodoo. Imagine me torching the ballet slippers of a rival dancer right before a company's tryouts. I'm pretty sure the police would get involved, and the crowd of spectators would be a jury of my peers.

"Hey guys, this is my cousin Mariana," Lilly gestured as she introduced me to her pack of friends.

It was at that moment I realized I had gone from being "Mariana Ruíz" to "Mariana Ruíz, Lilly's cousin." And she had only been here a week.

The girls smiled politely, and the guys raised their chins before turning their stares toward Lilly's chest. I couldn't really blame them; her cleavage was hard to miss.

"So, what, are you, like, new here?" Evan Casey eyeballed me as his lips pursed to the side.

The boy had gone to Sunday school with me for two years. We made our communion together. He knew quite well who I was. But being the captain of the wrestling crew with a muscle-bound image to protect, he couldn't dare acknowledge a lowly honors student like myself. It made me glad that I didn't have friends like his.

"No, Evan. I've lived in Spring Mills my whole life."

"Oh, seriously?" He snorted before elbowing his friend with a cocky grin.

"Yup. You sat next to me at St. Monica's. Remember that time Father Thomas reprimanded you for using the Lord's name in vain, and you started crying. They had to call your mom. I sat with you in the rectory until she picked you up. You remember, don't you?"

Complete silence. Puzzled eyes stretched wide as the snide grin washed from Evan's face. His nostrils flared with heated breath. I bit my lip to keep from smiling—that is until Lilly rippled with laughter.

"I'm sorry, Evan. But that's too funny," she gasped, giggling.

The crowd broke into chuckles, and Evan faked a grin.

"Oh, I, uh, must have forgotten. Whatever . . . It was a long time ago. And you look . . . different," he murmured, shrugging uncomfortably.

I paused and stared him straight in the eye. "No biggie. I knew it'd come back to you."

Just then, the varsity football team barreled out from behind the bleachers and burst through a "Spring Mills Rules!" paper banner the cheerleaders held taut. The last three boys, the senior captains, carried torches. They jogged down a dirt path lined by their teammates and faced the crowd.

"Hello, Spring Mills!" a captain bellowed into a megaphone.

The crowd ignited in cheers.

"It's football season, and we've got these wimps from down the road who think they're gonna come into our house next week and push us around!" he boomed to a mass of boos.

"But we're not gonna let 'em, are we?"

"No!" everyone shouted.

"That's right. 'Cause who we gonna beat?"

"Thorndale!"

The crowd erupted in thunderous claps. Guys body-slammed into one another and pounded their chests. Even without much experience with football games, let alone pep rallies, I could see how people could get caught up in this.

"Spring Mills!" *Clap, clap.*

"Ti-gers!" *Clap, clap.*

The mob howled in unison as the captains lowered their flames to the pile of wood. As soon as the first sparks flew, cheers swept through the student body.

It was a lynch mob if ever I saw one.

Lilly and her friends continued chanting as my eyes scanned the crowd. I spied Bobby, standing on the opposite end of the inferno, his digital video camera pressed to his eye. In that moment, he looked like a real filmmaker, slowly weaving his shoulders and extending his long legs to get the perfect shot. He was probably the one person in attendance who found the entire spectacle as odd as I did.

All of the sudden, thick, gray smoke pillowed up from the burning wood. The chalky scent filled my nostrils and water swelled in my eyes. I lifted my hands to cover my face from the airborne debris.

"God, who's that loser with the camera?" I heard Evan ask.

My shoulders instantly tensed.

"Who? Where?" asked Evan's buddy, Scott Piper.

"The dork with the glasses over there. He's filming this like it's some stupid project," Evan continued.

My pulse began to spike. It was obvious who they were talking about, and it might as well have been me. I didn't belong here either.

"I know, I hate it when losers like that try to ruin things. Get a life, buddy," Scott replied. Scott had also attended our Sunday school classes, though clearly all those lessons on "do unto others as you'd have done unto you" were wiped from both their memories.

I peeled my hands from my face and saw Evan glaring and pointing at Bobby.

"I know, maybe if he had one, he wouldn't have to film other people's. It's pathetic."

I dug my pink-painted nails into the heels of my palms as my dark eyes squinted. I glanced toward Bobby as he looked up from his eyepiece. He lifted his chin toward me and smiled.

"Is that freak smiling at us?" Evan asked, punching Scott's arm and nodding toward Bobby.

"What, is he gay?" Scott joked.

"Homo."

"Why don't you two shut up?" I snapped, shoving Evan's arm.

He jerked back and scrunched his brow.

"He's smiling at *me*," I spat with sudden fury. "And he's not 'gay,' or a 'freak,' or a 'loser.' God forbid someone doesn't play sports in this school."

"What's your problem?" Evan puffed his chest and stepped toward me, emphasizing his height.

I didn't budge.

Lilly quickly leapt beside me and threw her slender arm in front of my chest like a mom protecting her child.

"Evan, why don't you back off," Lilly suggested.

A crowd of heads turned.

"Don't look at me. She's the one spazzing. Man, you let someone hang out in the big leagues for one night . . ."

"The 'big leagues!' Are you freakin' kidding me?" I mocked. "You guys are so full of yourselves."

"Yeah, and you brains think you know everything," he barked.

"She knows more than *you*," Lilly shot back. She stood on her toes and thrust her face toward Evan.

The crowd took a collective inhale.

Evan's gray eyes sharpened to daggers. If we were guys, he would have slugged us.

"What's going on here?"

I looked over and saw Bobby standing behind the pack, his

shoulders slightly hunched. A camera dangled from his wrist and confusion filled his face.

"Nothing. Bobby, let's go."

I marched over, clasped his hand, and stormed away. Before I knew it, he laced his fingers in mine and squeezed my palm. Lilly was right behind us.

Chapter 12

The next day, I felt embarrassed. I knew Evan had no right to say what he did, but I also could have toned down the lecture a bit. The scene swirled in my brain, and each time it did, it left queasy currents pulsing in my belly. It's not that I cared what those jerks thought of me, but I preferred it when they *didn't* think about me. Now I'd be "that girl who made a scene at the bonfire."

But it wasn't just them. I couldn't stop thinking about the way Bobby's fingers laced with mine. The whole scene gave me a rush, and I didn't know what to make of it. But before I could contemplate further, Lilly knocked on my door. I knew her knock already—four gentle taps.

"Madison's here," she said through the thick wood.

I placed my hairbrush back on my vanity. "Okay. You ready?"

"Yeah. You sure you want me to go?" She opened my bedroom door.

"Of course." I slid my auburn hair into a leather headband and gazed at my reflection.

"Hey, are you cool with everything? 'Cause last night was pretty intense. And I know you're still fighting with your parents about Teresa, so I really wouldn't be offended if you didn't want to deal with my issues with Madison right now," Lilly stated with sincerity.

I stood up from my vanity and smiled. "I'm fine, really. Let's just go."

We bounded down the steps and out the front door to Madison's waiting sedan. The candy-apple paint sparkled with a freshly washed gleam. She had only had the car three months, and I think she'd washed it more than a half dozen times.

I opened the back door and climbed in.

"Oh, I didn't know your cousin was coming," Madison stated, frowning into the rearview mirror.

"Good to see you too, Madison," Lilly snipped.

"Oh, it's no big deal. We're just shopping. I figured you'd already have plans." Her blue eyes glinted with insincerity.

"Lilly's never been to Suburban Square, or any other American shopping plaza for that matter. I figured who better to initiate her."

"Cool." Tweetie, her Chihuahua, popped out of her giant purse.

"You're bringing your *dog?*" Lilly said with attitude.

"Of course," Madison snapped quickly, as if every socialite needed a two-pound dog to shop with. (She may have been right.)

"Anyway," Emily interrupted, twisting her neck to look back from the passenger seat. "Are we shopping for anything in particular?"

"Are we ever?" I asked.

"No," Madison and Emily replied in unison.

"Shopping is a professional sport in Spring Mills," I whispered to Lilly.

"Gee, and I thought football was exciting."

The Square was mobbed. Not surprising considering that it was an outdoor shopping complex in an upscale community, on a warm day, and there wasn't a cloud in the sky. We strolled down the sidewalk past high-end children's stores, kitchen gadget shops, men's tailors and women's boutiques. Our first stop was always the makeup counters.

We strutted into the high-end shop. Its hardwood floors shined under the dangling spotlights. Tall black walls of shelves were stocked with blushes, lipsticks, powders, and foundations, representing every luxury brand found in the latest glossy magazines. A collision of perfumes filled the air with a mix of tangy fruit and flowers.

"Hi, Caroline." Madison waved to the clerk behind the counter. Tweetie barked hello from his leather tote.

"Madison, darling! Great to see you. You know we got in some new fall colors. I just have to show them to you. You're gonna *love* them."

The spiky-haired blond waif dashed off to fetch the bounty as I strolled to the lip wall. Every shade in nature, and several never intended for human coloring, was displayed in sticks, mattes, glosses, creams, and stains. Lilly plucked a tester of purple glitter gloss and peaked at the price.

"Twenty-six dollars! For *one* lipstick! Are you nuts?" she asked, a wrinkle popping between her brows.

"It's *gloss*, not lipstick. And, yup, that's about what you'll pay here," I answered as I ran my finger over a tub of sheer peach.

"You can buy, like, five lip glosses anywhere else for that price."

"Not in this brand," Madison explained as she sauntered over. "See, the glosses you wear, what are they? Wet 'N Wild?"

She and Emily giggled. I could tell Lilly didn't get the joke.

"Anyway, the cheap glosses rub off in less than an hour. But *these* glosses," Madison continued, as she slid the wand out of the deep mauve tube, "these will last until you eat. And even then, some stays on. Trust me, they're worth the money."

"You have to reapply less. And they're not sticky," Emily added.

Lilly dropped her chin and gawked at them. I knew there was no language barrier, maybe just a culture barrier built on status. Madison grew up surrounded by money; four lipsticks for one hundred dollars seemed like a bargain to her. To Lilly (and most of the world), makeup was not a major purchase. It was something you bought in the same store as your toilet paper and your greeting cards.

Just then, the sales clerk returned with a wire basket full of cosmetics.

"Is this your friend?" she asked.

We nodded.

"I'm Lilly." She smiled meekly.

"Oooh, love the accent. Very exotic," Caroline greeted her before clutching my cousin's face. "Beautiful skin . . . You know, let me show you this new highlighter we got in. It'll really brighten up your skin tone and make those cheekbones pop."

Caroline rifled through her basket until she found a tiny iridescent bottle.

"You know to do this right, we really need to remove all of your makeup," she suggested. "These colors just aren't working. The pinks and purples clash with your complexion. You want to show off those freckles, not hide them!"

"I know," Madison agreed. "Cool tones are all wrong for her."

"She's right," Caroline continued as she thrust Lilly onto a tall, white plastic stool. "You're an 'autumn.' "

"A what?" Lilly asked, her forehead clenched.

"Relax, honey. We don't want wrinkles," Caroline warned with a wag of her finger.

"Maybe we should try that gold shadow," Madison suggested.

"Yes! With the bronze liner!"

"And the mocha gloss."

"But with the coffee pencil, just to plump them up."

"Brown mascara?"

"No, brown-black."

"And some eyebrow shadow."

"With a slightly higher arch."

Madison and Caroline shifted into a language that was incomprehensible to most people, Lilly included. Yes, Lilly wore a lot of makeup, but it was clear she had no training. Having lived with her mother, I knew she didn't have a positive influence when it came to makeup application. Mrs. Sanchez wore blue eyeliner and matching cobalt shadow. I was lucky Lilly didn't coat herself with fuchsia frosted lipstick on the first day of school. My mom, on the other hand, preached the less-is-more method. Her makeup bag consisted of an SPF moisturizer, lip gloss, mascara, and tweezers.

"Mariana," Lilly whispered, swatting at me with the back of her hand. Caroline was already soaking cotton balls with makeup remover. "They're expecting me to pay for this, *verdad*? Because I don't think my mom's monthly checks are going to cover it."

Caroline paused immediately and glared at us. Then Madison gently placed her French-manicured hand on Lilly's shoulder.

"It's on me. Consider it your welcome present."

Lilly looked at Madison, and after a few moments, they both smiled. It was the first time the two of them had expressed anything other than forced civility toward one another. I took a deep breath, and my smile spread from ear to ear. Finally, Lilly was getting a glimpse of my real best friend. Sure Madison had her over-the-top, spoiled princess moments, but she was also the most generous person I knew. She couldn't go into Philly without putting money in the hands of every homeless person we passed. And she was loyal to the core. She'd take a bullet for me if she could, just as I would for her. It was like I was finally getting my life back.

Nearly an hour later, Lilly was sporting a newly improved cosmetic look, which cost Madison's dad about two hundred dollars (not including Madison's charges, like a state-of-the-art eyelash curler and a hydrating Tahitian facial mask). We headed to a local café, predictably bustling with a mix of students and soccer moms. The smell of coffee and chicken soup filled the air, and the buzz of classic rock poured from the sound system. It was a typical Saturday.

We plopped down at a small round table, meals in hand. Emily and Madison ordered veggie wraps, while Lilly and I split a turkey club and a chicken Caesar salad (with the full-fat dressing). I already knew Madison wouldn't eat more than a morsel while in public view. I think Tweetie's travel water dish and dog

chow constituted more nourishment than what her owner consumed on a daily basis.

"I can't get over how pretty your eyes look. Maybe I should
wear more makeup," I stated as I stared at Lilly's freshly lined
lashes, her lids were shaded in deep neutral tones.

"No. I like that you don't wear makeup. It's your 'thing,' " said
Emily as she chewed.

"Consider yourself lucky. If I didn't wear cover-up, I'd look
like one of those 'before' pictures in the acne infomercials,"
Madison joked.

I scanned Madison's peachy complexion. It looked airbrushed
it was so perfect.

"Madison, you know you don't have a single pimple."

"Thanks to Dr. Cohen. God bless him."

Half our high school saw a dermatologist. Our parents had such
stellar medical coverage that a visit to a doctor and prescribed
medication cost less than buying an over-the-counter treatment
at the local pharmacy.

"Madison, you know, thanks for paying for all that stuff. It was
really nice of you. . . ." Lilly said, as she caressed her polished
cheek.

"Hey, it's the least I could do." Madison grinned.

Just then, the bells jingled above the café doors. I swiveled my
head and saw Betsy Sumner stroll in with Evan and Chad behind
her.

I elbowed Lilly and gestured toward the door.

"Oh, hey, Betsy!" Lilly called, waving wildly at her friend.

I kicked her shin under the table.

"Um, do you not see who she's with?" I whispered.

"Oh," Lilly grumbled as she caught a glimpse of Evan.

"What? What's going on?" Emily asked, twisting her neck toward the entrance.

Betsy was already strutting toward our table. Her friends stayed
in the doorway.

"Hey, Lilly!" Betsy cheered as she approached. "Um, Mariana." She stared at the wall as she addressed me.

"Hi, Betsy." Lilly smiled. "You know Madison and Emily."

"Oh, hi."

Madison and Emily faked grins, and Tweetie growled on cue as if she could sense Betsy's insincerity (good dog).

"Hey, by the way, don't worry about Evan. I think we're gonna eat somewhere else. I don't want any trouble."

"Trouble? Why would we start trouble?" Madison asked, shaking her head.

"Because of what happened last night."

Madison blinked at her.

"At the bonfire," Betsy stated, stretching her eyes.

My friends' faces shot toward me as I bit my lip. I hadn't yet told them what had happened. I was trying to forget about it altogether (and trying to avoid an argument for not inviting them).

"Anyway, they said they'd let it go. I mean, you were just defending your cousin." Betsy glared at me. "So don't sweat it. They're still cool with *you*, Lilly."

She smirked, swished her dirty blond waves over her shoulder and spun towards the door. I caught Evan snarling at me like an opposing football player. If he had had a torch, he would have used it.

"What the heck was that?" Madison asked.

"It's nothing," I mumbled, shoving a forkful of lettuce into my mouth.

"It kinda looked like something," Emily added.

I glanced at Lilly. She shrugged, then turned her focus back to her sandwich.

I told Emily and Madison the whole story. Everything from my spontaneous decision to attend the bonfire to my retelling of Evan's Sunday school horrors to overhearing him ridicule Bobby. They listened, in stunned silence, until the end.

"Evan and Scott just started ripping on Bobby out of nowhere?" Emily asked.

"Pretty much. They called him a freak and a loser and all this crap."

"They don't even know him," she stated, withdrawing her arms from the table and folding them across her chest.

Her body stiffened. I opened my mouth to respond, but Lilly interrupted.

"So, Mariana defended Bobby in front of all those guys. It was pretty cool."

"Well, if Lilly hadn't jumped in I think Evan would have lost it," I stated. "You should have seen his face."

"So, what happened after that?" Emily asked, one eye squinted. "Did you go home?"

I looked at Lilly.

"Yeah, well, sort of. Bobby drove us."

I stared at my plate.

"Oh," Emily whispered.

"Well, we couldn't exactly ask Chad and Betsy to take us. They're Evan's best friends," I explained.

"So Bobby drove you home," Madison confirmed, speaking up for the first time. "Did you mention Emily?"

"Mad!" she hollered, swatting at her.

"What? It's a logical question. If Mariana's in a car alone with the guy you like, I'd think she'd bring you up. You did, didn't you?"

I had a feeling Madison already knew the answer to that. And truthfully, I didn't know why I hadn't. I could claim that I was so rattled by what had happened that I wasn't thinking clearly, but that wasn't true. Actually, as I sat in the passenger seat next to him, all I could think about was how confident he looked when he laced his fingers in mine and marched us back to the car. It was all rather exciting.

"I *don't* like him," Emily murmured.

"It was a crazy night," I explained, fiddling with the toothpick in my sandwich.

"Yeah, sounds like it. Too crazy to even pick up the phone, huh? God forbid you invite us," Madison snapped.

"I didn't think you'd want to go. You hate football."

"You still could've called," Emily added. "We always invite you everywhere."

Their eyes drooped as the corners of their mouths turned down. I knew I should have included them. But I liked the idea of doing something with just Lilly. She lived in my house yet I felt like I never saw her. I missed how things were in Utuado.

"Guys, I'm sorry. You're right. I should have invited you."

"Yeah. And you should have at least told us what happened this morning. I can't believe we had to hear it from Betsy Sumner." Madison tossed her pale blond locks.

"I said I'm sorry."

She grunted. Clearly, she didn't believe me.

"I mean it, really. I should have called."

Neither Madison nor Emily said a word. They stared in opposite directions.

"Look, she's apologized. What else do you want her to do? It's not that big of a deal," Lilly scoffed.

Madison flung her head toward my cousin.

"Good thing she's got you to defend her, huh?"

And with that snotty accusation, Madison pushed out her chair, snatched her tiny barking canine, and stormed out of the café.

Chapter 13

It didn't blow over. At least not right away. We caught up with Madison after we paid the bill. Predictably she was in a clothing store with an armful of purchases headed for a dressing room. After thirty minutes of hearing me plead my case and insist my attendance at the bonfire was not premeditated nor an intentional act to exclude her, she softened.

Lilly, however, bore the brunt of her anger. Madison spent the rest of the day criticizing every article of clothing she touched. "God, Lilly, do you have any taste at all?" she gagged when Lilly's hand dared to brush a pair of white denim jeans. "Do they not have fashion in Puerto Rico?" Tweetie even snarled loyally at my cousin as if Madison had trained her for the task. (She probably did.) For the most part, Lilly took the insults as a favor to me. But I could tell she was dangerously close to her limit, and I convinced Madison to take us home.

By morning, when I called Madison, she seemed relaxed. I didn't bring up the bonfire and neither did she. She, instead, decided to focus back on my birthday party, which I still hadn't agreed to host. She offered to do all the planning and even ask her event planner Gayle to pull a few strings to secure a location. Part of me wanted to agree (the last thing I needed was another obstacle in our friendship), while the other part didn't want to host a rerun of her micro-detailed soiree.

"What's the big deal? Just throw the darn party," Lilly suggested, as she lay across my bed flipping through her algebra book pretending to do homework.

"You of all people should understand. How much did you want to have your *Quinceañera*?" I asked as I typed my assignment on the Boston Massacre. (Maybe I could have a colonial theme with guests dressed like Minute Men carrying super-soaker muskets?)

"Yeah, but this is different. It's an actual party. You don't have to wear a pink dress or go to church."

"But there's still all the pressure to be 'awesome.' And let's face it, I'm not an awesome kind of girl." I peered up from my laptop.

"And Madison is?"

"She had Orlando Bloom sign her guestbook, didn't she?"

"So? Why does a Sweet Sixteen have to be this star-studded event? Why can't it just be a birthday party?"

"And why can't a *Quinceañera* just be a birthday party? Because it isn't."

"Well, maybe that's how your party can be different. It can just be a party. I was talking to my mom. . . ."

"You discussed my birthday plans with your mom?"

"You discussed my *Quinceañera* plans *at length* with my mom. Are you kidding?"

"Good point."

"Anyway, she was thrilled to return the favor. And she said that you should be true to yourself. No poofy dress, no grand entrance, no crystal ballroom, just food, music, and friends."

"Don't forget family. I have the foreign *tia* flying in any day now." I rolled my eyes.

"Then don't invite Teresa! It's not like your parents can force you."

"Uh, clearly you don't know my parents. . . ."

I stared at my homework trying to focus on anything other

than party plans. Only the next question was on the Boston Tea Party, very fitting. I wondered if I tossed a bunch of lattes in the Delaware River, if it could pass as a Sweet Sixteen. It would be a whole lot easier.

"Hey, remember right after your parents showed up in Utuado, you joked that you'd throw a Puerto Rican fiesta? Maybe you could do that?"

"I was kidding."

"So? It doesn't have to be a joke."

I spun around in my desk chair. Lilly's ratty hair was tied in a bun on the top of her head, and she was wearing my old Dance Camp T-shirt and cut-off stretch pants. I used to sleep in that outfit. Now she did.

"We have, like, three weeks," I said, shaking my head.

"That's all you need. Between us and your mom, we can pull this together. Come on, look at all the work you did for my *Quinceañera*. It's my turn now."

I tossed back my head and dug my fingers into my hair. I still didn't have much of a guest list, but if I didn't have much of a party then at least it wouldn't matter. And a backyard locale would mean I wouldn't have to dress up. Plus, my family really couldn't cause too much damage. They already had the big post-Utuado confrontation at the barbeque, how much worse could it be? It's not like I would actually invite Teresa and expect them to hang out with her.

I yanked myself back upright and peered at Lilly.

"Fine. Let's do it."

Three days later, I was drowning in details. I had barely gotten the announcement out of my mouth before my mom hit the phone. She actually had a party rental place on speed dial, and within the hour, she had the tent, chairs, tables, and dance floor booked. The caterers were a bit trickier. As soon as we mentioned Puerto Rico, they assumed we wanted tacos, burritos, and enchiladas. Lilly grabbed the phone and launched into a lengthy discussion about the cultural differences between Mexico and

Puerto Rico, but I'm not sure it helped. At the end of the conversation, the caterer asked if they could still serve shrimp quesadillas as an appetizer.

But they weren't half as resistant as my friends. Madison and Emily had choked on their lunches when I broke the news on Monday. I had to wave the Spring Mills cafeteria monitor off as he dashed over to test out his freshly honed Heimlich maneuver skills. I had never seen someone gag so much on a sip of water.

"What?" Madison, shrieked between gasps of air as she coughed.

"A Latin theme? Like Ricky Martin?" Emily wiped her mouth from where she had hacked up her pretzel bite.

"No, not Ricky Martin," I answered. "Just Puerto Rican food and salsa."

"You mean tortilla chips? Who cares about tortilla chips?" Emily tilted her head.

"No! Salsa the music, not the dip!"

"Well, excuse us for not having much exposure to salsa music," Madison mocked between coughs. "We do live in America. I doubt many kids here will be jumping out of their chairs to hear some weird foreign music."

"Oh come on, it'll be fun."

"It's not in English."

"But the dance is really fun. Trust me, you guys'll love it."

"Doubt it," Madison mumbled as she sipped her water.

"So," Emily interjected. "Where are you having it?"

"At my parents' house."

They both groaned and rolled their eyes. Annoyance hummed between them.

"Seriously, Mariana, I realize you weren't here this summer," Madison's voice was calm and serious, "so you haven't been to as many Sweet Sixteens as Emily and I. But please, don't do this to yourself. Jackie Cash threw her party at her mom's house. It's practically an estate, and it still sucked. Why? Because how much fun can you possibly have in a tent peeing in portable toilets? And that wasn't the worst part. She played the Macarena. The Macarena, Mariana! One Spanish song ruined her party, and you're actually thinking of basing an entire theme around that crap!"

The conversation didn't get much better after that. Madison spent the rest of the day trying to convince me to book the lovely banquet hall her event planner had found available. She made a detailed list of reasons why my suggested party plans were as appealing as a presidential address, down to the fact that Lilly and I were the only "sort of Hispanics" in the whole school. Only she didn't realize that she had nailed my entire rationale. After sixteen years of enduring not-so-clever Spanish nicknames, I figured I might as well live up to my image. I was sick of apologizing for my last name. If the Irish could turn a saint's birthday into a universally celebrated drinking holiday, then I could make a Sweet Sixteen centered around salsa music.

So, eventually, Madison admitted defeat (or at least refocused on damage control). She was now helping Lilly, my mom, and me finalize the plans. Gayle contributed a list of local bands that played Latin music, and we were all logged onto computers rating their skills. Lilly was stationed in my dad's den, Madison and I were at the kitchen table, and my mom was scanning magazines. (She wasn't into music.)

"Okay, these people suck," Madison moaned as we listened to the third band in a row attempt "*La Copa.*" "I didn't know the song could be sung worse, but these fools managed it. I mean, if all they do is Latin music, you'd think they'd be better at it, right?"

"I don't know. They're not that bad," I whined, staring at my computer as a group of dirty old men in brightly colored outfits gyrated to Ricky Martin.

Truthfully, they weren't half as bad as the musicians who had played at Lilly's *Quinceañera*—a detail I had shared with Madison via e-mail while I was still in Puerto Rico. I was greatly regretting that decision now as my best friend ignored every suggestion my cousin made. "Tropical hick-town chic is not the look we're going for, 'kay?" Madison mocked as if it were a fact not an insult. Of course I couldn't really expect her to understand the benefits of a family-centric, homespun affair—the girl imported chocolate from Switzerland for her melting fondue fountain, and her L.A.-based band was slated to appear on the "Late Show" next month.

"Mariana, have you thought about serving the drinks with little umbrellas?" my mom asked as she examined a magazine spread.

"No, mom. Can't say that I have."

"Don't bother. Lucy Silver did it at her party in July, and the guys ended up using the sticks as little weapons. A kid almost lost an eye," Madison stated.

"Mmmm." My mom nodded.

I had already shot down a sombrero-shaped birthday cake, a professional flamenco dancer, and a candy-filled piñata in the shape of a coqui frog. (My mom thought she could craft the papier mâché herself. I was half-tempted to let her try, so I could videotape the scene and send it to Vince.)

"How about serving the fried bananas as a dessert rather than a side dish? Maybe with some melted caramel sauce?"

"They're called plantains, mom."

"Martha has an interesting recipe in here. . . ."

"Oh! You know what? We could do a mini dessert spread." Madison's eyes beamed as they met my mom's. "Have a tiny fried banana on one plate, a tiny dulce de leche on another . . ."

"That's fabulous. And if we serve it on the ivory china . . ."

"With little silver spoons . . ."

"Exactly!"

"We could even do mini fruit salads . . ."

"Or sliced pineapple."

"Rum cake?"

"Maybe, depends on how it's served," my mom suggested.

"Maybe in mini custard cups?"

"Or tiny flans?"

I left the room, taking the laptop with me. I was certain they wouldn't notice. By the time I got back, they'd probably have spent another grand of my father's money. He was currently hiding in the family room—the last thing he wanted was to be included in any party conversations, unless they pertained to the budget.

"So, how's the search going?" I asked Lilly. Her brown eyes were glued to the screen as yet another band belted "*Bailamos.*" The lead singer had to be older than my father and about twice his weight.

"A couple of these bands are okay. But I don't love any yet."

"Yeah, I don't think anyone does."

"How's everything out there?"

"I think the Southern Hemisphere could spontaneously combust, and my mom and Madison would still be focused on my party."

Lilly chuckled. "Now you know how I felt this summer."

Lilly had left all of her *Quinceañera* plans up to her mother until I stepped in. I single-handedly saved the girl from wearing a bubblegum frock with a thick yellow-gold rope necklace. But we were in Utuado; our options were limited. Here in Philadelphia, we seemed to be suffering from an overabundance of party options, from tropical centerpieces, to colored tablecloths, to silver serving bowls, to Latin music.

Lilly glanced back at the screen and clicked on another band's Web site.

"Hey, at least these people have some actual salsa songs on their playlist rather than just Enrique, Ricky, and Marc."

She downloaded their music files as I logged onto my e-mail from my laptop. Vince and Alex had both sent me messages.

I clicked on Vince's first. (I always read my e-mails in the order in which they were received—it was only fair.) A photo immediately popped up. It was a shirtless Vince surrounded by a wild crowd of guys in T-shirts, jeans, and baseball caps holding a funnel with a long plastic tube to my brother's mouth. His eyes were clenched shut, and beer was dribbling down his chin. Above it read: "I'm joining a fraternity, and I already broke their record! Only three seconds!" Clearly he was proud of his drinking accomplishments, and I didn't know whether to laugh or be embarrassed. But I definitely wasn't surprised. He might not be the brightest kid at Cornell, but I could guess he was one of the most popular.

Next, I opened Alex's.

> *Hola* Mariana!
> *¿Como estas? Estoy bien.* Puerto Rico's not the same without you and Lilly. School's boring. Just a bunch of stupid Americans—oops, sorry. How was your first day? Is Spring Mills everything you remembered it to be?
> I hear Teresa's moving to the States. Is that weird for you? I remember you had a hard time with everything here. I hope it's gotten easier. I asked Teresa to bring a surprise to your birthday party. I didn't want you to think I'd forgotten. Hope you like it.
> Miss you *mi amor.*
> —Alex

I read the e-mail three more times just to make sure I understood. *I asked Teresa to bring a surprise to your birthday party.* How did Alex know about my party (I hadn't told him yet) and who invited Teresa?

"What? *¿Que paso?*" Lilly asked, gawking at my shocked expression.

I wagged my head at the screen as my leg bounced.

"Is my house turning into the freakin' CIA or something?" I mumbled.

"What are you talking about?"

I didn't respond.

"Hey, did you hear me? I said I think I found your band."

I ignored her. Instead I stood up, grabbed my laptop, and charged into the kitchen.

"Dad! *Dad!*"

Chapter 14

I was finding it very hard to focus on chemistry the next day, considering there was a very real possibility that my uncle might attempt to kill his half sister during my Sweet Sixteen. It wasn't that I didn't find the proton numbers in atomic nuclei fascinating; it was just that they couldn't possibly compare to the atomic bomb that was my guest list.

It was Thursday afternoon, and as I tapped my pencil on my lab desk, my nerves spun into overdrive. I had to diffuse this situation. Only I couldn't rely on my father. When I had confronted him last night, he had accused me of being dramatic, *again*.

"Dad, would it have killed you to tell me that you were inviting some random *tia* to my birthday party?"

"Mariana, can you please not make a scene over this?" he griped, loosening his tie.

Lilly, Madison, and my mom were standing behind me in the family room. From the eye contact my parents were making, I could tell they had conspired together. My mom was probably waiting for the right moment to jump in and break up our argument, but I wasn't about to back off. Not this time.

I clutched my auburn hair in my fists, and I sucked in a long breath.

"Dad, I get that you don't feel the need to include me in all aspects of our family history. But would it kill you to maybe, just maybe, clue me in on the major events that do affect me?" I felt my heart thump in my gut as the words gushed out. "For example, shipping me and Vince off to Puerto Rico without saying 'Hey, by the way, you might run into my half sister,' was a bad idea. Not telling us that this same woman was moving across the bridge to Jersey was also a bad idea. But, at the very least, how could you possibly not think it important to inform me, *ME*, that you had decided to invite this ticking family time bomb to my birthday party?"

"God, Mariana, must you be so *dramatic?*" my father growled with an exasperated sigh.

Prior to this summer, he had never once accused me of being a drama queen, but now it was becoming a nickname of choice for his daughter. If he only knew what a real drama queen looked like (maybe he should spend some time at Madison's house), he would be grateful for how rational I was. But no, my father actually thought he had reason to complain about his difficult, "dramatic" daughter. Not that I dared point out how lucky he was to have me; it would only have made his facial vein pulse harder.

"Mariana. Hey, Mariana," Bobby grabbed my wrist and shook it slightly.

My eyes refocused on my chemistry classroom, and I realized everyone was gawking at me.

"I'm sorry, what?" I asked with a nervous cough, peering at Mr. Berk who was leering from a few feet away.

"I asked what element is represented by the symbol Pb," he bellowed as he adjusted his frameless glasses.

"Oh, um, lead," I answered, sitting up straight.

"Good, thank you."

Mr. Berk turned back toward the chalkboard and straightened his lime green bow tie. It was one of his many quirks. He was only in his thirties, but he seemed to find it clever to dress like a little old man. It was a shame, because I could tell that he'd almost be cute if he wasn't so odd. He had thick dark hair (rare for men these days), a tall, thin build, and pale hazel eyes. But once you added the bow ties, the zip up Mr. Rogers sweaters, the loafers with tassels, and the gray fedora hat, you got a guy who was justifiably single.

"What's up with you?" Bobby whispered. "You've been spaced out the whole class."

"I don't know. Random drama." I sighed.

"Your birthday party?"

"How did you know?"

I hadn't put together the e-vite yet. I wasn't planning on sending it until Sunday. Most teens at Spring Mills preferred to distribute birthday invitations over a weekend to preempt any uninvited castoffs from finding out and getting confrontational.

"Oh, I don't know. I must have heard it around," he said as he jotted his chemistry notes from the board.

"This is ridiculous. I haven't even invited anyone yet."

"Oh, sorry. I mean, I didn't think that I'd be . . ."

"No, it's not you. Of course you're invited. It's just . . ."

"No, you don't have to explain. I shouldn't have brought it up."

Ever since the bonfire, things between Bobby and me had been awkward at best. We had barely spoken all week. I didn't blame him for letting it drop—not too many students would want to rehash being called a "loser." But it was the hand-holding that had me tongue-tied. I kept reminding myself that he was a film-maker and that he was probably going for the cinematic effect: "Cut to the strong couple storming off into the dark night hand-in-hand." Only there was something about his touch that reminded me of Alex, and it kept me from sharing the detail with Madison and Emily.

When I had originally told Emily I was his lab partner, she had acted completely disinterested. When I had asked about their date this summer, she'd brushed me off. And when I would drop tidbits from our chemistry conversations, she'd glance away and look bored. I couldn't tell if she liked him, if she hated him, or if she was just genuinely over him. But he definitely touched a nerve. She had never had a problem talking about guys to me before. Of course, I had never had a problem asking her either.

"I don't think a lot of people know. About your party," Bobby whispered. "Emily mentioned it to me this morning."

My eyes whizzed up from my notebook, and I caught Mr. Berk staring at our table. We were supposed to be determining the number of neutrons and electrons in a series of elements using the atomic mass and proton numbers provided on the periodic table. All it required was a basic algebraic equation, but my mind wiped clean the minute Bobby mentioned Emily's name.

"I didn't realize you and Emily still talked," I mumbled.

"We don't. Not really. She just came up to me this morning."

"Oh, that's cool. I mean, she's my best friend. . . ."

"I know," Bobby whispered, cutting me off. "I know."

He dropped his head, throwing his dark blond hair into his eyes as he focused on his work. I wanted to say something, but I felt like the conversation was over. I turned my focus back to chemistry and finished my problems.

After class ended, I sped into the hallway and collided with a jock. His shoulder crashed against mine, sending me stumbling back. I quickly tightened my grip on my books and found my balance. I wasn't about to give him the satisfaction of dropping everything I had into a heaping mess on the ground. By now I had the defense down pat. It was the third time it had happened today.

Evan and his totally unoriginal friends had been "accidentally" bumping me as retribution for the showdown at the bonfire. They didn't body slam me, just strategically nudged me with their massive physiques when I crossed their paths. None of them said anything, and it probably wasn't obvious to the classmates around that I was an intentional target, but I was well aware of the intimidation technique. Vince used to pull it on me at home. Every time he and my dad had a blowout and I didn't take his side, Vince would spend the next week smashing into me on the way to the bathroom. Thankfully I knew Evan and his friends would eventually tire and back off. Vince always did.

I glimpsed back to see who hit me. It was Evan. He locked eyes with me and smirked like his actions were so clever. I smiled wide in return. At least I could annoy him by refusing to offer the reaction he so desperately desired.

He looked away first.

I turned and walked to Madison's locker. She was digging through her jumbled books and binders. School had been in session for less than a month, and already her space was a disaster zone. In contrast, my books were lined by height and color-coded by subject. My locker was always tidy.

"Hey, girls," I said as I approached.

"Was that Evan Casey who just slammed into you?" Emily asked.

"Yeah, he's such a dick."

"Well, you did kinda start it," Madison grumbled as she tossed a book in her bag. "Does Bobby know you're taking physical abuse for him?"

"Oh, please." I rolled my eyes. "If I could handle Vince, I can handle Evan. He barely grazes me. And speaking of Bobby, I hear you told him about my party." I shifted my gaze to Emily.

"Oh, uh, yeah. Why? Was I not supposed to?"

"Well, I'm not sending the e-vite until this weekend. But aside from that, I didn't think you guys were talking. I thought things were weird since this summer."

Madison and Emily briefly caught eyes.

"No, we're okay. I'm mean, we're not weird. Not because of that. Why? What did he say?" Emily's voice turned squeaky.

"Nothing, relax. He just said that he spoke to you. Why? Is there, like, something going on? Because I could talk to him if you want?"

"No!" Emily shouted. "It's nothing. I figured you already told him about the party since you guys are friends and all."

She reached into her purse and pulled out her cell phone. I

couldn't tell if she was actually checking her messages or if she just wanted to look busy so she didn't have to face me.

"We are friends in the lab-partner sense of the word."

"Do all lab partners defend each other's honor?" Madison asked. " 'Cause if so, Shelly Jaffe is seriously not pulling her weight. I've been sitting next to that girl for more than a month, and she's barely let me borrow a pencil."

"Very funny." I scrunched my nose at her.

Just then Lilly popped up at the end of the hallway. Usually she was at tennis practice by now.

"What's going on?" I asked as she walked over.

"Nothing, it's just I heard you invited Betsy's friends to your party." Her eyes narrowed.

"No, I didn't."

"Well, she told me she heard about it. She knew the date, the theme, everything."

I swiveled my head toward Madison. Her face was buried in her backpack.

"Uh, you got something you want to tell me?"

"I plead the fifth," she mumbled, still staring into her bag.

"Madison! This is a *small* thing. Why the heck are you blabbing about it?"

"Because it's a party! Spic, you've got to start inviting people."

Lilly's brown eyes bulged as her jaw collapsed toward the tile floor.

"What did you just call her?" she shouted, her forehead crumpled.

The muscles in my shoulders clamped down as I held my breath.

"What?" Madison asked with a breezy shrug.

"I can't believe you just said that. Man, and you're supposed to be her friend?"

Madison stepped back, looking Lilly up and down.

"I *am* her friend."

"Wow, I'd hate to hear what you call your enemies."

"Oh, please. You don't know me. You barely know *her*." Madison waved her wrist at me.

"Yeah, keep tellin' yourself that. At least, I'm not the one throwing around racial slurs. I have more respect for *my* friends."

All the saliva dried in my mouth, and my heart shifted to warp speed. I didn't know what to say. I had let Madison and Emily call me that for years. It was my fault as much as it was theirs. Of course, Lilly had every right to take offense. Unlike me, she had probably been on the receiving end of attacks like that before. She knew what that word meant.

"I didn't mean it like that," Madison snapped, rustling her shiny blond hair. "Stop making it into something bigger than it is."

"Oh, really? Well, try dropping the 'n' word in a room full of black people and passing it off as '*I didn't mean it like that.*' I'm sure that'd go over big." Lilly mocked Madison in the same "Back in Spring Mills . . ." voice she used to ridicule me this summer.

Madison's blue eyes immediately hardened. She stepped toward my cousin.

"It is *not* the same thing!"

"Yes, it is!"

"No, it's not! You're acting like I'm racist."

"No, *you're* acting like you're racist."

"Stop it!" I yelled, diving between the two of them. I thrust my hands in both directions. Emily silently watched.

"Look, this is my fault." I peered at Lilly. "Madison didn't mean it like that. I know how it sounds, but it's just a stupid nickname that got started years ago. I was too dumb to stop it."

I glared at Madison. "But I did ask you not to call me that anymore."

She rolled her eyes.

"*Chica*, why in the world would you let them call you that?" Lilly's eyelids fell as confusion gripped her face.

I blinked back. I didn't have an answer.

Chapter 15

Lilly made plans for the weekend without me—not that I was surprised. She and Madison needed some time apart. Plus, Madison's dad had followed through on his promise to score us Saturday night tickets to *Firebird*. We were seated on the floor, fifth row center, which is a blessing and a curse. From the close vantage point we'd observe every movement, every step of choreography, every intricate detail, but we'd also lose the magic. Ballet is an athletic dance (something Madison, Emily, and I knew very well). From up close, you can see the males strain to lift the ballerinas; you can hear the dancer's thud following every jump; you can see the company waiting in the wings behind the curtains. The fantasy was spoiled.

"Now, you girls have never performed *Firebird* have you?" Mr. Fox asked from the driver's seat.

"No, Dad."

Madison and I were seated side by side in the bucket seats of her family's SUV. Emily was perched on the bench seat behind us. It was the first time I hadn't sat in the back since school started, and it was only because I physically jumped in the car before they did. When Emily realized she had to climb to the back, she actually shot me a snarky look like I had broken an unspoken rule. I energetically ignored it.

"Well, the performance has gotten great reviews," Madison's mom added, twisting from the passenger seat. "Maybe you'll pick up some pointers."

Asking us to pick up "pointers" from a prima ballerina was about as realistic as asking a high school football player to "learn a thing or two" from Peyton Manning. We can either lift our legs that high, or we can't. You can't teach talent—not talent like that.

"So what's Lilly doing tonight?" Madison whispered, her tone biting.

"She's going to the football game."

"Figures."

The ethnic rumble on Thursday made yesterday's carpool quite interesting. I tried to convince Lilly that Madison did not mean offense, and that while it was a loaded term in Lilly's world, in my world the nickname was more ironic. Spring Mills wasn't exactly the Great American Melting Pot. With Vince gone, she and I accounted for the school's entire Hispanic population. She was well aware of my limited exposure to Puerto Rican culture. And since I had never taken my heritage seriously, I couldn't blame Madison and Emily for not treating it that way either.

Lilly, however, felt very differently.

"What up bitches?" Lilly hollered as we got into the car yesterday. (She had watched a "Real World" marathon and had clearly picked up a few things.)

Madison and Emily's heads immediately swung around.

"What, you think you're funny?" Madison barked.

"Don't take offense, hoe. I don't mean anything by it." She smiled.

"Oh, you're so clever." Madison crinkled her nose and squeezed her lips tight.

"What? It's just a word."

I tried to break it up, but they shot spiky comebacks at each other the rest of the day. Emily sat silently on the sidelines, acting like the entire dispute had nothing to do with her, when she was just as guilty as Madison of tossing around the insult. I wasn't sure if she was playing innocent or just not paying attention. Half the times I saw her lately, she seemed to have only one ear in the conversation while her mind was somewhere else.

"Now, do you girls know the story behind *Firebird*?" Mrs. Fox asked, jolting me back to the present.

"Oh, um, I think so," I answered. "It's a Russian fable about good versus evil, love conquering all. The usual. Except there's also a magic bird."

"Oh, okay. Well, that sums it up." Her father chuckled.

"Yeah, it's pretty standard. Bird dances, people turn into stone, they all come back to life at the end. Yadda yadda."

"You can see Mariana has a bright future as a dance critic," Madison quipped.

"Well, we all need something to fall back on."

We both giggled. It was the first time things had felt normal between us in days.

We pulled up to the Academy. From the outside, the building looked more like a Quaker Meeting House than a theater worthy of ballets, operas, and musicals. It was old and historic, constructed with brick walls so thick that even with the multiple lanes of traffic on Broad and Locust streets, not the slightest hint of street noise squeaked inside.

We hustled into the horseshoe-shaped theater trimmed with gold and red accents. A poetic mural covered the ceiling. The room was accented by Greek columns and a massive crystal chandelier. I nestled into my seat between Madison and her dad and tore open my package of Junior Mints. There was something about the theater that sparked a mint-chocolate craving in me. I never ate a Junior Mint outside of a cultural performance.

"So how long is this thing?" Madison's dad mumbled to her mom as I popped a mint into my mouth.

I knew he wasn't much of a ballet fan. I doubted he'd ever been to a performance aside from our recitals. It was nice of him to go out of his way to score the tickets. My dad would rather eat shards of shattered lightbulbs than sit through a ballet—my recitals included. He slept through half my solos. (Vince always relayed the exact time allotted before Dad started snoring.)

Vince's ball games were a different story. He'd travel to the ends of the earth to watch my brother play second base, and he was heartbroken when I refused to take up softball. My mother, however, was secretly thrilled. She bought my first pair of ballet slippers when I was three years old, certain I'd fulfill the dance fantasies she had never realized. (There was limited time for expensive extracurriculars while growing up in the projects.) I was her little ballerina.

"When does the curtain go up?" I whispered to Madison.

She glanced at her diamond-studded watch.

"Not for another fifteen minutes."

I stood up and stretched my legs. My last ballet practice left every muscle in my body sore. I rubbed the back of my neck as I stared into the balcony; almost every seat was filled. There was an elementary school class in the upper rows, tossing candy at one another, while a lonely adult flailed his arms wildly. I smiled and started to turn back around when my eyes clapped on a familiar face. My hand shot to my mouth as a snicker escaped my lips.

"Oh. My. God." I mumbled through my palm, swatting at Madison with my other hand.

"What?"

"You are not going to believe who's here."

Madison immediately shot to her feet. "Who? Where?"

I couldn't stop from grinning as my eyes locked on my target. He slowly raised his hand to his brow as if to conceal his identity, but it was way too late for that.

"Over there," I pointed, freeing my hand from my lips.

Emily was now out of her seat beside us. "What? Who are we looking at?"

"Evan Casey."

They followed my pointing finger until they spotted Evan and his white-haired grandmother seated about ten rows back.

"Omigod!" Madison chirped. "This is classic!"

"Guess he's not so tough now," I muttered.

Eventually he dropped his hand and raised his lip in a crooked sneer. It was a good attempt to cover his embarrassment; too bad his face was a brighter shade of red than the seat he was planted in.

The first act was amazing. Every time I attended a ballet, I itched to start practicing. I knew I'd never have a career as a professional dancer, but I thought it was amazing that there were people who did. They were paid to dance every day, while my father had to sit at a computer. I swore I would never sit behind a desk for a living. I didn't know what I wanted to do with my life, but I knew I couldn't possibly do that—especially when there were women who got to put on their ballet shoes for a paycheck.

"Why can't Madame Colbert put together choreography like that?" Emily asked, as she walked down our aisle toward the women's bathroom.

It was intermission.

"Because if she could, then she wouldn't be *our* instructor," Madison stated.

"Very true," I added. "And it's not like any of us can dance like them. Did you see her jumps?"

"Omigod. She looks like she's doing completely different moves than us," said Emily.

"I don't even want to think about what I look like compared to them," Madison muttered.

We worked our way into the lobby. A pale marble floor sat below dozens of sweeping archways framed with gold-trimmed glass panels. Sparkling chandeliers swung from molded ceilings lighting the timeless corridor. I felt like an adult dressed in my black pencil skirt surrounded by such sophistication.

We strutted toward the bathroom and, no sooner did we see the sign, than we crashed face-to-face with Evan.

"Well, look who it is!" I cheered, staring at Evan who was carrying a plastic cup of ice water. "Is that for your date?"

"Very funny," he snapped, staring off in the opposite direction.

I saw his grandmother in line for the ladies room. The line was about twenty women deep.

"Might as well get comfortable. Your date might be a while." I grinned.

"Evan Casey's a ballet enthusiast. If I had only known! We would have invited you to our performances," Madison glowed.

"Wait, maybe he's a dancer?" I teased.

"Or is this just a kickin' Saturday night for you?" Emily added.

"It could be the men in tights."

"Ah, Evan, is there something you want to tell us?" Madison beamed.

"Oh, shut up!" he cried. "So I'm at the ballet? Big deal."

A rash of pink swept over his face, and we all flooded with laughter.

"You like ballet!" I giggled.

"I do not! I'm here with my nanna."

"Your *nanna*!" Madison squeaked, still laughing.

"Stop it! It's her birthday! It's what she likes to do." His hands were waving frantically as he spoke, and I could barely look at his face, it was so burnt red.

"Okay, okay," I said, calming down with deep breaths. "But your macho act is officially shattered. No more body slams in the hallways."

He flicked his eyes toward me. "Then no more embarrassing stories in front of crowds."

"Well that depends, does this one count?"

My friends and I erupted in giggles once more. Tears filled the corners of my eyes. He pretended to ignore our reaction as he scanned the masses for his "nanna."

"By the way, where's Lilly?" he asked, glancing at the three of us.

Madison immediately stopped smiling.

"She's at the football game," I stated. "Where I thought you'd be."

"Do your friends know you're here?" Emily asked.

"No, and they don't need to," he said in a stern tone.

"Whatever, twinkle toes. Your secret's safe with me." I shrugged.

Just then, his creased-faced grandmother with salon-curled

hair waddled over. Her black dress looked older than I did, and her stockings were bunched around her ankles and tucked into dark orthopedic shoes. She touched the strand of pearls around her neck as she approached. Her nails were painted pink.

"Evan, are these young ladies friends of yours?" she asked, examining us closely.

I instinctively pulled at the hem of my skirt. It fell past my knees, but from the way she was looking at my bare legs I felt almost naked.

"Um, yeah, I guess. They go to school with me," he grumbled, clutching her arm to assist her balance.

"Oh, lovely. Are you enjoying the ballet?"

"Yes, of course," I replied. "We're all dancers."

"What?" she yelled, leaning her head toward us.

"We all dance ballet," I enunciated in my loudest speaking voice.

"Oh, wonderful! Evan used to dance! You should have seen him as a boy. So handsome in his tights. He had real promise."

She grinned with such pride that it took every ounce of willpower I had not to explode with giggles in her wrinkled face. I held my breath and chewed on both my lips to keep from smiling. Madison was not so restrained and immediately smacked her palm to her mouth and darted toward the ladies room. Emily was right behind her.

"Did I say something?" his grandmother asked, glancing at Evan.

His eyes were closed. No doubt he was trying to erase the last two minutes from his life. I could almost see him mouthing the prayer. He placed his fingers to his forehead, hung his head, and breathed slowly. I took it as my cue to leave.

"Um, I'll see you at school, Evan," I choked, before stumbling off and snorting.

I saw Madison and Emily holding my place in the restroom line. Tears were streaming down their faces as they bent over shivering. People might have thought they were writhing in pain if they didn't know them better. Only I did.

Chapter 16

I sat next to Madison on the ride home. I had figured that Emily would fight her way into the middle seat, only she immediately climbed in the back without a fuss.

Mr. Fox said he'd take us for ice cream on Main Street when we got back to Spring Mills. A new place had opened with a singing wait staff. I hadn't been there yet. It debuted while I was in Puerto Rico.

"So, Mariana, you can blend anything together. Oatmeal, Oreos, M&Ms, the works," Mrs. Fox explained.

"It's awesome," Madison added. "It's actually where Emily went with Bobby after the movie. Right, Em?"

I turned around, and Emily smiled faintly. She said nothing, so I didn't press it further.

"You girls wanna spend the night?" Mrs. Fox asked as we drove out of Philadelphia.

"Yeah, you should," Madison cheered.

I hadn't slept at Madison's since I got back from vacation. I used to spend half my weekends there, only lately the air seemed too tense for an all-nighter. Now, I finally felt like I was home.

I exhaled slowly, my stomach softening. "I'd like that. Lemme call my parents."

I dug into my leather bag for my cell phone. I had turned it off during the show. It was a cardinal sin to disturb a ballet performance. It was like screaming at a golfer right as he swung.

"Hey, we can finalize your birthday plans," Madison stated. "Maybe we should invite Evan now."

"Yeah, we know he can dance," I joked, glancing back at Emily. She was quietly gazing out the car window as the headlights zoomed past. I touched her arm.

"Oh, what?" Emily asked, startled.

"We were talking about Evan."

"Oh, that was hilarious," she said softly, her eyes bleached as her lids hung low.

I glanced at my phone. It powered up and let out a quick succession of beeps signifying messages.

The first was a text message from Vince:

> **Rush week is insane. Frat hangs with the hottest chicks! Downed 21 shots for bro's b-day. Luv college! LOL! L8R**

I shook my head at the screen, smiling. At least he was consistent.

Next, I dialed my voice mail.

> *"Uh, hola, Mariana. It's me, Lilly. Um, I'm at home, and you might want to get here soon. Something unexpected's happened. We have a visitor. Well, uh, Teresa's here. She flew in this evening . . . [deep breath] So yeah, get home. Soon. Hasta luego."*

I snapped my phone shut and stared at the back of the passenger seat.

"What? What happened?" Madison asked.

I looked toward her, then toward her father.

"Um, Mr. Fox, can you take me home?"

"You're not coming for ice cream?"

"I can't." I coughed nervously. "My family's in town."

We pulled into my driveway moments later. I could feel the

heightened energy as soon as I stepped from the car. It was like the entire area around my house vibrated with unknown mayhem. My shoulders pushed high, and my fingers constricted.

Madison and Emily took the news surprisingly well. Teresa was a subject they dared not touch. I was thankful they had known my family before it became a soap opera, otherwise I might have found the entire situation rather humiliating. At least I didn't have to explain myself to them, not about this anyway.

I opened the heavy red door to our freshly painted house. I could hear everyone congregated in the kitchen, and the scent of pizza swept through the air. As soon as I stepped inside, Lilly appeared in the doorway. She rushed toward me, grabbed my arm and dragged me into the living room.

"She was here when I got back from the football game," she hastily whispered.

"Did my parents know she was coming?"

"No. Apparently, this Carlos guy she's dating works for an airline and got her a last-minute ticket for, like, nothing."

"Well, why isn't she with him?"

"He's working tonight. He actually called your father and asked him to pick Teresa up at the airport."

"What? When?"

"Like an hour before her plane landed. They got here not long before I did."

"My dad must be freaking out."

"I don't know. Sort of. Your mom ordered pizza, and everyone's acting like it's totally normal."

"Welcome to my world."

I walked into the kitchen and instantly froze at the sight of Teresa. She was settled into a stool at the island, holding a slice of pepperoni, her dark auburn hair swept up on the sides. I didn't know why the sight of her shocked me so much. I knew what she looked like. I had spent time with her in Utuado. But something about seeing her in my house, in my kitchen, in my reality, stopped me in my tracks.

"*Hola*," she stated, with a tiny dimpled smile.

"Hi."

We moved onto the patio. It was a cool night, and Teresa, Lilly, and I were cuddled in sweatshirts and blankets while Tootsie sniffed Teresa's feet. (It was like he was trying to determine where the infidel came from.) My mom was in the kitchen brewing a vat of iced tea while my father whispered on the telephone behind closed doors. I figured that he was talking to my uncles, and I doubted that they would be happy to hear about our visitor.

While I knew Teresa was coming, I had assumed it was primarily to be with her new boyfriend. If Carlos didn't live in New Jersey, then there would have been no reason for her to leave Utuado. But the way she had sat in my kitchen, hanging on my father's every word, sent a strange vibe sizzling through my body. Something in her eyes expressed more than a simple "thank you for picking me up at the airport." It almost seemed as if she were waiting for a smile, a laugh, a touch, something to prove that she belonged.

"So where's Manny?" I asked.

Clearly her two-year-old terror was not in the country, or I was certain I would have heard his screeching all the way from the soundproof Academy.

"He's with my *mamá*. I wanted to have some time with Carlos before I brought Manny into it."

Lilly and I looked at each other. Just the mention of Teresa's mother, my grandfather's mistress, caused a softball to form in my throat. She was the evil woman who ruined my grandmother's life, not some nice lady's mom.

"So, tell us about this Carlos guy," Lilly suggested, rapidly switching topics.

"Well, we met online about a year ago. He lives in Williamstown. . . ."

"That's right across the bridge," I pointed out.

"So I hear. He works at the Philadelphia Airport."

"Did you see him when you came in?" Lilly asked.

"No, he handles baggage and couldn't get away. We thought he'd be able to; that's why we didn't call your father until the last minute. I actually thought Carlos was picking me up." Teresa looked at me with an embarrassed smile. "I'm sorry I didn't give your family more notice. It was all very rushed."

"Don't sweat it. Even if you did, my parents probably still wouldn't have told me 'til today." I chuckled.

"Well, your father's been very nice."

"Hey, he let me move here," Lilly added. "I think he's starting a whole Utuado migration."

"Yeah, well, try growing up with him."

Teresa peered at me curiously, her head sloped to the side.

"What? You don't know him," I stated. "Trust me, he gives new meaning to the word 'stubborn.' "

"Stubborn? Gee, I wonder who that sounds like?" Lilly moaned.

"What?"

"Do you even remember yourself in Puerto Rico? You didn't speak to me for two weeks."

"It was a misunderstanding."

"That you let go on forever because you're so freakin' stubborn."

"I am not."

"Then why did you give me the silent treatment?"

"Because you were rude."

"No, you were stubborn."

"I am not!"

"You wanna prove my point further?"

I snatched the lemon wedge out of my glass and chucked it at her. It smashed onto her shoulder, leaving a wet mark.

"Oh, you wanna go there? I'll go there." Lilly dug her fingers into her drink for an ice chip and took aim.

"*¡Chiquitas!*" Teresa yelled, rising to her feet. "*¡Para!*"

Tootsie barked on cue as Teresa stretched her arms wide. Lilly and I slowly placed our glasses back on the patio table and glared at each other.

"*I'm not stubborn,*" I mouthed.

She laughed and shook her head.

"So, tell me about your birthday party," Teresa stated calmly, her dimples showing.

I could tell that she liked spending time with us—her pale brown eyes smiled in a way that they hadn't in Puerto Rico. I couldn't imagine growing up without any siblings, with just my mom for company. In addition to her driving me absolutely bonkers, I'd probably spend my life with the constant realization that everyone else got to experience a sense of family that was denied to me. For as much as I complained about my crazy relatives, I wouldn't trade them for anything.

"Well, the big day's in two weeks," I stated.

"Is your family coming?" she asked in a soft voice, her hope squeaking through.

"You betcha," I groaned, staring at her sideways.

"I know your uncles have a problem with me."

"They don't know you," Lilly stated.

"No, I understand. *Esta bien.*" Teresa nodded, her shoulders slightly hunched. "Your brother, Vince, is he coming?"

"No, he's at college. It's his fraternity's rush week."

She squinted, her forehead creased with confusion.

"Trust me, you don't want to know," I mumbled. "It's just a bunch of beer and puking."

"So, are you officially inviting Betsy and them?" Lilly asked, perking up.

"Well, I don't want to, but I feel like I have to because they already know."

"So, what's the harm?"

"I don't like them."

"You don't like anyone."

"Not true."

"Okay, Miss Stubborn."

"Shut! Up!" I shouted, my eyes wide. Tootsie immediately jumped on all fours, barking to defend me.

"*Chicas* . . ." Teresa warned in a deep tone, holding up her palms.

"By the way, Lil, I almost forgot to tell you. Your precious boy Evan is a ballet freak." I curled my lips.

"What?"

"He was at *Firebird*. With his grandma."

"That's kinda cute," she whispered, grinning.

"Oh, don't tell me . . ."

"What?"

"The guy's a jerk."

"You don't even know him."

"I know he bad mouths my friends and rams into me in the hallways."

"So? You bad mouth his friends. . . ."

"Lilly!" My mouth dropped open.

"Relax. He's just a friend."

Teresa's brown eyes flicked between Lilly and me like a ping-pong match.

"Did you girls really just meet this summer?" she asked, inquisitively touching her chin with her index finger.

"Yeah."

"Why?" I asked.

"Nothing." She laughed.

I grabbed my iced tea and took another sip. Lilly and Teresa did the same.

Chapter 17

When Carlos picked up my *tia* later that night, she didn't invite him in for an introduction. She just rushed out of the house apologetically, almost as if she was worried about disrupting my family's evening any further. My parents quickly retired to their master suite without a word to Lilly or me, and they didn't mention her sudden visit for the duration of the weekend. The only thing discussed was my birthday, which also seemed to be the topic on the minds of the entire tenth grade population at Spring Mills High School. Because by the time I got to school on Monday, everyone knew about my upcoming party.

Apparently the e-vite I had sent to fifty classmates last night was forwarded to another two hundred by morning. Since they all received the e-vite, they all assumed they were invited regardless of the fact that it hadn't been sent by me. (Note to self: send only paper invitations in the future—harder to forward.)

I stood in the cafeteria line waiting for my wonton soup and debating how I should tell my mother to quadruple the catering order. Or was it still possible to uninvite the not invited? I could send a follow up e-vite officially denouncing their prior invitation. There had to be an e-card somewhere with *"You're Not Invited"* written in elegant cursive script and a succinct rhyming message to follow:

You got the card
But it wasn't for you
Don't come to my party
I did not invite you.

I was mulling over the wording as I stared at the vat of broth and dumplings glowing with the greenish tinge of the overhead lights. It was odd that I was willing to eat food in a school cafeteria that I would reject anywhere else on Earth. I snubbed my nose at half the meals my mom made from scratch, yet here I was about to slurp down artificially colored, sodium-laced chemical substitutes.

"Hey, Mariana, can you move it along?" Chad griped from the back of the line.

A gap had formed ahead of me.

"Sure, Chad. Thanks for monitoring the line for the rest of us." I glanced back to see if Evan was with him. He wasn't.

"Can't wait for your party next weekend."

My stomach tensed. The kid openly didn't like me, yet he planned to attend my Sweet Sixteen. Maybe if the Main Line offered more locations for teens to congregate, we wouldn't have to crash each other's parties.

I handed the cashier my money and carried my tray back to my table.

"Hey," I muttered as I plopped down.

Emily was already halfway through her yogurt, and Madison was munching on a celery stick. She had heard that raw vegetables didn't account for many calories. So she was now on a raw diet. (Like she needed to lose weight. If she shrunk down more, she'd be shopping in the children's department.)

"So everyone knows about my party," I whined, nodding at Chad.

"Yeah, the whole grade's talking about it," said Emily.

"Since when does 'everyone' know who I am?"

"Since you brought back a cousin who's the next Miss Spring Mills."

Madison rolled her eyes. "And since you decided to throw a party. You know people don't have anything else to do in this town."

"I can't believe Betsy's whole crew is coming," I griped. "And you know what's worse? I think Lilly has a thing for Evan."

"Oh, God, no!" Madison shrieked, slapping the table. "He's disgusting."

"Don't get me started."

I drummed my nails on the weathered wood and glanced around the cafeteria. Dozens of tables formed neat rows through the window-lined hall. It was the tenth grade lunch and of the more than 250 kids crammed into the massive room, I had only spoken to about half. And most of those conversations had taken place in grade school. The rest of the kids I merely passed in the halls or saw on the athletic fields. They were names and faces about as familiar to me as most celebrity couples.

"So how'd the Teresa meet and greet go?" Madison asked.

"Fine, I guess. She's seems normal enough. But I'm worried about my Uncle Diego. The last thing I need is a big showdown at my birthday party."

"Well, people will know you a lot better after that." Madison half-chuckled as she peered around the lunchroom.

"Gee, thanks."

"Mariana, there isn't a single kid in here without family drama," Emily reasoned as she gazed into her empty yogurt cup.

"You don't have family drama."

"Yeah, that's what everyone thinks. Until it falls apart," she whispered.

Madison and I nodded.

I could feel the goggles burning impressions into my cheeks and forehead. There was nothing worse than strolling the hallways after chemistry with red science-geek goggle lines. I pulled on the plastic protective eyewear hoping to give my skin time to breathe.

"Mariana, you know the rules about goggles. Keep them on at all times," Mr. Berk warned.

The man had nothing better to do than stand in front of the class waiting to pounce on any student who dared alleviate the goggle pressure. If the school board really wanted us to wear them, then they should get us more comfortable goggles. Or Mr. Berk should be forced to wear them as well.

"This lab is taking forever," Bobby whispered.

"A watched crucible never evaporates," I warned.

We were in the midst of a hydrate lab and tasked with finding the empirical formula of five grams of magnesium sulfate hydrate using any laboratory procedure available. Currently, Bobby and I were heating the hydrate in the porcelain "crucible" as Mr. Berk called it, or the "jar" as we called it. We had the lid slightly off hoping to burn off excess moisture. It was a classic tip I'd learned in my mother's kitchen. If you don't tightly cover the pot while heating pasta sauce, it dries up and gets crusty around the edges. Apparently, the rest of the class had gotten the same lesson from their mothers because they were all using the same technique.

"So your party's in two weeks. I think I can make it," Bobby grumbled, a pencil in his mouth.

He tugged on his goggles, which were uncomfortably placed over his black plastic glasses. If I found our eyewear uncomfortable, I couldn't imagine how he felt.

"You and the rest of the student body."

"Did you invite a lot of people?"

"No, but that doesn't seem to be stopping them from coming."

Bobby took his pencil from his lips and tapped it on the table. It was the first time he stopped chewing it all period.

"What's with you?"

"Nothing," he said abruptly, shifting the pencil's metal tip back into his mouth. "It's just, I mean, I was kinda, you know . . ."

I snatched the No. 2 from his hand and slapped it on the table. It left a small pool of saliva on the surface.

"Try talking without the lead in your mouth. It might help you form a sentence."

"Oh, sorry." His cheeks fluttered with pink.

"Why are you being so weird?"

I had never seen Bobby blush before. He actually had one of the quickest wits of anyone I knew.

"It's nothing. It's just, I'm having a screening of my documentary this weekend," he blurted out. "The one I made in Dublin. I just finished editing it. . . ."

"No way." I smiled, grabbing the crucible tongs and checking our experiment.

"And I was wondering, if maybe . . . you'd like to come."

"To see your film? Totally! When is it?"

"Saturday night. At my house."

"Sweet, who else is gonna be there? Because I don't think Madison or Emily have plans. I wonder what Lilly's doing. . . ."

"Oh," he interrupted, tugging at his curls. "Okay."

I peered over and put down the tongs.

"Oh, my God. I'm sorry. I thought it was a group thing. I'm so rude. Here I am complaining about people crashing my party and I go and invite a bunch of randoms to your film—"

"No, no. It's cool. I mean, they can come. If they want."

He stared at his worksheet.

"They don't have to. If you've already got too many people . . ."

"No, not at all. The more the merrier, or whatever."

"I'm sure they'd love to see it. You made a movie!" I cheered, punching him in his shoulder.

Only, apparently, I caught him off guard. His lanky frame wobbled on his lab stool, lifting two of the chair's legs off the ground and tilting his body backwards. His feet swung up and, before I could stop it, his whole body crashed on the floor, his arms swinging desperately in the process.

I knew I shouldn't laugh, but I couldn't help it. An involuntary burst of giggles shot out of me igniting the rest of the class. Mr. Berk darted over, but Bobby waved him off and slowly stood up. His cherry red face glowed as he took a mortified bow. The class clapped and cheered.

"That was graceful," he mumbled, before breaking into chuckles himself.

Chapter 18

Thursday marked Lilly's tennis debut. She had been practicing with the team for only a few weeks, but the coach thought it was time to throw her onto the court and see how she handled the competition. She was justifiably nervous. She had joined the team purely for social reasons, and I didn't think she had thoroughly considered what would happen when she was asked to play a match that would affect the team's record.

She begged me to come, and I in turn begged Madison and Emily, which was not an easy sell.

"She has a cheering section larger than the Philadelphia Eagles!" Madison pointed out huffily. "Why the heck does she need us?"

"Because she's my cousin, and my mom will kill me if I don't go. Plus, those boys aren't her friends. . . ."

"And *we* are?" Madison grunted.

I shot her a look.

Eventually, she and Emily caved, and we plopped ourselves onto the rickety wooden bleachers. The JV squad competed on the practice courts, which were boxed in with a metal chain-link fence to protect spectators. On the opposite side of the weathered stands sat Lilly's fan club—a half-dozen pimple-faced boys shaking homemade "Go, Lilly!" posters and waving Puerto Rican flags. It seemed more humiliating than flattering.

"When the heck is your cousin gonna play?" Madison whined, taking the last sip from her water bottle. The water had lost its chill long ago.

"I think she's up next."

Lilly was the final seed on the JV doubles lineup, which meant her match was dead last. Almost two hours of boring matches, and it looked like she and her partner, Juliet, were finally beginning to warm up. Juliet Downy, a freshman like Lilly, was about thirty pounds overweight and about as coordinated as an elephant. Since I'd been watching, she'd already knocked over a teammate's water cup, dropped the entire contents of her sport bag, and tripped into her own coach while she was arguing with a referee. The lovely, raven-haired, forty-year-old woman gracefully brushed off Juliet's clumsiness and continued her rant. I could tell she was used to the ineptitude.

I watched as Lilly bounced a ball on the court. Her reddish-brown hair was tied in a high ponytail; she wore a white terry sweatband around her forehead (a gift from Betsy), two more sweatbands on her wrists, and the adorable team uniform with a white collared shirt that clung to her breasts (even with a sports bra) and a tiny white skirt. She might not be the greatest tennis star, but she definitely looked the part.

"Oh, hey, she's up!" Emily hollered.

"Go, Lilly!" I shrieked, jumping to my feet.

"Yay!" Madison yelled.

I looked down to smile at my friends and caught a glimpse of Evan Casey standing just behind the bleachers. He was hovering in the shadows, his face blocked by the top row of seats. When I followed his gaze, his eyes were focused on my cousin, who was bopping on her toes with her back to the crowd. I gestured to Madison and Emily, who immediately turned around.

"Looks like Lilly's got another cheerleader," I whispered.

Madison rolled her eyes.

Lilly then clutched the ball for her serve. She was playing in the court right before us and was close enough to hear our conversation. Her fan club was off to the side. We all fell silent. She lifted her arm high and turned her face to spot the ball. Sun dripped into her hair as she tossed the ball high and swung ferociously. A whiz of green fuzz flashed toward the opposing team, soaring about three feet over their heads until it crashed onto the far back fence about a foot shy of clearing it. (If this were baseball, it would have been a homerun.)

"It's all right, Lil!" I screamed, clapping my hands. "You got another serve. Just get it on the court. You can do it!"

"Go, Lilly!" Emily cheered.

"You got it! You got it!" Madison clapped, rising to her feet.

Lilly twisted her neck to peek at us, then glanced at her fan club boys who were whirling around wildly calling her name.

She bounced the ball onto the court several times to regain her focus. Juliet turned to look at her.

"Come on, Lilly," she cheered, tapping her racquet with her free hand.

Once more, Lilly held the ball up high, tossed it into the air and swung with all her might. This time it beelined, with the speed of a major league pitcher, straight toward the referee. He swiftly lunged to the side, instinctively raising his hand to protect his head. She didn't hit him.

"*Mierda*," she cursed, shaking her head. "*Estupida.*"

Three boys seated in the row in front of us, decked out in red and black T-shirts to support the opposing team, suddenly turned to each other.

"Well, that explains a lot," the dark-haired teen mumbled.

His buddies smiled and grunted.

I glared down, squinted my eyes before glancing to Madison and Emily, but they didn't seem to notice the interaction. They were focused on the court. Lilly's deadly serves continued the entire game. Not one made it on the court.

Finally, the serve switched. A petite blond from the other side of the net tapped the ball gently, serving it into the correct box and sending it straight toward Lilly's partner. Juliet hustled over and swung awkwardly, barely clearing the net. The waiting opponent quickly made contact, volleying the ball back toward Lilly. I held my breath and crossed my fingers as her fans yelped and shouted, their Puerto Rican flags waving. Lilly smashed the ball with a massive follow-through, sailing it straight toward her opponent's head. The ninety-pound brunette flung up her racquet to protect her face but the force of the impact caused her racquet to shoot backwards, crashing into her nose. The ball ricocheted out of bounds, giving Lilly the point.

"I'm okay. I'm okay," the opponent whimpered, her eyes filled with tears.

"I'm so sorry," Lilly shouted.

The girl waved her off, blood dripping from her nostril.

"Did you hear the accent on that one?" the dark-haired teen in front of me hissed to his friend.

"Yup, dirty spic."

"I wonder when her raft came in."

The words hit me with abrupt force. My lungs froze as my body tensed. Out of the corner of my eye I saw Emily's face swing toward mine. Madison rested her hand on my arm.

"Mariana, why don't you sit down," she whispered, yanking me toward her.

Blood flushed from my brain as I plopped onto the bleacher.

"Did you hear what they said," I grumbled.

The blond-haired guy in front of us cocked his head slightly. He was obviously listening.

"Mariana, just drop it. Let's watch Lilly," Emily suggested quietly.

I glared at the backs of the guys' heads. They were white, clean-cut teens in khakis and jeans with brand-name sneakers. If it weren't for the opposing team's T-shirts, I could have mistaken them for students from my own school. They didn't look any different.

The blond guy twisted his cleanly shaven neck further and caught my eye.

"You know they shouldn't let people on the court who don't know how to play," he said loudly.

"Yeah, well, I don't think *those people* know how to do much of anything, except mow our lawns," his friend responded.

I jumped to my feet.

"Shut the hell up!" I shouted.

"What did you say?" the blond barked, rising to his feet.

"You heard me. Why don't you get out of here? No one wants to hear your crap."

"Says who? *You?*"

His friend stood up beside him. He had to be at least six feet tall.

Madison and Emily quickly popped to their feet, standing firm at my side while the fan club swarmed in.

"Says *us*! You can't insult the redheaded goddess!" a tiny pimple-faced boy shouted. He was holding a small Puerto Rican flag in Lilly's honor.

"Back off evildoer. You are not worthy of our Lilly!" a scrawny, five-foot boy added in a squeaky voice, a "Go Lilly" sign clutched between his fingers.

"Are you freakin' kidding me?" the jerk from the opposing school chuckled, scanning the guys up and down.

"Hey, clearly nobody wants you here." I cocked my head toward him. "Why don't you go back to where you came from and leave my cousin alone."

"Your cousin's the spic?" the blond grunted with a snotty grin.

"What gene pool did she fall out of?" his friend said nastily.

"*My* gene pool."

"You're not *Hispanic*." The guy laughed scornfully, like he thought I was kidding.

"Yes I am."

"No. You're not. I know a spic when I see one."

"You say that one more time . . ." Pinpricks of anger lifted the hair on my arms. My hands balled into fists. Madison gripped my shoulders as if she needed to hold me back—the guys were twice my body weight. I might be loud, but I wasn't stupid.

"Back off buddy, right now!" Evan shouted, charging over.

He puffed his well-toned, championship wrestler chest at them and thrust his face forward.

"I think it's time for you to go," Evan whispered with authority.

"Who the hell are you?"

"I'm the guy who's gonna kick your ass if you don't get out of here."

Evan was so close to the blond that I could see the spit from his mouth splash onto the guy's cheek.

"Whatever," the kid muttered, taking a step back. "This school sucks."

"Let's get out of here. We don't need this crap," his friend added.

The three guys grabbed their backpacks from the ground and turned toward the parking lot. They left without saying another word.

"Holy shit," Madison muttered, staring at Evan.

He locked eyes with me, then he turned toward Lilly, who was standing on the opposite side of the fence staring at us. Apparently the match had halted after her opponent took a racquet to the nose. Lilly had heard every word.

"Hey." She gazed at Evan.

"Hey."

Her face lit up with a luscious look before she briefly glanced at me. My heart was still thumping rapidly and, before I could say a word, the referee blew the whistle to restart the match. Lilly turned her focus back to the game.

Evan sat down next to us.

Chapter 19

The next night, my parents had planned a family dinner. It wasn't just for the immediate family to sit around the table and discuss our day over roasted chicken; no, my mother invited my two uncles and my new *tia* Teresa.

She said that since Teresa was moving to the States, the proper thing to do was to officially welcome her to the family. My father didn't comment on the affair, but I knew that if he wasn't supportive of the idea, then the dinner wouldn't happen. This meant that on some level he must want to get to know his half sister—which is partially why he sent Vince and me off to Puerto Rico. He wanted to reclaim his roots, and it seemed like those roots were following him across the ocean.

I was currently hiding in my room with Lilly and Tootsie, absorbing a few moments of peace before the guests arrived. It had been more than twenty-four hours since her tennis match, but the inevitable loss didn't faze her in the slightest. All she could talk about was Evan.

"It's just the way he stood up for me..." she stated, her brown eyes dreamy.

"*He* stood up for you? Don't forget the skinny redhead who got in their faces first," I snipped as I dug through my closet for a cardigan.

"Oh, yeah. Sorry. But I already said thank you to you."

"Still. I thought I was pretty hard-core."

"Yes, you were very scary."

"Those guys were shaking."

"Absolutely petrified."

Lilly smiled as she swept on another coat of nude lipstick—a gift from Madison's Suburban Square makeover. Ever since the shopping excursion, Lilly's look had gone from thick and cakey to sheer and nude. It was a definite improvement that shined all the way to her added boost in confidence. She didn't even wear her miniskirts anymore. She said it was no longer "the look she was going for."

I pulled my black sweater over my tan short-sleeved top and checked my reflection in the mirror. Tootsie barked his approval as I smiled.

"You know, I defended your honor," I said as I smoothed my black wide-leg pants.

"Well, you also defended *your* honor. . . ."

"It was weird. It was the first time I was ever offended *not* to be considered Puerto Rican."

"Ah, my little girl is growing up," Lilly cooed.

"Shut up," I said, tossing a pillow at her as I plopped on the bed. "You don't want to mess with me. I'm tough."

"Oh, yes. I'm sure given the choice between you and Evan, those dicks would much rather have fought Evan," Lilly mocked.

"So you like him?" I asked, an eyebrow raised.

Lilly smiled. "Betsy says he's a good guy. . . ."

"Ah, the magnificent Betsy. I still can't believe you're friends with her."

"Why? She's nice!"

"She is; she's just 'Betsy Sumner.' She kinda rolls in a stratosphere more fitting for Lindsay Lohan than the lowly ole Ruíz clan." I smirked.

"Well, I'm not a Ruíz."

"No, but you are a girl who'd never stepped foot outside of Puerto Rico before a few weeks ago. I mean, how are you dealing with all this? I know I forget to ask sometimes because every-thing just seems so easy for you. . . ."

" 'Cause I have *you*." She grinned, nudging my arm.

"Trust me, I have nothing to do with your celebrity status."

"Oh, please!" She rolled her eyes as she sat at my desk and fastened my new black sandals onto her feet. She swore she had nothing to go with the black dress she was also borrowing from my closet. "Seriously though, I like it here. A lot. It's different, but it's fun. It's like a never-ending vacation."

"Don't you miss your parents?"

"Eh, a bit. But you guys have supplied enough family drama to keep me occupied."

"You got that right," I moaned. "I swear we're *this close* to get-ting our own reality show. 'Coming up next week, find out if Uncle Diego busts a coronary over his long-lost sister, da-da-da-daaaaaa . . . .' " I joked in my best newscaster voice.

Just then I heard the front door swing open and a heavy set of footsteps strut into the foyer. I glanced at Lilly.

"It's like they heard me," I teased.

The dining room was staged as if we were having a Thanks-giving feast. All of my birthday planning paraphernalia had been cleared out: the brightly colored tablecloths, the linen napkins, the votive candles, the place cards, and the magazine cutouts of floral centerpieces. In its place was the good wedding china and the crystal glasses imported from Prague. Five low arrangements of burnt orange roses and calla lilies filled the expanded dining table, and the buffet was covered with dozens of stainless steel serving platters, all simmering above blue flames.

I sat between Teresa and Lilly. My uncles Diego and Roberto were across from us, joined by my aunts. They had left their kids at home. Too bad I wasn't as lucky.

"These potatoes are fabulous, Irina," my Aunt Stacey noted as she bit into a tiny roasted wedge.

"Thank you. I got it out of a new cookbook. Remind me to show it to you before you leave."

"Yes, please do so." My aunt fiddled with the other four potato fragments on her plate. They matched her tiny slice of chicken. "Mmm, good."

The room fell silent again. I could hear the buzz of the chandelier light bulbs overhead. I scooped a forkful of chicken and gravy into my mouth. Lilly was glaring at her plate refusing to look up. I think she was trying to zone out the uncomfortable tension that gripped us all.

"So Mariana, I heard you went to the ballet," my Aunt Joan commented, trying to keep the dull conversation going.

"Uh, huh," I mumbled. "We saw *Firebird*."

"Now, I don't think I've ever seen that. Is it new?"

"It's from the early 1900s."

"Oh, I see. I'm sure *you've* never danced it, right?"

"No," I said, tightly clutching my fork to prepare for her next statement. I already knew what was coming.

"You know my David plays *all* the classics. You should have heard how his conductor went on and on about him."

My Aunt Joan never made it through a visit without praising the modeling escapades of her thirteen-year-old daughter Jackie or the saxophone accomplishments of her fifteen-year-old son David. She thrust them into the limelight every chance she got, but God forbid her niece or nephew scored some attention. If I got straight A's, it was because I wasn't in private school; if I won the lead in a ballet recital, it was because there wasn't much competition. The worst was when Vince got into Cornell. She made sure everyone knew it was "just because of his athletics." There was a brief moment during Easter dinner last year when I thought my mother might actually slug her.

"So, Mariana," my Aunt Stacey interjected. "Your sixteenth birthday's next week. Are you excited for your party? I know we're looking forward to it."

"Uh, yeah. It should be fun." I smiled politely, stabbing a piece of meat as I clenched my teeth.

This dinner was turning into a slow torture. No one wanted to speak to Teresa, so instead my aunts flooded me with benign questions to maintain the appearance that we all got along. I wished I was old enough to drink. At least then I could drown out the monotony that was my family.

"You have a lot of friends coming?" my aunt asked as she cut her tiny slice of chicken into even tinier morsels.

"Yeah, I guess," I replied, staring at her miniature portions of food. "You want some gravy?"

"Uh, no, no." She shook her head.

From what I'd heard, my Aunt Stacey had stopped eating after she gave birth to her only child, my cousin Claire. Apparently, my Uncle Roberto wanted more kids, but my aunt could never get pregnant again. (My mom said it was because she couldn't eat enough to nourish herself let alone another person.) So every time I saw her, I watched her waste away further. No one asked her about it, nor commented on the issue to my uncle. But I knew they thought the same thing from the not-so-subtle glances they shot at her plate. The worst was when she sneezed; I half expected her to break a bone.

My mom dropped her fork and glared at my father, who was seated at the opposite end of the long table. They never moved their lips, but I swear they were having an entire conversation telepathically. I was pretty sure I understood the interaction, assuming they were saying something along the lines of "Wow, this is awkward. Why the heck did we force everyone to do this?"

"So, Lilly, I heard you had your first tennis match yesterday," my *tia* Teresa said, speaking for the first time since we sat down to eat.

All eyes flicked toward her. It was like a light finally sparked in the room. I perked up.

"Yeah, I lost though," Lilly stated.

"But you did great," I cheered, nudging her arm.

"I hit a girl in the face." She giggled.

"Well, she should have ducked." I chuckled.

Lilly laughed. No one else found it funny. They just glared at us silently. A clock ticked in the background.

"Mariana almost got into a fight," my cousin blurted out.

"Lilly!" I screeched, my eyes stretched.

She shrugged as if she didn't know what else to say. I could tell the dreary dinner was taking its toll on her too.

"It wasn't a fight," I mumbled.

"You didn't tell us about this," my father said sternly, wiping at his dark mustache with his linen napkin.

"That's because there's nothing to tell."

"These racist jerks were calling me names."

"Lilly!" I kicked her under the table.

"What do you mean 'racist?' " my father asked, his brow furrowed.

My uncles' eyes flew toward us.

"Nothing. These guys just said some stuff and I asked them to stop. That was it."

"They were total *pendejos*," Lilly added.

Everyone chuckled at the curse word, mostly because it was true.

"All these years and nothing has changed." My Uncle Roberto shook his head.

"I can't believe there are still people who think that way," my mother stated.

"They think that way because their parents think that way," my Uncle Diego spat. "There are a lot of bad parents in this world."

He glared at Teresa as he spoke, ice in his eyes.

"Good thing we're all more mature than that," I stately sweetly, staring at him.

Everyone stopped eating, and my uncle sighed so loudly it almost sounded like a shout. I could see my sarcasm wasn't lost on them.

"So, Teresa, tell me about your new house," Lilly jumped in. "Do you like Carlos's place? Is it nice?"

Teresa smiled and took a deep breath.

"Yes, everything's *muy bueno*. Carlos has been very sweet. I can't wait for my son to meet him. I think we'll be very happy here."

"So who's the father?" my Uncle Diego asked with the tact of a homeless person.

Teresa coughed slightly, her hand on her chest.

"Oh, um, a former boyfriend."

"So you guys weren't married?" he grunted.

I glared sharply at my uncle.

"Um, no," she responded meekly.

"I guess the apple doesn't fall far—"

"Diego!" my father interrupted.

"What? It's just an observation. Unless she's ashamed of her child . . ."

"Oh my God!" I snapped. "What's wrong with you?"

"Excuse me!" my uncle hollered, rising to his feet.

While I didn't know Teresa and really had no reason to defend her, I still couldn't stand the blatant hatred sweeping off my uncle. Clearly my father wanted to get to know this woman, and I wanted him to have that opportunity. Only his brother seemed determined to destroy the relationship before it started.

"Little girl, I don't need to answer to you," my uncle hissed.

"No, you don't need to answer to anyone. Do you, Diego?" My father pushed out his chair and stood up. "You always know what's best . . . for everyone."

My father cleared his throat and left the room.

Chapter 20

I sat on the front porch swing with Teresa as she waited for Carlos to pick her up. My aunts and uncles left before dessert. My father's storming off seemed to signify the end of the evening. My Uncle Diego never apologized, and my father never said good-bye to his guests. This was my model of maturity.

"I hope you're not too upset," I stated softly.

"No, it's okay. I kind of expected something like this to happen," Teresa said as we gazed out at my dark suburban street.

"Then why'd you come?"

She shrugged, saying nothing.

A couple of flies hovered around our faux antique porch light as I swayed on the wooden swing. Something about the scene reminded me of my great aunt and great uncle's place in Utuado. I half expected to hear the coquis sing. Teresa said that my cousin Alonzo had moved to San Juan with José not long after we left the island, and that Aunt Carmen and Uncle Miguel were bragging to the entire town about how well my family was doing in the States. I missed them.

"You should know that your father invited me to your birthday *fiesta*," Teresa stated. "But that was before tonight. And now I'm not sure if it's a good idea. . . ."

I didn't know how to respond. Part of me didn't want her to attend. Realistically, my Sweet Sixteen would go a whole lot smoother without her there. (An Uncle Diego death match was not exactly on my list of entertainment.) But if I couldn't muster up the courage to disinvite the two hundred-plus students crashing my party, then I couldn't exactly rescind her invitation.

"You're more than welcome to come. . . ."

"Really?" she asked quickly.

I didn't expect her to be so eager.

"Sure." I nodded, a little taken aback.

"Thanks. I'd really like everyone to meet Carlos." She smiled wide. "And the party sounds like fun."

"Actually, I could care less about it," I admitted.

"Why?"

"Because I didn't want to have a party."

"So, why are you?"

Teresa looked at me without the slightest bit of judgment. Almost as if she were a psychiatrist there to listen. I took a deep breath.

"It was so important to everyone else that I have a Sweet Sixteen. My mom acted like I would be denying myself this great adolescent experience. My friends acted like I would be denying *them* this great party experience. . . ."

"What about Lilly?"

"She really didn't care either way. She's the only one who probably understood," I explained.

Lilly was currently upstairs finishing her algebra homework. And I was glad she wasn't around. It gave me time to vent.

"She didn't want her *Quinceañera* anymore than I want a Sweet Sixteen. But even still, she talked me into having something with this whole Puerto Rican theme. And now it's being blown out of proportion. All these kids are coming who I didn't invite—probably just to be near Lilly. She's been hanging around with these jocks. I mean, I want her to have her own friends and all, but I also don't want to have to hang out with them, you know?"

Teresa nodded calmly as she absorbed my words. Then she took a slow breath.

"Mariana, you know what it's like to be the stranger in a strange place. That's how Lilly feels right now. She might not show it, but I'm sure being here, in your school, scares her."

"Lilly's not scared of anything. She became the most popular girl in Spring Mills within an hour."

"Even still. Even with all those friends, *you're* the one she wants to spend time with. You're the reason she moved here."

Her chocolate eyes fell slightly as she spoke, and a chill ran down my forearm.

Just then, a set of headlights appeared at the end of the dark street. Teresa stood up. It was Carlos. She grabbed her purse and walked toward my driveway.

"Tell your parents I said goodnight," she said, clutching the car door handle.

Carlos smiled and waved at me from inside the vehicle. His gray hair surprised me. He looked older than I expected, maybe in his late forties, with a salt and pepper beard and mustache, and weathered lines around his eyes. I grinned back.

"Teresa, I'm glad you came," I called after her.

She looked into the car at her new boyfriend.

"So am I."

I logged onto my e-mail after Teresa left. There was a message from Vince with three photo attachments. I quickly opened it up.

The first picture showed my Ivy League-educated brother standing in front of a muddy pond, buck naked with one hand in front of his crotch and the other holding a bottle of wine to his mouth as he guzzled. The second image showed him hoisting a beautiful blond girl on his shoulders as they 'chicken fought' another couple on the grounds of an exquisitely maintained vineyard. The third photo showed him on a bus with dozens of guys (who I could only assume were his fraternity brothers) while he puked into a Doritos bag.

I laughed as my hand covered my mouth. It boggled my mind that he wanted me to see this stuff, and it seriously concerned me that these boys represented some of the smartest students in the country. These were our nation's future presidents, CEOs, and lawyers. And with all this technology, I was guessing that these soon-to-be high-powered professionals would one day find themselves hit with a lot of blackmail.

His message read:

Wineries rock! The fraternity I'm rushing took us on this tour of the Seneca Lake Wineries. We finished a case of chardonnay on the bus before we even got to the second vineyard. I was sooo tanked. We had these chicken fights on the lawn and some girl almost broke her nose. She yacked up red merlot and it splashed all over my leg. So me and this dude jumped in the irrigation ditch naked. It was freezing! And I soo sliced up my foot on a rock. The winery totally kicked us out.

But the brothers got me a bottle of wine because of it. I seriously shouldn't have drunk it, 'cause I spewed chunks on the bus all the way back to campus. It was awesome, though. I can't wait 'til I'm initiated!

Later!

—Vince

I smiled as I stared at the screen. After the night I'd had, this was exactly what I needed. It was like he knew.

Chapter 21

The next night we headed over to Bobby's to view his documentary debut. Prior to leaving, I had assumed that Lilly, Madison, Emily, and I would be among dozens of other Spring Mills students supporting his Dublin masterpiece. Only we were now seated on the couch in his basement in between his Grandma Abigail and his Uncle Lester. There was a gathering of other aunts, uncles, and cousins plopped around us on the floor and only two other students from our high school—photography club presidents Wyatt Benson and Jackson Dilks.

Madison hadn't stopped digging her nails into my arm since we had arrived, and Emily just looked embarrassed to be included. Her face fell when I told her that Bobby had invited me to the screening, even when I insisted that he had extended the invitation to all of us. I almost had to drag her through his front door earlier, and now she was seated on the couch, not speaking, and staring at her folded hands.

Lilly, however, was taking the whole thing in stride. She sat on an armchair, engrossed in a conversation with Wyatt over whether digital photography could ever really replace the quality of print images. This coming from a girl who still uses disposable drugstore cameras.

"But with Photoshop, don't you think you have more range with digital pictures?" Lilly asked, chomping a handful of pretzels.

"Not necessarily. You can have any roll of film made into a CD these days, still giving you those options. But with film, you have more natural colors and skin tones. And don't even get me started on black and white. The mood you can create with darkroom techniques . . ."

Lilly nodded like she understood his views to the point that I thought she should really consider a career in the theatrical arts. I'd have to mention it to Bobby, in case he ever made the switch from documentaries to major motion pictures.

"When is this thing going to start?" Madison droned as she nibbled on a chip. I knew she was desperate if she was eating junk food to keep busy.

"Soon, I guess."

"Do you even know what the film is about?"

"I'd assume it's about Ireland, right?"

Bobby's two preteen cousins were playing foosball in the "playroom" off to the left of where we were seated. Half his relatives were packed in the tiny room cheering with a level of excitement most actual soccer games would not be worthy of, let alone a bunch of plastic figures on metal sticks. Only right now I was half-tempted to join them. If it weren't for Madison's nails in my forearm, I probably would have dozed off long ago.

"When can we leave?" she grumbled, her nails plunging deeper. I wiggled my arm free and rubbed my skin.

"It's not my fault this is boring," I said softly. "He made it seem like it would be some big movie premiere with lots of people."

"Yeah, lots of old people."

She scanned the room, waving her hands around. "Check out his grandmother. I think she is going to the bathroom in her pants," she whispered, pointing. "Look at her face."

His gray-haired grandma was sitting serenely on a wingback chair with an expression of pure contentment.

"She's either peeing or she's medicated." Madison chuckled.

"Shut up." I smiled and covered my mouth.

"Could you imagine wearing granny diapers and just peeing whenever, wherever you wanted?" Madison continued with a mischievous grin.

"Shhh!" I murmured, a giggle slipping through my fingers.

"Just think of all the time you'd save not waiting in line for the bathroom."

"But do you think they change them each time they go?" Emily chimed in. "Because it's kinda gross just to sit there in your own pee."

"Or worse . . ."

"Oh, that's disgusting!" I groaned.

"But it does explain why old people smell funny."

"Madison!" I half-whispered, half-yelled.

The three of us were giggling so hard tears spurted down our cheeks.

"What'd I miss?" Lilly asked, diving into our conversation. "Please tell me, because it seems a lot more fun than 35-mm film exposures."

I was so giddy I couldn't get out the words before Bobby's dad sauntered down the stairs toward his mother.

"Nanna, is everything going all right? You need any help?" he asked.

Madison and I broke into another round of hysterics. I wiped at my eyes and tried to swallow the snorts, but I couldn't control myself. Emily had a much better grasp on her composure. She chewed her lip and rapidly turned away.

"You girls seem to be having a good time," Bobby's dad said as he approached.

He looked so much like his son, with a tall, thin build and a pointy nose; only his blond curls were darker and cropped short against his head. He wore wire-frame glasses with jeans and a corduroy blazer. Even if I didn't already know he was a German professor at Penn, it would not have been hard to figure out.

"Um, we're fine," I choked as I tried to calm down.

"Yeah, it was just, uh, Emily said something funny," Madison lied.

Emily instantly covered her face with her hands, and I could feel the embarrassment pulsating off her.

"Emily?" Mr. McNabb muttered, peering at her.

She slowly lowered her palms and gazed at him through her long eyelashes.

"Um, it was nothing," she mumbled. "I just said something stupid."

Mr. McNabb stared at her with such intensity that I wondered if Bobby had mentioned Emily's name before. Maybe he had told his dad about their date this past summer. Or maybe he did really have feelings for her. My gaze shifted between the two of them.

"Um, uh," his dad stuttered, his shoulders squirming. "I, uh, hope you girls have a good time tonight."

"Thanks for inviting me," she said politely, her brown eyes fixed on his face.

"Yeah, me too. Your house is really nice," I added.

Madison and Lilly nodded in agreement.

"No problem."

Mr. McNabb spun off towards the playroom just as Bobby entered the room. The mood instantly lifted as everyone simultaneously ceased what they were doing to look at him. Their expressions seemed more like those of fans gawking at a celebrity, than relatives bored by a kid's low-budget student film.

"Hello, everyone," Bobby said, sounding very official. "Glad you could make it."

Guests immediately filed out of the playroom to take their seats on folding chairs and pillow cushions plopped on the plush-carpeted basement floor. Bobby's mom and dad sat alongside his grandmother, right beside the jumbo flat-screen TV.

Bobby ran his hand through his curls, tilting his head toward the recessed lights, before letting his fingers slide slowly down his neck. It almost looked like a prerehearsed pose, and if it was, it was rather effective. For a moment, he appeared deep and artistically tormented. When his green eyes turned to me and he smiled, I felt oddly drawn to him in a way I usually felt when watching male dancers execute intense ballet moves with effortless power. It was the look of talent. And I had never seen such confidence in my locker buddy before.

"I'd like to take this time to thank you all for being here, since this is probably the closest I'll ever get to a real audience. Thanks, Mom." Everyone smiled and laughed on cue. "Tonight I'm going to debut the documentary I made in Ireland featuring the struggle between the Catholics and Protestants as shown through the lives of two very real teenagers. Having grown up in a country where God is a controversial word, it was interesting to see two people, my age, who believe so strongly in opposing religious views, views that to most of us don't seem a whole lot different. God's a big deal."

Everyone cheered and applauded.

"Please don't. You're wasting your time. God doesn't oversee the upper middle class. We pray to Bill Gates," Bobby stated with a deadpan expression.

Everyone roared again.

It was a pure blend of self-deprecating humor and thought-provoking insight. My heart melted. I didn't even need to see the movie to know it would be great. He was great. He had already sold me on the film.

"Now if my stage hand could dim the lights. *Mom.*" Bobby waved toward the switch, and everyone chuckled. "We'll begin. I hope you enjoy *God Save Ireland.*"

The documentary was amazing. The way Bobby was able get those teens to open up was impressive. Plus his use of historical footage with current Irish music perfectly illustrated the situation, but with a modern, youthful perspective. Even the editing was remarkable, just fast enough to keep the viewer engaged, but not so fast that it felt like an MTV segment. It more than made up for the hour of foosball and granny panty discussions we had to endure waiting for it.

"I can't believe Bobby, Locker Buddy Bobby, made that," I muttered.

"Apparently, there's more to him than just his locker," Lilly stated.

"I've always seen him with his camera. I guess I always thought it was just a geeky hobby," Madison added.

"He's really talented," Emily stated.

I looked at her. She smiled and shrugged.

"I mean, didn't *you* think it was good?" Emily asked quietly, staring at her black boots.

"Good? It was freakin' amazing! He's going to be famous one day—full out Oscar nomination. Without a doubt."

"What was that?" Bobby asked, startling me.

He was standing so close, I could feel his breath on the back of my neck. A shivery thrill crept through me, and I spun around.

"I said that you are America's next great cinematic genius. Scorsese better watch out."

"I prefer Woody Allen."

"Professionally or socially? Because I don't think you want to follow his lead and marry your stepdaughter," I joked.

"So, I have children now!"

"Of course, you're a famous filmmaker with a mansion in Bel Air."

"What happened to my being a starving artist in the Lower East Side?"

"I thought that before I saw your movie. Now I think you're going to be a fat, pampered Hollywood director tormented by his sudden fame and the pressure to please his investors."

Bobby chuckled. "I'm glad you liked it."

"No, I loved it."

He gazed into my eyes, saying nothing. I couldn't stop smiling. That is until Lilly indiscreetly coughed beside me.

"Oh, right," I shook my head. "We *all* loved it. Right, girls? Em, why don't you tell Bobby what you thought of the movie?"

"Oh, um, I, uh, I really liked it," she stammered. "You did a great job."

"Thanks." He nodded at her.

"So, Bobby, are you gonna show this to other people? Because it's really good," Madison asked.

"I don't know. I might enter it in a few contests or something. . . ."

"What about showing it at school? I mean, if we can have an assembly to celebrate our losing football team, I don't see why we can't have a screening of your film. Maybe we should talk to Dean Pruitt?" I suggested.

"We?" he said, raising an eyebrow. "You mean you'd help me?"

"Totally. Dean Pruitt and my dad are tight. How do you think Lilly got here?"

I caught Madison and Emily exchanging an odd stare.

"You guys wanna help?" I asked.

"No, I think you've got it handled," Emily stated quickly.

"You sure? It could be a cool project. And I bet I could talk the soon-to-be-famous director into thanking us in the program." I smiled at Bobby.

"I'm sure you could," Madison mumbled under her breath.

"Well, I'll help!" Lilly cheered. "Clearly tennis isn't my calling, so I need to start looking into some other activities before I lose all self-esteem."

"Great. I'll stop by the office on Monday and see if Pruitt'll meet with us. We can discuss strategy tomorrow. . . ."

"We're going shopping tomorrow," Madison interjected. "Your Sweet Sixteen dress, remember?"

"Oh, crap. Well, then we'll figure something out," I said before turning to Bobby. "I'll give you the lowdown at the lockers Monday morning."

"Great. Thanks for your help. Seriously."

"No problem. But if I ever get the urge to don a tutu and perform *Swan Lake* center stage in the Spring Mills auditorium, you better help me hook that up."

"It's a promise."

Chapter 22

The next day, I sat in Madison's car cruising the parking lot. There were more than sixty shopping days until Christmas, yet every spot was occupied. Of course, this wasn't an ordinary shopping complex with a modest parking lot, two anchor stores, and a single aisle of stores connecting them. No, this was King of Prussia, a mall known for being one of the largest in the country (though it didn't have an amusement park or anything). With eight department stores and several hundred boutiques, it was somewhat of a local shopping Mecca, which Madison prayed to often.

"All right, I'm about ready to just give up, park across the street and walk it," Madison huffed, as she spun down another packed lane of cars.

"Why don't you head over toward Bloomingdale's. There's usually more parking on that side of the mall," Emily suggested.

"But then I'll get lost getting out of here. I only know how to exit from Macy's. The last time I tried to go a different way I ended up halfway to the Poconos before I figured it out."

"I can get you home," Emily insisted.

"You don't even have a driver's permit."

"Is it my fault that my birthday's not 'til May?"

"Okay, young buck. Wait 'til everyone starts turning twenty-one; then it'll really suck to have the last birthday."

"Yeah, well wait 'til everyone turns thirty, then I'll be the envy of all of you."

"Wait! Right there! There's a spot!" I hollered, pointing toward a large, middle-aged woman loading an armful of bags into her trunk.

"Thank God!" Madison sighed, turning on her blinker.

A large SUV with a blond female driver pulled up from the opposite direction also attempting to claim the spot.

"I will seriously kick some ass. . . ." Madison muttered, flashing her high beams at the twenty-something driver until she pulled away. "Yeah, you better run."

A few minutes later, Madison parked the car, and we all jumped out and headed toward Neiman Marcus. My mother had handed me my father's credit card before I left and whispered something about how having the party at home was saving them loads of cash, so I could feel free to spend away on the dress. She would have jumped at the chance to be included, but something about having my mom in the dressing room with me was beyond humiliating. I still hadn't forgotten my eighth grade graduation fiasco—she had told the saleswoman helping me that I was difficult to shop for because of my "tiny little nibblers." Considering two years had passed and my boobs still hadn't sprouted past the training bra stage, I could only imagine how my mom would describe them this time around.

We hopped on the escalator to the second level. The marble floor shined. A pianist played live music on the baby grand. Madison knew the layout of the mall and every shop in it better than most war generals knew their battle plans. She was on a mission, and it would be accomplished by dinnertime.

"Okay, first thing we need to consider is length," Madison stated as she strolled confidently toward a rack of gowns. "Do we want short or long?"

"Short, definitely," I stated.

"Dress or skirt?"

"I don't care."

"Then definitely a dress."

I scanned the store. It had only been thirty seconds, and I was already positive I wouldn't find anything I liked. Unlike Madison, I was not born with the shopping gene. I hated trying on clothes, taking my shoes on and off, pulling my jeans up and down, creating a scientifically certified electrical experiment with the static in my hair. But thanks to Madison's last-minute check, I was at least more prepared for the ordeal.

"All right, here's the deal. Wear slip-on high-heeled shoes with no socks, so we can get an accurate take on the length and style. Wear a button-down shirt to avoid snagging your hair. And no jewelry. We need a blank slate," she had stated earlier.

Lilly immediately separated from the pack to peruse a collection of colorful dresses on the other side of the department. Emily attacked the opposite sides of racks Madison was scanning, and I watched.

"Do you have a preferred neckline?" Madison asked as she fondled a navy halter swinging from its hanger.

"Ideally something that doesn't draw too much attention to my lack of feminine attributes."

"I wouldn't worry too much about that. Look at Debra Messing. She's one of the best dressed women on the red carpet and she's got your same 'tiny little nibblers.'" Madison chuckled.

"Must you remind me?" I rolled my eyes.

"You can always wear a water bra," Emily stated.

"Yeah, and I can just see a fork accidentally perforating a boob during dinner. Could you imagine? I would forever be known as 'Niagara Falls.'"

"No, how 'bout 'A River Runs Through It'?" Emily joked.

"Or 'Waterworld,'" I added.

"Hey, don't knock 'em. Those bras work." Madison lifted a white strapless dress.

"You do *not* own a water bra!"

"Uh, yeah. You should have seen my boobs at my party. We're talking Pamela Anderson prior to getting her implants removed."

"I thought she had them put back in?" Emily asked.

"Oh, I don't know." Madison shrugged.

"Anyway, I don't even think a water bra will help me. Seriously, the day I have cleavage will be the day Vince takes the oath of office."

"How is he anyway?" Emily asked.

"You mean aside from the pictures of him funneling beer and swimming naked?" I raised an eyebrow. "Seriously, I'm not sure he's found his classes yet."

"We should go visit him," Emily suggested.

"Road trip in the Audi!" Madison cheered. "I love it!"

"Well, he did mention he's getting 'initiated' in a couple weeks. He actually asked me to come up."

"Perfect!" Madison smiled, holding up a chocolate brown satin dress with an asymmetrical neckline and enough beading to make a 'mother of the bride' proud.

"Please tell me you're not talking about the dress. . . ."

"Too much?" she asked, tilting her head as she stared at it. "Anyway, I was talking about the trip. Count us in."

Just then, Lilly strolled over with an armful of colorful creations ranging from canary yellow to bright coral.

"All right, I found some. Let's hit the dressing room!"

"Do you have anything there that wasn't thrown up by the Care Bears?" Madison snapped, flicking her hand at my cousin.

"What? You haven't even seen them yet."

"Actually, I can see them quite well. I think I'll need sunglasses to look any closer."

"Since when is color out?"

"Since the eighties ended."

"Mariana . . ." Lilly whined with a frown.

"I am an equal opportunity shopper," I stated. "I will try on anything that's brought to me. Once I'm naked I don't care how many dresses I zip."

"Well, we don't have time to play games." Madison curled her lips to the side.

"Sure we do. Plus, I have no idea what I'm looking for. I might as well try on everything."

Lilly beamed as she grabbed my hand and dragged me toward the fitting room. I could already tell it was going to be a very long day.

Exactly one hundred and four dresses later, after we visited four department stores and a half-dozen evening gown boutiques, I finally found a dress I liked. Only it wasn't an instant success with the team.

"But it's black," Emily moaned as I posed in front of three full-length mirrors angled to show my bodily imperfections from every possible view.

"I thought you guys hated color," Lilly snipped.

"I know, but black is so black. It's blah. It's the color of death and mourning."

"No, it's the color of sophistication," I rebutted as I turned to look at my butt.

The dress was loose fitting and fell straight to my knees with no defined waist. I called it a tube dress, while Madison called it a 1920s flapper-style cut. It had a modest V neck accented with ruffles to plump my petite chest and a matching hint of ruffle at the shoulder. Starting a few inches below my waist was a series of five ruffled pleats, ending just above my knee. It was subtle, it was modern, it was comfortable, and it wasn't over-the-top attention-grabbing. It was exactly me.

"But it's not very Puerto Rican," Madison stated. "It doesn't fit your theme."

"The designer's name is 'Rodriguez!' That's about as Hispanic as you can get," Lilly stated, shaking her head. "I don't get you guys. We've tried on so many dresses my eyes are bleeding. This is the first one she's actually smiled in. Please, let's call it a day!"

"Lilly does have a point." I twirled to showcase my swishing ruffles. "Plus, I can dance in this and not feel self-conscious."

"As long as you like it," Emily stated.

"You do look great," Madison added.

And with that I put on my street clothes for the last time of the day, paid the nice cashier, and stumbled out of the mall. That should have been the end to an exhausting day, only it wasn't.

I foolishly invited my friends inside to show my mom the dress, hoping their opinions would influence my mother's reaction. (She can be hard to please.) We barely got through the front door, when she came traipsing out of the dining room with an armful of designer paper.

"Thank God you girls are here!" she shouted, her blond hair sweaty and unwashed and her eyes hovering above deep circles. I saw our poodle cowering under a coffee table, clearly hiding from my mom's crazy energy. "We need to cut out all of the place cards. I picked up a paper cutter at the store, but I'm having trouble with the blade. It just won't cut straight. And I need to put all of these fuchsia and tangerine votives in the glass holders. I started to glue-gun the lime ribbon on the stainless steel vases for the centerpieces, but I'm only halfway done. And we need to finish tying bows on these donation favors."

"Donation favors?" Madison asked. "When did we decide on that?"

"This morning. Sylvia from the museum knew of this amazing charity in Philadelphia that works with underprivileged Latino students. It fit the theme."

"Perfect," Madison cheered. "Gifts to charities are very chic party favors right now."

"I know. I like it so much better than minipiñatas."

Madison nodded while Lilly and I looked at each other and tried not to laugh. I swear sometimes I thought that Madison and I were switched at birth; she definitely fit in with my mother better than I did. The two of them could talk for hours about china patterns and color schemes. I wasn't even present when they settled on the fuchsia, tangerine, and lime palette. (Though just to annoy them I called the colors pink, orange, and green. Their eyes froze and their fingers clenched every time I said it. I still found the reaction amusing.)

Madison immediately followed my mother into the dining room and got to work. She swept a sheet of hot pink opalescent paper into the cutter and sliced a perfectly straight line with ease. Despite having enough money to hire people to handle these details, my mother insisted that a few homemade projects would give the party "a personal touch." Personally, I'd rather see someone else hot-gluing ribbon. But heck, what did I know? It was only my party.

Lilly, Emily, and I obediently followed her into the dining room.

"Looks like you guys will probably be staying for dinner," I muttered. "Do you mind?"

"You kidding? It's Sunday. My parents will be ordering C14 and C22 from China Fun in about an hour. I'm not missing anything," Madison stated.

"My dad went to work today, so I'm sure my mom is off having a good time elsewhere," Emily grunted.

"She should hang out with *my* mom. She's probably a few martinis deep by now," Madison joked.

"I wish I was," my mother mumbled, before snapping her head up. "The dress! I have to see the dress! Did you get one?"

I smiled and darted toward the foyer where I left the dress hanging in its plastic garment bag. I pranced into the room and unzipped it triumphantly.

"Oh, baby, I love it!" my mom squealed. "It's perfect. It's fun, age-appropriate, gorgeous—just like you."

She grabbed me in an awkward hug with tears clinging to her eyes.

"Wow, Mom, it's just a birthday party. It's not my wedding."

"I know, I know," she sniffed. "I need a tissue."

She left the room, and I plopped down at the dining table with my friends. Madison was busy cutting the place cards, Lilly and Emily were tackling votive candles, so I grabbed some ribbon and tied bows around the "In lieu of favors . . ." scrolls.

"I see the infamous Teresa is seated at the head table," Madison said as she lifted her seating card. "She's seriously coming?"

"Yup. Even after the crap my uncle pulled at dinner."

"She's just a glutton for punishment, isn't she? Unless . . ." Madison trailed off.

"What?"

"Ya ever think she just wants cash?"

"For what?" I yelped.

"Thirty-five years of back child support from your deadbeat grandpa."

"Madison!" Lilly shrieked. "The woman wants to get to know her family."

"Sure she does. . . ."

"All right, drop it," I stated, mulling over the insinuation. "I don't know what she wants, but I prefer to steer away from the conspiracy theories. Anyway, I don't want my mom to hear."

The room quieted as everyone returned to their projects.

Madison waved another place card in the air. "Oh, so looky here. Bobby McNabb, Table 5. That's prominent placement."

"What? He's one of the few people from Spring Mills I actually invited. I'd like to think he'd get seated above Evan Casey. . . ."

"Hey! Don't knock Evan," Lilly interrupted.

"Sorry, Lil. But your boy Evan's at Table 17. Ouch," Madison mocked.

"Mariana!"

"What? Lil, I barely know the kid."

"He stopped you from getting your butt kicked at my tennis match."

"No, I was defending your honor, and he jumped in uninvited. Big shocker."

"Just like you defended Bobby's honor?" Emily asked, cocking her head.

"Well, yeah," I snipped. "What, am I just supposed to keep my mouth shut when jerks bad-mouth my friends?"

"So your little crusade to get his film shown at school, are you doing that 'just as a friend?' " Madison asked.

"Of course."

"Because I don't remember you guys being close friends before," Emily noted.

"Why are you making such a big deal out of this? We're lab partners, we have adjacent lockers, that's it."

"Dude, he invited you to a family function," Madison added.

"No, he invited *all of us* to his movie screening."

"No, he invited *you*. Unfortunately for him, you dragged us along." Emily sighed.

"Emily, seriously, if you like him, just tell him. Because *you're* the only one he's asked on a date. No reason to get all drama-queen about it."

Emily's eyes shot up from the tangerine candles.

"Wow, you sound like your father," she snipped.

A surge of alarm clenched my chest. All those years I thought Vince was so much like our father and that I was the odd kid out. Could I seriously be turning into my dad?

"Oh, my God. I can't believe I said that," I mumbled.

"Whatever," Emily shrugged. "I just wish you'd be a little more honest about what's going on with Bobby."

"And I wish you'd do the same."

She turned toward me and we stared at each other, dead in the eye, for the first time in a long time.

"All right girls! How we doin'?" My mom gleamed as she returned to the dining room.

The tension was so substantial that I was surprised she couldn't feel it from upstairs, but she jumped right into her designated crafts as if nothing odd was occurring. She grabbed a vase and slowly began adhering a ribbon to its base. I turned back to the project I was completing and let the conversation drop. So did everyone else.

Chapter 23

When I saw Bobby standing at his locker Monday morning, he looked different. I felt almost embarrassed—like he could tell that I'd discussed him with my friends over the weekend, and even worse, that I'd been thinking about him (a lot) since his film screening. I didn't know whether to act like his screening was no big deal, or whether I should acknowledge the spark I felt between us. Of course, I could have been imagining the spark. I could have distorted it in my mind into something that it wasn't, or I could just be letting my friends' reactions get to me.

"Hey, Bobby. Long time, no talk," I joked as I swung the dial on my locker.

"Oh, yeah. I haven't seen you in ages." He smiled as he looked up from his book bag. "So how was shopping?"

"Huh?" My forehead wrinkled as I glanced at him.

"Yesterday, for your Sweet Sixteen dress. You said you were going shopping."

"Oh, yeah. Right. Glad to see you were listening." I chuckled as I took out the books I had packed over the weekend.

"I'm always listening."

"Ew, Big Brother."

"I wouldn't go that far," he stated, shoving a few spiral note-books into his bag.

"Anyway, Lilly and I went to Dean Pruitt's office this morning, and his secretary said we could stop by after school to discuss Spring Mill's first-ever film festival."

"Oh, it's an entire festival now!"

"Well, sort of. If we can find any other kids who've completed movies. But I was thinking at the very least we could display some student photography in the halls, maybe do a screenplay reading, what do you think?"

"I think that you thought a lot about this," he said, gazing at me so intently that for a second, he reminded me of Alex.

A quick flash of Alex and I kissing near the waterfall in Puerto Rico flickered in my head. I hadn't e-mailed him since Teresa came to town, and I knew he was dying to hear about my family's reaction. But as I saw with Madison and Emily this summer, it's hard to keep long-distance friendships going. Even if he and I were a lot more than friends. I missed him, but I knew that keeping in touch would never move him any closer to Spring Mills. Sometimes I wondered why we bothered to communicate at all, because it only reminded us of how we would never really be together again.

"Mariana? Hey, Mariana." Bobby snapped his fingers, startling me. "Where'd you go?"

"What? I'm sorry," I said, shaking my head. "Anyway, Lilly and I are meeting with the dean after school, and I think you should come with us. I'm sure he'll want to speak with you."

"Yeah, absolutely."

I could feel his eyes burning into the side of my face. But I didn't return his stare.

Madison and Emily joined the campaign. I knew they would. Madison couldn't stand being left out of anything, though she did warn that the timing was inconvenient given all the work still to be done for my party on Saturday. But I assured her (more times than I could count) that the party would go off without a hitch and that the film festival probably wouldn't occur for quite a few months even if the dean agreed.

"All right, so what's the plan?" Lilly asked as she walked over to my locker.

"The plan is to ask the dean and see what he says," I responded as I slammed my locker shut. Madison and Emily were already waiting patiently beside me.

"That's it? We need to have more to our pitch than just a simple 'ask'," Madison stated.

"Like what?" I leaned back on the lockers as we waited for Bobby.

"Well, Bobby's our big selling point. We need to stress the importance of his movie to the overall psyche of our student body. Touch on America's void in understanding foreign cultures. And emphasize the lack of support for the arts at our academic institution," Madison said as she scanned her text messages.

"*Caray*. Did you just come up with that?" Lilly asked, expressing her disbelief.

Madison chuckled and looked up from her phone. "No, my dad's in marketing. He just texted me that strategy. I left him a message about it an hour ago."

I giggled. "Gotta love Mr. Fox."

"At least one of our parents is useful," Emily added.

When we were in middle school, Madison, Emily, and I insisted that we should be able to perform a *Nutcracker* routine during our school's Christmas pageant. There were already plans to have a holiday play, two chorus performances, and a visit from Santa Claus, so we thought it only fair that we should get to add our ballet rendition to the lineup. Only the principal insisted that the schedule was predetermined and that there was no time for another event. Madison immediately informed her father, and he formulated a strategy to highlight the importance of our contribution to enhancing dance appreciation among the local preteen demographic. He wrote out an entire speech we were to give our principal with a half-dozen visual aids (photos of us performing at our last recital contrasted against images of hoochie dancers in rap videos). The principal had no choice but to agree—plus if he didn't, he knew he'd probably have to sit through the whole pitch again, only this time given with conviction by Madison's father.

"My dad said to ask Bobby to bring a copy of his movie to give to the dean—as an advance screening, of course. And he should bring photos from his trip to Ireland to improve the dean's visual connection to the project."

Just then, Bobby turned the corner and walked toward us.

We quickly gave him a brief recap of Mr. Fox's strategy and in turn, he yanked two photos of Ireland from his locker door and grabbed a burned copy of his movie from his backpack. We headed to Dean Pruitt's office, and his secretary quickly escorted us in.

After a ten-minute razzle-dazzle presentation, including all of Madison's father's advice, the dean finally got a word in edgewise.

"So Mr. McNabb, you'd like to hold a screening of your movie?" Dean Pruitt confirmed, as he leaned back in his brown leather desk chair and tapped his silver pen on the oak desk in front of him.

"Yes." Bobby nodded.

"Well, all right then. I think it sounds like a wonderful idea. I'll talk to Suzanne and see where we can fit it on the calendar. I'm thinking it might make a good send-off before Thanksgiving break," he stated, as he made a notation in a leather-bound notebook.

I smiled widely at Bobby, then glanced at my friends, who looked just as happy.

"Is there anything else?" he asked, noticing we were still in the room.

"Oh, um, no. Nothing. That was it," I stammered as we all stumbled to our feet and swiftly exited the office.

"Nice work," Madison whispered, elbowing my side.

"Yeah, thanks," Bobby added, resting his hand on my shoulder as we walked past Suzanne, the dean's secretary.

I glanced down at Bobby's hand and he quickly pulled it away—thankfully just moments before Madison spun around.

"All right, now that that's over with, let's move on to the more important stuff—party plans. Has everyone responded?" Madison asked, grabbing my arm and dragging me away from Bobby.

"Yes, everyone I invited plus a few dozen extras. The seating chart is officially set."

"Perfect, so how are we gonna handle your entrance?"

"Um, it's at my house. Unless you wanna show up an hour early and watch me walk down the stairs, there will be no entrance."

"*Mariana!*"

"I agree with Madison," Emily stated as we strolled out of school and toward the student parking lot. "You need to start getting into the spirit of the day."

"And what spirit would that be?" Bobby asked.

Emily bit her lip. "Um, well, this *is* her party. She's the host. If she doesn't psych herself up to have fun, then the entire thing is gonna suck," Emily explained, tugging at a lock of her dark mocha hair.

"Emily's right," Lilly stated. "I went to this *Quinceañera* once where the girl was completely miserable. Trust me, she ruined her own party."

"I'll have fun," I confirmed, as I spotted Madison's car ahead. "As long as you don't pressure me into having fun."

"Fine," Madison huffed as she unlocked her car. "Bobby, you need a ride?"

"Uh, no." He gestured to a beat-up black sedan across the lot that looked as though it had seen its prime more than dozen years ago. "My parents didn't buy me a new car for my birthday."

"Don't feel bad. I'm sure if my father has his way I'll be getting a savings bond on Saturday."

"Ah, the gift that keeps on giving."

"Yeah, whatever."

I peered up at him as my stomach swished. Something about the scene, him standing over me in front of a parked car, felt like the end of a romantic evening. As he looked at me, saying nothing, I half expected him to lean down and kiss me. I quickly looked back and saw that all my friends had piled into the car.

"So, I'll, uh, see you tomorrow," I cheered as I climbed into Madison's car, killing the moment.

As soon as I shut the door, she swiftly pulled away.

Chapter 24

When I got home, I had the distinct urge to e-mail Alex. He had been popping into my head a lot lately, and the more things pushed forward with my party, the more I wished he could be there with me. So, after dinner when Lilly headed into her room to finish her math homework, I plopped in front of my laptop. As soon as I logged onto my e-mail, I saw two messages in my inbox. One from Vince and one from Bobby.

I opened Vince's first. (It had arrived two hours before my locker buddy's.)

Hey! I scored $20 today because one of the brothers didn't think I'd streak my English Comp class. It was freaking hysterical! I wore this crazy ninja mask, and bolted down the center aisle, my junk flappin in the breeze, until some dude blocked the exit. I had to turn around, go back out the front door, run naked through the arts quad, by a daycare center and into the woods. Thank God I still had my clothes in my backpack. It was classic! Everyone's talking about it! You gotta visit!
—Vince

I placed my hand on my forehead as I shook my head at the screen. At least he didn't send a picture.

I clicked open Bobby's e-mail.

> Hi Mariana,
> I wanted to thank you again for everything you did today. It was very cool of you to set up that meeting with Pruitt. I would have never done that on my own.
> I hope things aren't too crazy with your birthday plans. I'm looking forward to your party. Now that you've met my family, I think it's only fair that I get to meet yours.
> See you in school tomorrow.
> —Bobby
> P.S. I'm glad my locker ended up next to yours.

I read his message again. It was friendly, not flirtatious. He was simply thanking me for my help, which was an appropriate response. I was certain there were tons of etiquette books out there promoting this polite policy. He probably meant nothing more by it than what it said—a straightforward, uncomplicated thank you.

Only as I read it for the third time, I couldn't stop my leg from bouncing. And by the fourth read, I couldn't stop smiling. I decided not to share it with Madison or Emily. And part of me knew that if it were just a friendly message, I wouldn't need to be secretive. I decided not to focus on that part of my brain.

I clicked on the button to compose a new message. I didn't know whether to write to Vince, Bobby, or Alex. A blank message field popped up. I placed my cursor in the "To:" field and paused.

"Dear Alex . . ."

Chapter 25

By Wednesday, my birthday was all anyone could talk about. My mother had turned into a complete party-planning nut. I had called Vince begging him to come home. (He couldn't; he had midterms. Apparently, he was actually going to classes.) He said he'd try to finagle himself into a false emergency by Friday afternoon if I really wanted to call things off this weekend. But I figured it was no use. Even if he did land in the hospital (no doubt because of an alcohol-related incident), my mother still probably wouldn't cancel the party. One of my parents would stay behind to ensure the event continued just to torture me. (Of course they'd think they were doing me a favor.)

At this point, I was certain that there was something fundamentally wrong with me. I was turning sixteen. My birthday fell on a Saturday. It was supposed to be a monumental moment, something I'd remember forever. But all I wanted to do was bypass the weekend and go straight to Monday. The idea of spending an entire day as the center of attention, being perky and amusing for hordes of virtual strangers, having dozens of eyes watching my every move, made my palms sweat. I was grateful I had ballet. It gave me an excuse to avoid home—and my mother.

"All right ladies, let's begin," Madame Colbert ordered, snapping me back to the present situation.

I was seated on the ballet studio floor beside Madison and Emily. We were in final auditions for parts in our upcoming performance of *Sleeping Beauty*. Everyone was gunning for the role of Princess Aurora, but personally I would have been happy just to be a fairy godmother. The idea of granting girls' wishes seemed very appealing at the moment.

Emily was at center stage. She was the last to perform—Madison and I had completed our auditions nearly a half hour ago. We each had to dance Princess Aurora's famous solo from Act I's birthday scene. Madame Colbert used that one choreographed sequence to determine all the parts in the ballet (except for the roles of Aurora's father and her prince in shining tights—we only had two guys in the class, so they always got the two male roles unquestioned).

The spotlights gathered on Emily as Tchaikovsky's classical score filled the background. Her body moved to the music with perfect timing. Her flexibility was stunning, her extension exquisite, her elevation amazing, but her emotional connection felt a little off. Her passion looked more like furor than the joy of a princess celebrating her sixteenth year. (Not that I had much room to talk. For some reason, I couldn't muster up enthusiasm for the role either.) When Emily finished, she sent a wake of sizzling energy through the room. Madison and I gave her a standing ovation.

Madame Colbert stood from her metal folding chair and glanced at her clipboard.

"Girls," she said, flicking her eyes toward the twenty of us seated on the polished wood floor. "I just need a moment to confirm my decision. I'll be back with the assignments soon; please wait here."

Our instructor left the room as Emily trudged over, panting. She slumped down beside us.

"Em, you were awesome," I stated, as she stretched her back like an angry cat.

"Seriously, you nailed it," Madison added.

"No way," she said, slowly rolling up. "Mariana, you were the best audition all day."

"Are you kidding? I'm no Princess Aurora. Trust me, I should be the last girl in the world cast to dance for joy at a sixteenth birthday party."

My friends laughed.

"True, you might have a hard time selling the role," Emily joked.

"I think I'd be more believable as the wicked fairy who ruins everything."

"Hey, don't knock it. That's a good role," Madison stated.

"I'm not," I said. "I actually think I'd make one heck of an evil fairy."

"Oh, please," Emily whined.

"I'm serious. I wish I had someone to curse me so I could prick my finger and sleep through my party."

"Oh, Mariana, you're so *dramatic*," Madison mocked.

"You do not want to quote my father right now," I said, with a raise of my eyebrow. "I think he's gonna flip when he realizes how much my mom spent on the caterer."

"That bad?" Emily asked.

"Let's just say I never realized chicken and rice could cost so much. I won't even get into the price of the individual *dulce de leches*."

"Hey, it's your sixteenth birthday!" Madison cheered. "You only get one. Live it up."

"I wish I had your enthusiasm."

Just then, Madame Colbert reopened the door to the studio. She gracefully floated into the center of the room, and we quickly sat up. I watched my fellow ballerinas in the mirrors. They fidgeted, fluttering their knees as they sat cross-legged or tightening their buns over and over. Everyone was wearing full stage makeup, bright red lips, and thickly-lined eyes, hoping to appear more convincing as Princess Aurora.

Sleeping Beauty would be the biggest production our studio had ever undertaken. We would even be doing some of Marius

Petipa's original choreography from the nineteenth century production. Madame Colbert had even rented out a local theater to
showcase the ballet. It was to be her studio's shining moment.

When we joined with Madame Colbert more than ten years
ago, we were three of only a dozen students. Now she had five in-
structors and an army of ballerinas. She even taught a ballet boot
camp on the weekends for anyone interested in getting into
shape with a ballerina's workout. My mom took the class once; it
wasn't pretty. She jumped and stretched about two beats behind
everyone else, never fully following instructions or understanding the difference between a flexed foot and a pointed one. I
clearly did not inherit my talents from her. Afterward, I had to
ask that she never take the class again for fear it would negatively
impact my instructor's view of my abilities.

"All right girls, I have to say I'm very impressed with all of
you." Madame Colbert lowered her clipboard to her side. "You
clearly took this audition very seriously, and I saw some real talent up there. You should all feel very proud."

We collectively smiled and nodded our heads. I watched in
the mirror as Emily chewed her thumbnail. I had never seen her
so nervous. Usually she took these auditions in stride; we all did.

"Okay, clearly you've all heard that Gabriel will be our Prince
Florimund and Drew will play Aurora's father, King Florestan."

We all clapped obligatorily, even though the male dancers
weren't even present. There was no reason for them to sit
through the three-hour female audition rounds when their auditions took all of fifteen minutes. Madame Colbert had made her
decision as soon as she selected the ballet.

"Now, for the female lead. This was a tough decision, but I
wanted someone who could capture the grace of Aurora. It wasn't
all about power or passion or even technique. It had a lot to do
with body movement, how she flowed in between the steps, the
beauty she expressed through the dance."

Madison and I looked toward Emily and smiled. I reached
over and squeezed her thigh as she wrung her hands together.

"Mariana Ruíz, congratulations!" Madame Colbert cheered, clapping with delight.

All eyes turned to me as the girls erupted in applause. I watched Emily's hands unclench. She slowly placed her palms on her thighs as her head slumped toward her chest. A fellow ballerina leaned over and hugged my shoulders from the side.

But I kept my eyes locked on Emily.

Finally, she took a deep breath and turned to me. "Congratulations," she whispered with a fake grin.

I mouthed, *"I'm sorry,"* but she had already turned away.

"Emily Montgomery will be the evil fairy Carabosse," Madame continued in an ominous tone. "The way your body exploded and contorted during auditions, I thought perfectly portrayed the fury in Carabosse's curse on Aurora's sixteenth birthday. Well done."

Our instructor applauded and smiled at Emily, who was digging her nails into her legs so hard I thought she might draw blood. I rested my hand on her back, but she squirmed away, shaking me off.

Madame Colbert continued through the list of fairies and queens. Almost the entire production was cast in minutes.

Finally she noted, "And Madison Fox will be our Puss 'n Boots. Congratulations."

Madison's face fell to the floor, her shoulders sinking.

"Puss 'n Boots!" she whined quietly.

"No, Mad, it's good. You have a solo at the end, during the wedding scene!" I stated in my perkiest voice, clapping for her like I really did believe it was a good role.

"But Puss 'n Boots! How do I tell people that?" she shook her head.

"It's better than the wicked witch," Emily shot back, standing aggressively.

She marched over to her sport bag and shoved her feet into her sneakers.

"Come on, Em, you know Carabosse is a huge role. You're the

first person on stage; you have a bunch of solos," I said, my face locked in the same unnatural grin I had pasted on when the parts were first announced.

"I guess I'm just nobody's princess."

"Em, don't be like that."

"No, it's okay. It's your birthday, your role, your life. I'll just keep hanging on the sidelines. It's where I belong anyway. I mean, really, did I actually think something was going to work out for me? How stupid am I?"

"Em. . . ." I moaned, my eyes sad.

"No, don't worry. I'll go to your party. I'll have fun. I mean, everyone just loves Mariana!"

She grabbed her bag and stomped out of the studio door as my stomach recoiled from the verbal sucker punch. I had never seen her get so angry, and I couldn't believe it was over a ballet performance. She had never cared this much about dance before.

Chapter 26

By Saturday morning, it was party central. The caterers had already arrived and were drenched in sweat. I hadn't even gotten a shower, yet there were already hordes of strangers buzzing around my house, setting up the tent, the chairs, the buffets. The party didn't start for another nine hours.

I popped a bagel in the toaster and plopped down at the island with a glass of cranberry juice. I didn't care that I was still wearing my electric blue flannel pajamas with tiny flying pigs, nor that my matted hair was frizzed in hideous waves, nor that my fuzzy pink slippers had multiple rips in the soles from overuse. I was going to sit in my kitchen and eat breakfast like I did every Saturday morning.

"Excuse me, miss. We need some rags. Do you know where some extras are?" asked a twenty-something guy in a white oxford button-down and black pants.

"Aren't you with the caterer?" I asked, sipping my juice as I waited for my bagel.

"Yes."

"Then shouldn't you bring your own rags?"

The guy's eyes squinted, then he groaned and spun in the opposite direction.

"Not my fault you came unprepared," I noted under my breath.

"Mariana! You're not in the shower!" my mom hollered as she raced into the kitchen, fastening a dangling diamond hoop to her ear.

She was perfectly styled as if she had been up for hours. Her blond hair was swept up in a loose French twist, her emerald dress was freshly ironed, and her makeup added a beautiful radiance to her fair complexion. She looked like the star of the party.

"Mom, it's ten A.M. I have plenty of time."

"But it's *your* party. It's gonna take a long time to get ready."

"How long does it take to put on ChapStick?"

"Mariana, this is important. You're gonna get a little more done up than you do for gym class."

"How do you know what I look like at gym class? I could be one of those skanky girls who wears poom-poom shorts and cherry lipstick to play kick ball."

"Yeah, sure." My mom shook her head.

I suddenly heard Tootsie barking from behind our basement door.

"Mom, did you lock our dog in the basement?"

"Of course. I can't have him running around with our guests."

"He can't be in there all day! What if he has to pee?"

"The caterers are watching him," she said as if it were obvious.

I doubted the renowned chefs expected dog-sitting to be a part of their high-class party duties. But for what she was paying them, I assumed they'd put up with just about anything (and I was certain she'd push those boundaries).

She looked out toward the tent in the yard. "Oh, no! They're putting the dance floor on the wrong side! Can't these people get anything right?"

She darted toward the sliding glass doors and charged into the yard. I could hear her yelling even after the doors slid shut behind her.

"Ah, *mija. Feliz Cumpleaños*," my father said as he strolled into the kitchen.

"Hey, you remembered it's my birthday. I think Mom forgot. She's acting like this is some occasion to showcase her party planning skills."

"Oh, cut her some slack. You know she loves this stuff." My dad opened the refrigerator and pulled out the egg carton. "Eggs?" he asked, shaking one at me.

It reminded me of my Great Uncle Miguel and my first morning in Utuado. That breakfast with him, when everything was still so foreign and scary, was the one thing that reassured me I was going to be okay.

I smiled at my dad. "No, I'm fine."

I grabbed my bagel from the toaster and dipped my knife into the cream cheese. I had barely gotten a layer slathered when Lilly stumbled into the kitchen.

"God, is it party day already?" she asked, wrinkles from her sheets still pressed into her face.

"Yup. Look familiar?" I asked as I bit into my breakfast.

Lilly shrugged.

"This is exactly how your house looked before your *Quinceañera*."

"Except minus every luxurious detail." Lilly grabbed a box of sugared cereal from the cabinet.

"Not true. Your party was amazing."

"Uh, yeah. Sure." She grabbed a bowl and the carton of milk and sat down beside me. "Mariana, you have a crystal chandelier in your tent."

"So?"

"You're serving plantains on designer china."

I blinked back.

"You have a twelve-piece band."

"You had a band!"

"Not with three different lead singers!"

"Still, your party was very nice."

"And your party will be off the hook."

"I may need you to remind me of that, so I don't drown myself in my bath water."

"Oh, stop being so *dramatic*!" she mocked.

We both looked toward my father. He glanced at us with a wrinkled brow, his eyes confused.

"What?" he asked, pumping his shoulders.

Lilly and I both laughed.

"Nothing," I muttered. "You can go back to avoiding the *drama.*"

"Thanks, I believe I will."

Lilly and I finished our breakfast together. It was probably the last moment of peace I'd have for quite a while.

A few hours later, I sat at Madison's mercy. She had already completed a round of under-eye concealer to hide the dark circles I didn't know I had. Then, she moved on to foundation to cover facial imperfections that never bothered me before. Then, she added liquid bronzer to give my complexion a summer glow in October. And now, Madison was dusting my skin with powder to prevent any unwanted shine. (Apparently there was a distinct difference between a "glow" and a "shine".)

"Who in their right mind wears this much makeup?" I asked when I glanced in my bathroom mirror. "I look like a drag queen."

"You do not!" Madison quickly corrected.

"You can barely tell you're wearing anything," Emily added. She was smiling as if her rant at ballet practice never took place. She seemed happy. I just hoped it was legitimate.

They had both arrived right after lunch. I had stepped out of the shower, and there they were seated in my room with their dresses hung in garment bags on the back of my closet door. They said they were my 'extreme makeover squad.' I didn't realize I needed one.

"The goal here is for you to look like you, only better," Madison explained, as she took out a giant palette of eye shadows.

"What's wrong with me actually looking like me?"

"Because you look like that every day. Today is special. It's your Sweet Sixteen." Madison smoothed her long brush over a swatch of mocha powder.

"You need to stand out," Emily said as she ironed my dress.

"You know I hate this, right? I think tinted ChapStick is too much."

"Well, that's why *I'm* here." Madison snatched another brush from her extensive collection and continued the endless procedure.

It took hours. And by the time the sun began to fade, I was sprayed, teased, colored, shaved, and scented. My hair had been straightened by Emily to create a gleam I didn't know my follicles were capable of, then Madison applied a fresh coat of clear polish to my fingers and toes, while Lilly walked on the pavement out front to break-in my new heels. Madison had indiscreetly excluded her from the pre-party preparations.

"Um, sorry, Lilly," she had said. "But Mariana told me about your *Quinceañera*. I mean I'm sure it was fun and all, but I really don't think you're the best judge of 'American taste.'"

Before I could say a word, Lilly left the room to "break in my shoes" (and curse silently in Spanish). Despite her anger, she looked amazing. She was wearing a dress I had sported to my cousin's wedding last year, only her boobs actually filled the purple halter-top to a swelling perfection. It was like the dress finally got to be what it was always meant to be.

Emily was decked out in a red strapless number that made her legs look a mile long, and Madison's blond hair was swept up to showcase the jeweled turquoise straps on her otherwise nude cocktail dress.

I, however, hadn't yet been permitted to put on my party clothes. Apparently, there was a fifteen minute waiting period following my deodorant and body moisturizer application (to avoid transfer stains). Madison was clocking it.

"Okay, five more seconds and we're good," Madison stated, staring at her watch.

I immediately lifted my freshly ironed dress, clutched a pair of underwear from my dresser, and headed into the bathroom to change.

"What are you doing?" Madison asked, glaring at me.

"You said it was time."

"No, not that."

"Please don't tell me I have to get dressed with my 'team' present." I gripped the door handle.

"No. What are you doing with that underwear?" she asked, horror spread across her face. "Do you see what she's holding?"

She looked at Emily.

"Is that a cotton thong? With a bow?" Emily asked, as if I were holding an automatic weapon.

"Uh, yeah. Why?"

They both shook their heads at me. Then Madison reached into her overnight suitcase and pulled out a shopping bag.

"I thought you might need these. I can't believe you don't have them already."

She held up the largest pair of flesh-colored granny panties I'd ever seen. They looked like eighties bicycle shorts with a waistline that had to reach my boobs and an equally horrific three-inch crotch.

"Are you kidding?"

"Do you know nothing about panty lines?"

"Yes, I do. That's why I'm wearing a thong."

"With a bow!" Madison shouted.

"It will protrude right through the fabric of the dress," Emily explained.

"You need something to hold you in and keep your butt tight," Madison added.

"Since when does my butt need extra tightening?"

"Trust me. These suckers work wonders."

Madison handed me the hideous, parachute-sized panties, and I disappeared into the bathroom. More than five minutes of sucking and heaving later, I got the nylon torture traps up and slipped my black dress on top of them. I smoothed fabric over my stomach, which did look inhumanly flat, and turned toward the full-length mirror. It was the first time I caught a glimpse of myself with my full, quasi-professionally styled Sweet Sixteen look.

I smiled.

Chapter 27

All of my guests arrived on time—my family, my friends, and my not-so-friends-who-invited-themselves-anyway. I was standing by the bar, alone, soaking in the scene. The tent swept high above us in white silk waves. Dozens of round tables with tangerine and fuchsia tablecloths popped against green and white orchids, lilies, and hydrangeas—their fragrance melting with the smell of seafood hors d'oeuvres. Votive candles glowed around each floral arrangement, accented by white china and lime green napkins. It was a tropical paradise in suburban America.

The cocktail hour was almost over (which in the underage-drinking world meant ginger ale and Shirley Temples). Guests filled more than two hundred chairs waiting for dinner to be served and the festivities to begin.

My 'grand entrance' had occurred about an hour ago when I walked into the kitchen, amidst dozens of bustling wait staff, to get a handful of pretzels to settle my stomach. The fact that Betsy and Evan were the first guests I saw did nothing to help my nerves.

"Hey, happy birthday," Betsy had cheered as she handed me a pink present with a giant white bow.

"It's from all of us," Evan mumbled.

"Oh, Mariana, you're ready!" Lilly shrieked as she ran into the kitchen from the den. "I was just going to tell you that the first guests had arrived."

"I, uh, see that," I grumbled, through a mouthful of pretzel bites.

Lilly halted a few feet in front of me. "Oh, my God."

"What?" I asked, still chewing.

"Nothing. It's just, you look . . . Wow. *Bonita*."

Lilly beamed as she ran over and hugged me, squishing me tight.

"Oh, no! I'm wrinkling you!"

"Don't worry about it," I said, as I grabbed a bottle of Evian from the fridge.

"No, but really, you look amazing," Lilly stated again. She lifted a disposable camera to her eye. "I have to take a picture for Mom. After everything you did for my *Quinceañera*, she'd kill me if I didn't send a photo from your Sweet Sixteen."

"Ah, and how are the Sanchezes?" I asked, smiling for the photo.

"Wishing they could be here. They sent gifts!" Lilly cheered. "I tossed them in the pile with the others."

Lilly gestured toward my living room, which was serving as a gift receptacle. It was the one clear benefit of the party.

"You do look nice," Betsy added with fake enthusiasm.

"I like your shoes," Evan said, staring at my peak-toe pumps with gold studs.

"Gee, Evan, I didn't know you cared." I tilted my head and grinned at him.

He smirked back.

That was the last thing I remembered before the ambush of people came through the front door. I was hugged from all angles by a swarm of relatives and passing students, all headed toward the sizzling rhythms drifting from the tent in the back.

The band was currently in its Latin jazz, cocktail music phase. There were no lyrics, so my guests probably hadn't yet figured out that they were in for a night of popular Spanish music. Most of these kids didn't know me very well, which probably meant that after tonight they'd think I was some crazy, wannabe Latina—like those newscasters who look like Malibu Barbie but who pronounce their names with ethnic accents. Before this summer I barely spoke Spanish, I let my friends call me by an ethnic slur, and I resented being labeled "Hispanic" on standard-ized tests. Now here I was serving Puerto Rican food with the sounds of salsa in the background.

I popped another shrimp cake into my mouth. I had been standing by myself at the bar hoarding appetizers from passing waiters for several minutes. None of my guests seemed to notice me.

"Mariana!" Lilly yelled as she ran over. "I've been looking for you."

"I've been right here," I told her.

"Why are you alone?"

"I don't know. Why not?"

"You're supposed to be having fun."

"Really? I must have missed that part."

"All right, that's it. Let's go!" Lilly grabbed my arm and yanked me from my resting place.

"Where are we going?"

She dragged me straight to Bobby, who was talking to his pho-tography friends.

"Wait here," Lilly said before running toward the band.

I shuffled my feet and peered up at Bobby. He wore a plat-inum button-down shirt and a silver tie. His curly blond hair was slicked back and his normal two-day-old scruff was shaved clean. He looked like a grown-up.

"Hey." I lifted my chin.

"Wow," he replied, eyeballing my ensemble. "You look amaz-ing. I wouldn't have recognized you."

"Gee, thanks. Do I look that bad normally?"

"You know what I mean. I've just never seen you so dressed up before."

"Same goes for you."

"Well, I thought the occasion deserved a little more than old corduroys and a beat up T-shirt."

"Truthfully, I'd rather be wearing the cords right now."

Bobby pulled on his tie. "So would I."

A few moments later, Lilly darted back and grabbed both of our hands. Her light brown eyes were electrified as she yanked us onto the dance floor.

"We're going to kick this party off," she stated.

She left Bobby and me staring at each other with confusion on the parquet floor as she ran off in search of Evan. She pushed him onto the floor and nodded at the band. Immediately the twelve-piece ensemble ripped into a fast salsa rhythm with the thunder of brass trombones and pounding bongos.

"What the heck is this?" Bobby asked, staring at me open-mouthed.

Lilly grabbed Evan in a standard ballroom dance frame, then looked toward us.

"The girls lead, the guys follow," she cheered.

Lilly's hips swiveled as her feet rock-stepped and kicked. Evan looked stunned but kept up surprisingly well (those formative years in ballet must have paid off). He stepped from side-to-side as quickly as he could with a solid sense of rhythm.

I gazed at Bobby. "You wanna give it a whirl?"

"I don't know what to do."

"That's okay. Neither did I the first time."

With that, I bent my right elbow, and he clutched my palm. I placed a hand on his shoulder while he held my waist (which was extra firm thanks to my monster spandex panties) and we lightly swayed to the music. We locked eyes as he tried to move his legs in time with mine.

"Don't worry about your hips," I stated. "That'll come later. Just try to feel the music."

Bobby smiled nervously and kept stepping and swaying in a circular pattern as we moved across the dance floor. We weren't

exactly on beat, but we could've been worse. At least he was trying.

"See, you're a natural."

"Yeah, right!" he joked, just before nipping my toe.

We slowly found our flow, our hips waving together in time
with the music. As the rhythm slowed, Bobby spun me under his
arm and pulled me back for the final note. I opened my mouth to
offer a compliment but was interrupted by a clash of applause.
We turned toward the dining tables to see the entire crowd on its
feet, hooting enthusiastically. Lilly swiftly ran over, clasped my
hand, and pulled me to center stage.

"Ladies and gentleman, the birthday girl!" she screamed to a
roar of cheers.

My face filled with heat as I scanned the collage of faces in the
tent, all smiling and clapping. Then I did what any trained ballerina would do. I bowed.

Chapter 28

I sat with my family at dinner—not just my parents, but everyone. I was surrounded by my uncles, my aunts, my cousins, and of course (just to complicate things), my new *tia* Teresa and her boyfriend Carlos.

"So, Mariana, I didn't realize you knew how to dance merengue," my Aunt Stacey stated as she nibbled a lettuce leaf.

"It was salsa," I corrected through a mouthful of chicken.

"Oh, there's a difference?"

"Yes," Lilly stated, grinding her teeth as she smiled as politely as she could.

"Okay." My aunt stared down at her tiny collection of Puerto Rican food.

Neither of my aunts were Latina, and neither was my mom. The Ruíz brothers unilaterally married outside their culture, which today wouldn't be as huge a deal, but twenty years ago, it caused quite a stir. My mother's Polish father wasn't exactly liberal-minded. He gave my father such a hard time, convinced he wasn't good enough for his daughter simply because he was Puerto Rican, that both my parents have sworn numerous times that Vince and I can marry whomever we want. My Aunt Joan's Irish parents and my Aunt Stacey's Italian family had similar reactions to their multicultural marriages. The only saving grace was that they were all devout Catholics, which at least gave the families the traditional weddings and baptisms they desperately desired. I still went to church every weekend with my parents, and so did all my cousins.

"I love your dress," my cousin Jackie stated. "Dior?"

"No, Robert Rodriguez." I nodded.

"Oh, I should have known. You know, he worked for Dior."

I shook my head with an oblivious expression. Jackie was thirteen going on twenty-eight (never thirty; she already intended to lie about her age). She was tall, blond, thin as a rail and obsessed with fashion. She had been shopping in designer women's boutiques since her growth spurt in the fifth grade. Every spare weekend she spent at modeling agencies waiting for her big break. She was certain that if she didn't get onto a runway soon, she'd be too old to enter the business. Apparently, fifteen was over the hill.

"Jackie has such a great eye for fashion," my Aunt Joan cooed. "You should have seen how impressed these photographers were last week during the shoot for her new headshots. She could name every label of every garment on the studio's rack!"

Jackie gave a smug shoulder roll as her medically enhanced lips curled in a perfected grin. I rolled my eyes at Lilly, who was staring at my cousin's collagen-packed pout. Jackie was the only girl I knew who asked for plastic surgery for her thirteenth birthday. And my Aunt Joan is the only mother I knew who would actually agree to such a request.

"So, Mariana, any other plans for your birthday?" asked my Aunt Stacey.

She was eating salad for dinner—just a small plate of tomatoes, lettuce, cucumbers, and sprouts (with no dressing, and she picked out the orange slices). My mother had ordered enough food to serve half the state of Pennsylvania, and my aunt was eating a side salad.

"Nope, no other birthday plans," I muttered, spearing a piece of sauce-covered chicken with my fork. "This is pretty much all I can handle."

"Mariana doesn't like being the center of attention," my mother whispered.

"Isn't that a little odd for a ballerina?" my Aunt Joan countered.

"It's different when you're on stage. With the spotlights, you can't see anyone."

"Really? Because I'd think performing would attract a lot more attention than a little birthday party. At least if you were any good." She fake-laughed as she spat out the last line.

"You sure looked relaxed while you were dancing with that boy," my Uncle Diego muttered, glaring at my father, who didn't look up from his plate.

"Is he your boyfriend?" my Aunt Joan continued in her sweetest tone.

"Bobby's just a friend from school. . . ."

"Still, you didn't seem to mind the attention then." My Aunt Joan bit into a green bean and smiled wide.

I narrowed my eyes. Lilly clutched my arm in support.

"You kids and your contradictions," she went on, shaking her head. "You don't want attention, but you throw a big party; you don't want the spotlight, but you dance in front of crowds. I just can't keep up!"

"Well, Mariana likes to dance," Teresa snapped, speaking up for the first time.

My Aunt Joan flicked her eyes toward her husband's half sister. Her lips drew tight. "With all due respect, I don't think you could possibly know what Mariana likes."

My Uncle Diego grabbed his wife's hand.

"I know because I asked her how she felt about this party," Teresa said, lifting her linen napkin from her lap. "Did *you*?"

"Wow, you pop up during their *unsupervised* frolic through Puerto Rico, and now you think you're an expert on our family?"

"I didn't say that."

"You know, you really don't need to say much of anything. I think we all know enough about *you*."

All eyes spun toward Teresa. She immediately stood up and rested her napkin gracefully on the table. She lightly squeezed Carlos's shoulder, then walked away.

"You know, this is hard for her too," Carlos stated, rising from his chair. "Would it kill you to acknowledge that? Because she deserves better than this."

"Tttsst," my Uncle Diego hissed, aggressively shaking his head.

"You know, you're the ones acting like you're sixteen."

And with that, Carlos marched off after my *tia*.

Lilly and I chased after them without a word to anyone at the table. It didn't matter what my grandfather did with her mother; no one deserved to be treated that way—especially not at my birthday party. I was embarrassed to be related to my family.

When we found Teresa, she was in the powder room in the downstairs den, despite the fact that my mom had rented a collection of luxurious trailers to serve as extra restrooms for the guests. I guess it helped that Teresa had joined us for a family dinner—she knew the layout of our house and the best place to hide.

"She's in there," Carlos stated as we rushed in.

He was standing in the doorway to the den, pointing toward the bathroom door on the back wall. He glanced around the room nervously. I sensed that he was afraid to invade my father's home office.

"Did she say anything?" I asked as I walked into the dimly lit room.

He took one step inside and stopped. "She's not speaking."

Lilly knocked on the dark wood door to the bathroom.

"Teresa? Teresa, it's Lilly and Mariana."

No response. Lilly tried the door handle. It was locked.

"Teresa, it's Mariana. Look, I'm sorry my family sucks so much."

Still nothing.

"Thanks for trying to stick up for me. My Aunt Joan has some serious issues. Trust me, it's not you, it's *her.*"

I heard the faucet turn on inside. Then she blew her nose.

"Teresa, if it makes you feel any better, Mariana's friends don't like *me* very much. I know what it's like not to fit in," Lilly stated.

"That's not true!"

"Yeah, it is." Lilly sighed. "You saw how they acted before the party."

"That's just because Madison's so into makeup and stuff. It's, like, a calling."

"So? I still could've helped you get ready."

"I don't think she meant to be rude."

"I do. The girl made me break in your shoes!"

"I thought you wanted to break in my shoes. . . ."

"For a half hour! Come on."

"It was a big help," I muttered, staring at my feet.

"Yeah, well, I hope your feet are very comfortable."

"Actually, they are. Thank you."

Slowly the bathroom's doorknob rotated, and the door creaked open. Teresa stood there, her eyes bloodshot and her nose pink.

"You girls . . ." she mumbled, shaking her head. "You fight like *hermanas.*"

"Or distant cousins," I joked.

We all chuckled.

"Really, I'm sorry for what happened back there," I stated.

"Don't apologize for them," Teresa said softly as she turned off the bathroom light and stepped into the den. "You shouldn't apologize for other people's actions."

"She's right," Carlos added, strolling to his girlfriend. "But it was very nice of you to come looking for her."

He looked at my *tia* and grinned slightly before wrapping his arm around her.

"*Esta bien,*" he whispered to her.

They hugged like a couple who had been together for ages. She pressed her head against his chest as his bearded chin rested on her head. Who knew you could find all that on the Internet?

"My family," I murmured, "we're a stubborn group."

"Yeah, you are," Lilly huffed.

I snarled at her before breaking into a smile.

"We're stubborn," I continued. "But we're good people. They'll prove that to you eventually."

"Mariana, I know you mean well. But I don't think I belong here," Teresa stated with an exhausted sigh.

"Yes, you do. I invited you."

"Hey, you're more closely related than I am," Lilly quipped.

"This is true. She's, like, my third cousin."

"And you're her half aunt. That has to be a higher ranking."

We both snickered.

"I have to accept that they may never accept me. And that's okay." Teresa closed her eyes and rested her head on Carlos' shoulder. "I have my own family now."

"They will. In the end, they will."

She looked at me with weary eyes. I could tell that she wanted my family to want her, even if she acted like it wasn't important. She wouldn't have come to my party if she didn't, nor to the family dinner, nor to Lilly's *Quinceañera*. She sought us out even after we offended her repeatedly.

"Let's go back to the tent," I stated.

She shook her head.

"Come on, Teresa. It'll be fun. There's dancing. And have you taken a look at the crowd? No one else can salsa. We'll look like rock stars," Lilly added.

"She makes a good point," I said. "And I hate to do this, but it *is* my sixteenth birthday. I can pull the guilt card here. You can't run out on a birthday girl."

Teresa offered a small grin and stood up straight. Her dark round eyes passed between Lilly and me.

"Fine, I'll go. But only because of the dancing. These people are gonna look like *idiotas.*"

"See! Now that's the spirit!" Lilly cheered.

I nodded at her, and then we all walked back into the party together.

Chapter 29

No one was dancing. When we returned to the tent, all of my guests were seated at tables staring at the stage as if they were watching a classical orchestra. Even my own family wasn't strutting their stuff, and I was certain my father and uncles knew how to salsa. My father listened to Spanish radio in the car, and he had Spanish CDs in the den. Yet there he sat at his daughter's birthday party, sulking.

"Wow. Are your friends always this exciting?" Lilly asked as she glimpsed at my yawning guests.

"Well, in their defense, they've probably never heard this music before," I said.

"And God forbid people in Spring Mills try something new."

"Hey, don't knock my people."

"Well, I think it's time for your people to meet *my* people."

Teresa and Carlos were standing silently behind us. I glanced at my family seated stubbornly at the table. Their eyes blazed in our direction, searching for signs of trouble. I only wished they were as good at talking as they were at staring.

"All right, why don't you track down Madison and Emily, and I'll track down Betsy and them?" Lilly suggested as she scanned the massive tent.

I nodded and took off toward my friends' table, weaving through the crowd. When I finally saw them, they were drumming their nails on the silk tangerine tablecloth and staring at the band with the enthusiasm of a pack of patients in a doctor's waiting room. Their mothers sat beside them engaged in conversation that I could hear from a few feet away. They were practically screaming over the din of the music.

"So, you're writing a novel?" Mrs. Fox asked Emily's mother.

"No, it's an anthology," replied Mrs. Montgomery.

Madison's mom stared blankly at her, her blue eyes lifeless.

"I'm editing an anthology of poetry. I'm a poetry professor," Mrs. Montgomery repeated.

"Oh, that's nice. So it's a book of your poetry?"

"No, it's a collection of various poets."

"Yourself included?"

"Of course not."

"Well, why not? It's *your* book."

Mrs. Montgomery shook her head and, as I got closer to the table, I could tell she was clearly annoyed with the conversation. Madison's mom was my mom's best friend. The two volunteered together at an art gallery, sat on the boards of several charities, planned numerous fundraisers, and socialized as a regular pastime. Emily's mom traveled with an academic crowd. Aside from her father's coworkers, I didn't think I had ever seen a friend at the Montgomerys' house. They were too busy working.

"Hey, everyone," I said as I stood before the table.

Madison and Emily slowly turned their heads.

"Oh, hey." Madison sighed.

"Mariana, you look beautiful." Mrs. Fox beamed. "I just love the dress. Your mother told me all about it, but it looks even better than I imagined."

Madison's mom was glowing in a gold dress and matching jacket that probably cost more than most people's rent—in Manhattan. Her pale blond hair flowed to her shoulders matching the shine and hue of her daughter's locks, which was logical given that they shared the same colorist. No one would guess that she was in her mid-forties, and I doubted she would ever admit it. She'll be thirty-nine until the day she dies.

"Thanks, Mrs. Fox. And you look amazing! Are you still doing yoga?" I asked.

"Three times a week. Your mother switched to pilates, but I don't think it has the same effect on the body. I bet she'll be back within a month."

"I'm sure she will. And Mrs. Montgomery, thank you for coming. You look nice."

She offered a bored smile, as if she knew it was an empty compliment. Emily's mom was forty-eight and looked forty-eight. Her dark brown hair fell in long, natural waves with a hint of frizz that never seemed to bother her. Her weathered skin shone through her lack of makeup, and her navy dress was long, loose and more appropriate for a picnic than a formal party. But that was who she was. She talked about smoking pot in the seventies and hitchhiking across the country, while her husband donned a suit to go to Little League games and spouted Wall Street Journal headlines at social events. Somehow they created Emily.

"Um, guys," I said. "I was wondering if you wanted to help me get the dance floor going?"

They dropped their chins and stared at me like I had just suggested they get a root canal and skip the Novocain.

"Come on," I whined. "Give it a try. You guys are the best dancers here. If you can dance ballet, you can pick up salsa."

"And what are we supposed to do? Salsa in circles around each other?" Madison droned.

"No, we'll find partners. Look at all the guys that showed up." I waved at the dozens of teenage boys surrounding us. "They're all bored. They'd probably love to dance."

"Yes, because most teens just jump at the chance to embarrass themselves." Madison snorted.

"Girls, this is Mariana's birthday, and I think you owe it to her to give this a try," Mrs. Fox said as she rested her French-manicured hand on Madison's arm.

"She's right, Emily. It's about time you tried something new," added Mrs. Montgomery.

"Oh really, Mom. Well, why don't you show me how it's done? You go out there," Emily suggested.

"With your father?" She snorted.

"It would be a start. Or is there someone else you'd rather dance with?"

Mrs. Montgomery's face shot toward her daughter. Emily cocked her head and raised her eyebrow in an expression I usually only saw on Madison.

"I think your father is a little busy talking stock reports with Mr. Fox." Mrs. Montgomery gestured toward the bar where the two men were standing with tumblers in hand. They sipped their dark liquor, engrossed in conversation like they couldn't hear the roar of the band.

"Your mother's right, Em. Unless you know how the Nasdaq closed on Friday, I doubt you'll be able to interrupt *that* conversation," Mrs. Fox joked, her palm on her spray-tanned chest.

Emily looked away, breathing hard.

"Okay, how 'bout this," I said, jumping in. "If I find us dance partners, will you girls give it a whirl?"

Madison sighed, slumping forward as she flopped her elbows onto the table. "Fine. But they better know how to dance."

I glanced quickly at Emily, who nodded halfheartedly. That was all the confirmation I needed. I darted through the tent toward Lilly.

"All right, what do you got?" I asked, as I quickly approached my cousin. Evan was right beside her. "Madison and Emily will only dance if we find them partners."

Lilly looked at Evan.

"What?" he asked.

"Will your friends dance?"

"Chad and Scott? Are you serious?"

"Well, *you're* dancing."

"So?"

"So doesn't that make it cool?"

"Not to them."

"Come on, can't you talk them into it?" Lilly batted her lashes at Evan as her glossed, dewy lips grinned with seduction.

"Fine." He shook his head and trudged toward his buddies.

"Okay, you handle this. I'm gonna find Bobby. Meet me at Madison's table?" I stated, already walking away.

I rushed toward Bobby, who was standing with a pack of his friends yawning. Thankfully, it wasn't hard to convince him to dance. He looked almost relieved at the suggestion. I swiftly dragged him over to Madison and Emily, who seemed less than thrilled to see us.

"What are we gonna do, split him in three?" Madison snipped, flicking her hands in the air.

"Relax. Lilly's got it taken care of."

I craned my neck and glimpsed Evan, Chad, and Scott clustered around her. Knowing Lilly, the guys were probably fighting over who got to dance with *her* first. But regardless, I was certain she'd be able to talk them into a little salsa. She could talk guys into anything.

"Oh, great. Chad and Scott," Madison whined, following my gaze. "What? Were bin Laden and Hussein busy?"

"They're not that bad."

"Easy for you to say." Madison looked to Bobby.

He was standing silently behind me, and I noticed that Emily's gaze was locked on the condensation dripping from her water glass.

"Em, now that I've shown Bobby what to do, maybe you guys could dance?"

Her face snapped toward mine, her eyes bugged, and her jaw swung open. Clearly I had said the wrong thing, and I noticed her mother looked equally horrified.

"Oh, Mrs. Montgomery. Have you met Bobby McNabb?" I asked, gesturing toward him like Vanna White presenting the new car. "He goes to Spring Mills with us."

Emily's mom stared at Bobby in a way that seemed disapproving, which was odd because the woman usually preached against prejudging people. Maybe those opinions only counted for people who hadn't shown an interest in her daughter.

"Uh, hi," Bobby stated, waving his hand.

"Hello," she said, then turned toward Emily, who was again deeply absorbed by her water glass. "Mariana, are you and Bobby dating?"

I jerked my head back slightly. I expected embarrassing questions from my nosy aunts, but I usually held Emily's mom to a higher standard.

"Um, no. We're just friends."

She straightened her shoulders and rested her chin on her hand like a seasoned professor waiting for more explanation. I was getting nervous.

"We're lab partners," I added.

"And Mariana's locker's next to mine," Bobby said.

"So all of you hang out a lot?" she asked, gesturing toward Emily. "I mean, I know you two went out this summer. . . ."

"Mom!" Emily screeched, snapping her head up.

"What? You did, right? I just thought you guys didn't hang out anymore. . . ."

"Mom, please! Stop talking," Emily ordered, her pupils enlarged.

Bobby took a few steps back as if he thought that would hide him from the uncomfortable situation.

"Fine, fine," Mrs. Montgomery muttered. "I just want to know who your friends are."

"Well, now you do. Does that change anything?" Emily quickly stood up from the table, shaking the china resting on it.

Fighting with your parents is never fun, but fighting with them in front of other people (especially a boy) takes the revolting confrontation to another level. I could feel Emily's humiliation as if it were my own. It was the same way I felt every time my family attacked Teresa.

Madison jumped to her feet, licking her lips, prepared to charge off with her best friend. But Lilly cut them off in their path.

"All right! Let's dance!" cheered my cousin as she strutted up to Emily and Madison, a slew of guys on her heels.

I tried to catch Lilly's eye to express the awkward tension she was cutting into, but she remained oblivious. She was too busy tugging at her halter straps to prevent the guys around her from catching a free peep show (though it looked like they were already satisfied).

"Now, Chad and Scott have agreed to give it a go in the first round. But loads of other boys are just dying to become salsa kings. You girls ready?"

Without a word, Emily marched over to Chad, clutched his hand, and pulled him onto the dance floor. Clearly, she was ready.

Three songs later, and the floor was filled with Spring Mills students. Lilly had taken it upon herself to swipe the band's microphone and offer a five-minute impromptu lesson about the intricacies of hip swiveling. Once the first song was over, enough people felt confident to at least attempt the rhythmic sway. Bobby and I were leading the way along with Teresa and Carlos.

For the first time all night, everyone was having fun.

The brass trombone blared with pounding beats, making it hard to hold a conversation. Sweat poured down my back, and the temperature in the tent rose despite the caterer's extra fans. I closed my eyes as Bobby's hand pulled on my hips. For a second, I almost felt like I was back in Utuado, and it was Alex's arms around me.

"Ya mweally mwood at mwis," Bobby shouted. My eyes snapped open.

"What?" I yelled, leaning toward him.

He pressed his lips against my ear. "You're really good at this."

His breath felt hot and moist, almost like a kiss. A tingle tread down my neck.

"Thanks!" I said, smiling.

I looked over and saw Lilly bouncing between partners. Evan, Chad, Scott, and two other guys were taking turns spinning her across the floor, their eyes locked on her chest. Madison and

Emily rocked next to her, dancing with whomever wasn't winning Lilly's attention. Currently, Lilly was spinning under Scott's arm, Emily under Chad's, and Madison under Evan's. For two people who claimed not to like each other, Evan and Madison were dancing rather close. All grievances must have melted away when their hips pressed tight. It was the power of salsa.

I motioned toward my friends.

"They look like they're having fun!" I yelled.

"Whah?" Bobby asked.

I shook my head, signaling it wasn't important enough to repeat.

We kept dancing as the lead singer crooned in Spanish. I had no idea what he was saying. Song lyrics were always harder to understand, because the words slurred together too rapidly to catch. But he did keep repeating *"Baila, Baila, Baila!,"* which I knew meant we should keep on dancing. And we did, all except for my parents, who were still willfully seated at their table with my aunts and uncles. They looked like kids stuck in 'time out,' they were pouting so much. Technically my mom and dad were hosting this party, so their perfect etiquette should dictate that they at least take one whirl around the dance floor.

I looked up at Bobby. "I'm gonna go talk to my parents!"

"Whah?"

"My parents!" I screamed, pointing toward their table.

Bobby nodded and grabbed my hand, offering to come along. I smiled as I looked down at his fingers laced in mine. Then I quickly glanced at Emily, who was sweaty and busy dancing with Chad.

Together we made our way to my parents' table. They barely looked up.

"All right, what's up with this?" I asked, glaring at my mother. "The hosts of the party can't be spoilsports."

"What do you mean?" she asked as if she had no idea what I was talking about.

"Would it kill you to have a little fun? I know you both can dance."

"We're letting the kids have their fun. We don't want to intrude," said my mom.

"Who says you're intruding? There are adults out there!"

My Uncle Diego grumbled, then shot a look toward my Aunt Joan. She squinted her eyes knowingly.

"Oh, don't tell me this is about Teresa!" I yelled, wrinkling my brow. "What, because she's dancing means that you can't? Do I have to draw a line down the center of the tent?"

"Mariana . . ." my father warned sternly.

"Don't even think of calling me dramatic," I interrupted. "Because if there *are* any drama queens at this party, they're sitting at this table."

"Is that how you let your daughter talk to you?" my Uncle Diego barked.

"Don't talk to me about my parenting."

"Well, maybe someone should."

"What's that supposed to mean?"

"It means that if you hadn't sent your teenage kids off without a chaperone this summer, none of this would have happened. Like you didn't know she lived there."

My father's dark eyes heated as the vein in his forehead began to thump. My hands immediately slimed with sweat, and I released Bobby's palm. He took a few steps back, removing himself from the impending altercation. Thankfully, that gave me one less thing to worry about.

"Actually, I wouldn't know where she lived. *You* made sure of that," my father hissed.

"Oh, please. You want me to apologize for protecting you? Yeah, I'm such a horrible brother."

My Uncle Diego rose to his feet and instantly so did my father.

I looked around the table; everyone was motionless. Even my Uncle Roberto sat mute. Four grown adults refused to step in and stop this. All my mother did was hold her breath, her hands in prayer formation in front her mouth.

"Well, excuse me for not instantly hating this woman like you do," my father ranted.

"How could you not?"

"Because she's done nothing wrong!"

"Tell that to her *mother*!" my uncle shouted.

"Her mother's not here!"

"No, she sent her *dirty bastard daughter* here instead!"

Everyone took a collective inhale, his words ringing in our heads. I turned to gauge exactly how low class Bobby thought my dueling family was, but instead I was smacked with the sight of Teresa. She was standing just a few feet behind me, next to Bobby, with tears collecting in her eyes and a present in her hand.

"I, I, wanted to give a gift . . . to Mariana. From, uh, Alex," she said through a smothered sob, her devastated eyes glancing at me, then at my uncles. "I, I should go."

She spun around and ran toward the tent's exit. This time, I didn't follow her.

Chapter 30

"I can't believe I missed all that!" Lilly cried, leaning back on my bed's fluffy pillows. "You know what? Don't worry about your family right now. Your party was awesome."

"Yeah, it was," Madison added as she crossed her legs on my floor, her pink and orange plaid pajamas hiking up her shins. (Only Madison would have pj's to match my party's color scheme.) "Who knew salsa would be such a hit?"

"I knew," Lilly stated with a smug smile.

"The dancing was cool," I said, then looked at Madison. "And you guys kicked butt. I told you ballet was all the training you'd need."

"Totally. It was a piece of cake."

"Hey, don't forget who taught you your moves," Lilly said, tauntingly. "Maybe I should take ballet. I could be a natural at this dancing thing."

"You can't *start* ballet at sixteen," Madison quipped.

"I'm fifteen. And why not? I started tennis."

"Yeah, and how's that working out for you?"

"Exactly. I can't be any worse at ballet than I am at tennis."

I pulled my knees into my chest as I rubbed Tootsie's head. He was finally liberated from the basement now that all the guests had left. A poor, barely-out-of-high-school waiter looked exhausted as he handed me the leash. I was guessing that my giant poodle wasn't easy to keep quiet amidst the hectic festivities. Tootsie was now dozing quietly at the foot of my bed as my mind drifted back to Teresa—tears hugging the corners of her eyes. I couldn't shake the image from my head. She had looked like she had been punched in the gut, and the vision of her crumbling face still made me wince.

"God, ya know, my uncle, he was awful tonight," I murmured.

"I'm sorry," Lilly whispered.

"At least no one saw," Madison offered optimistically.

"Bobby saw."

After Teresa stormed out, the night felt over for me. Guests stayed for another hour, but I didn't go back onto the dance floor. I was no longer in a salsa mood. My aunts and uncles grabbed their coats and took off moments after the confrontation. My Uncle Diego snarled like someone owed *him* an apology. Never mind that he had tried his hardest to ruin his sixteen-year-old niece's birthday party (such a picture of adulthood). My mother busied herself with cleanup instructions for the caterer, with the help of Madison and Emily's moms, who politely pretended not to have heard the screaming fit that spread across the tent. My dad conveniently joined the men at the bar and drowned himself in bourbon without a single word of explanation.

If my friends and I attacked each other like that at one of my parents' parties, you could bet that my father would never let me hear the end of it. He would lecture until there wasn't a breath in his lungs. I'd watched him do it numerous times with Vince. But no, because they were adults, they seemed to have a free pass to scream and curse no matter what humiliation they caused. Shouldn't it be the other way around? Given their age, shouldn't they be even more mortified by their actions?

"Hey, Bobby couldn't have been any cooler," Lilly counseled. "When I got over to you guys, he really looked concerned. He didn't seem weirded out at all."

"How would you know what Bobby looks like weirded out?" Madison asked.

I turned toward Emily, who was quietly seated on the floor, her back resting on my closet door. She had spent most of the night dancing with guys she barely knew, and didn't like, the day before. I thought she was having a good time, despite her tiff with her mother, but now she seemed back to the sullen state she'd exhibited since I'd come back from Puerto Rico.

"I don't need to know *Bobby*, I know *guys*," Lilly said, wagging her head.

"Yeah, you sure proved that all right." Madison smiled condescendingly. "Exactly how many guys did you *know* back in Puerto Rico?"

"What's that supposed to mean?"

"It means you sure got popular here pretty darn quick."

"Maybe that's because I'm not a stuck-up snob," Lilly muttered.

"Yeah, I'm sure *that's* what the guys are attracted to." Madison glared at my cousin's chest, which was bulging from her tank top. Lilly instantly pulled at her neckline.

I swiftly sat up and flung my hands toward both of them. "Stop it! I really don't need any more crap tonight."

Lilly and Madison nodded begrudgingly.

"Sorry," Lilly grumbled.

"Me too," said Madison.

"So, what the heck am I supposed to do now? Just pretend like my family's not falling to pieces?"

"Do you have a choice?" Emily piped up, her voice faint.

We all turned to her, so surprised she had joined the conversation that we expected her to continue with something deep and meaningful. She simply stared back.

"Well, yeah," I said. "I could confront my father. I could reach out to Teresa. I could make my parents talk some sense into my uncles. . . ."

"Mariana, it's not your place to fix your parents' problems," Emily reasoned.

"Gee thanks, Dr. Phil."

She rolled her eyes and slumped back onto the wall.

"Hey, so what did Alex get you anyway?" Lilly asked, changing the subject.

I chuckled. "A stuffed coqui frog and an 'Everyone Loves Puerto Rican Girls' T-shirt."

"Classy," Madison mocked.

"Very Alex," Lilly stated.

And truthfully, I loved the gifts. I'd never had a boy buy me a present before, and just the fact that he'd remembered and planned far enough in advance to get the gift to me on time, made me feel special.

Just then my cell phone rang. It was hooked into its charger on top of my desk. I wasn't expecting any calls after midnight.

"Who the heck?" I said, strolling over. "Vince."

I flipped open the phone and walked into my bathroom for privacy.

"Hey," I said.

"Happy birthday, Birthday Girl!" Vince cheered.

"You're a little late. It's after midnight."

"Well, it's the thought that counts. Plus I didn't want to disrupt your party. How'd it go?"

"Fine until Mom and Dad started a royal rumble."

"Oh, God. What now? Teresa?"

"Yup. Aunt Joan did her best to mortify the woman. . . ."

"Let me guess—Teresa sucks and '*David's in a new marching band!*'" he said, mocking my aunt's tone.

"You guessed it. Anyway, they're all freakin' lunatics. Uncle Diego called Teresa a 'dirty bastard child' loud enough for the entire party to hear."

"Dude, he's losing it," Vince groaned. "But seriously, let it go."

"How can I?"

"Because, think about it. If we found out Dad had an affair and some other kid hidden away, I think we'd hold a grudge too."

"I know, I know. But it sucks. And it's embarrassing."

"Please, wearing last year's shoes is embarrassing in Spring Mills. Why don't you get out of there? Come visit during initiation. . . ."

"Yeah, I got your e-mails."

"I'm telling you, this place is awesome," he said with a burp.

"Are you drinking right now?"

"Dude, it's Saturday night. I'm wasted. We had this monster kegger at the frat and afterward we all went up to the house's towers and chucked things off. I seriously launched a desk three stories. It shattered like sawdust."

"You better not fail out."

"I won't." He sighed, burping even louder. "Anyway, initiation's next weekend. There's a party, and you can bring your friends. Tons of people'll be there: relatives, alumni, the works."

I paused, considering the offer.

"Mom and Dad probably feel really guilty right now. They'll go for it," Vince added. "And you can tell them that you're coming for a 'campus visit.' "

After a quick minute, I hung up the phone and charged back into my bedroom. My friends were still in the same positions they were when I left. Their eyes flicked toward me as soon as I entered the room.

"Girls, we're going on a road trip."

Chapter 31

By Wednesday, the plans were made. Madison would be driving to Ithaca, thanks to a GPS device her parents installed to help her navigate and to help them track us via satellite. We were mandated to have our cell phones charged and turned on at all times, and Vince would be held solely responsible for keeping us alive while there. If anything happened, my father intended to prosecute him to the fullest extent of the law (if Madison or Emily's parents didn't kill him first).

Vince was right. My dad felt so guilty, he barely argued when I brought up the trip. He simply called Madison and Emily's parents and worked out the details. He even called Lilly's parents in Puerto Rico to explain the plans to them; they were thrilled their daughter would be visiting an Ivy League school. They, along with my Uncle Miguel and Aunt Carmen, had sent me a gold necklace with a crucifix for my birthday. It wasn't exactly my taste, but I knew it must have taken Lilly's mom weeks to pick out. My cousin Alonzo's gift probably didn't require as much thought. He sent me a bottle of piña colada mix to commemorate my one drunken night in Utuado. Of course, he didn't send the alcohol that went with it, but I understood the gesture.

Emily and Madison took the prize for the best birthday gift. They bought me a video iPod with loads of memory and a coordinating stereo. As expected, my parents offered a generous savings bond and a tasteful ring featuring my birthstone, an opal.

I fiddled with the new white-gold ring as I walked toward my locker. Bobby was already standing there. We had barely spoken since my party, aside from minor chemistry-related conversations. This was actually the first time I had seen him at his locker all week, which led me to believe I was being avoided. My guess was that my family drama fell into the "too much information" category. Not that I blamed him. He wasn't my boyfriend. It's not as if he were obligated to stand by me.

"Um, hey," I muttered as I swung my locker's black and white dial.

"Hey," he said, not looking over.

"Look, about my party. I'm sorry you had to see that. . . ."

"You don't have to apologize," he said, looking toward me.

"But, everything that happened. It's just . . ."

"Complicated," he finished, nodding his head like he understood.

"Yeah, and well, a lot of stuff came out while I was in Puerto Rico. . . ."

"Mariana, you really do not need to explain anything to me."

"But you've been so quiet lately." I bit my lip.

"No, God. That has nothing to do with you. I'm not mad at you or anything."

"Oh, because, I just thought . . ."

"I had fun at your party. With you." He smiled as he tugged at the straw-colored hair on the back of his head. "I should have called you. . . ."

"No, no. It's okay." I turned back to my locker.

"I mean, I *wanted* to call you. I want to get together. You know, do something."

"Well, I'm actually not gonna be around this weekend."

"Neither am I."

"I'm going to Cornell."

"So am I."

My forehead scrunched as I peered at him. "Seriously?"

He nodded, his eyebrows shoved high.

"I'm going to visit Vince . . . for this initiation thing."

Bobby broke into a laugh, his neck tossed back revealing his bulging Adam's apple. When he lifted his head, his smile was wide.

"I'm going to the same thing! My dad's an alum at one of the fraternities. He's trying to get me to apply to Cornell and give up the whole NYU dream."

I laughed with him, genuinely amused. "Wow, small world."

"So is it just you?" he asked, as he slammed his locker shut.

"No, me, Lilly, Madison, and Emily. Your whole film festival crew."

He nodded as his lips drooped down. "That's cool," he said, but his eyes drifted elsewhere.

I could tell he was contemplating something I had said, but I couldn't determine what. He hadn't seemed to mind being around Emily before, but maybe her mom's bringing up their date had more of a discomforting effect than I had realized. Or maybe he really did like her. Suddenly, he shook his head as if he had just realized that I was still standing in front of him.

"You know," he continued, changing topics. "Dean Pruitt picked the date for the festival. It's the Friday before Thanksgiving week."

"That's great. We'll *all* help," I said, cautiously. "We might get busy with ballet. We have a performance right before Christmas. But, we'll make time."

"Cool." Bobby tossed his backpack over his shoulder, looking deep in thought once more. "Uh, see you later."

For some reason, when he left, things felt as awkward between us as before we talked.

Chapter 32

The next day, as I pulled my sport bag out of my locker, my muscles ached. I was headed to our fourth ballet practice of the week. Madame Colbert had accelerated the schedule to make sure she had chosen the right dancer for each part. So far, Emily hadn't shown any direct animosity toward me or the secondary role she was asked to play. Her practices for Caraboose were challenging and intense, and she really nailed the dark emotions of the character. Probably because they mimicked the moody personality she'd adopted in the past few weeks.

Only today's practice was set to focus almost entirely on Princess Aurora's sixteenth birthday scene, which featured my largest and most demanding solo. The last thing I wanted was to dance Emily into another gloomy mood, and these days I didn't know what was going to trigger the blues.

I smashed my locker shut and started my trek toward Madison's to catch my usual ride. All the time we spent in the car this week was devoted to discussing our Cornell plans. Madison bought an entirely new wardrobe for the occasion, claiming she needed to "look collegiate." This included new jeans, tight yet casual sweaters, European leather boots (not sure how they tied in), and a fresh crop of makeup in neutral tones so she wouldn't look like "a made-up high school girl." I, on the other hand, hadn't spent a moment contemplating my soon-to-be-packed attire. I was visiting my brother. The boy had seen me at the breakfast table with greasy hair and an unwashed face. I didn't need to impress him or any of his friends. Bobby was a different story. But I doubted I would see him. He'd be with his dad, and I was sure they'd have their own schedule.

From down the hall, I spied a group of teens gathered in front of Madison's locker, chatting and flirting. As they dispersed, I caught a glimpse that stopped me in my tracks. Madison was standing with her hand resting on her locker door gazing up at Evan Casey as he leaned in with an easy grin. Their eyes were locked and their bodies were angled comfortably toward each other. Only it was the way they were smiling, with a mix of shyness and flirtation, that made me pause. A wave of anxiety sped through my bones.

I took a long breath and slowly walked toward them.

"Hey," I said, loudly. "Hope I'm not interrupting anything."

Evan immediately straightened his shoulders, and Madison turned away.

"Um, no. Evan was just telling me how much fun he had at your party. I told him you'd be here in a second, so he could tell you himself," Madison said as she stared at the contents of her tote bag.

"Uh, yeah. It was a blast. I loved all that Spanish stuff," he said.

"Yeah, you're a pretty good dancer," I said, stepping toward him with an innocent grin across my face. "I guess *Lilly's* a good teacher, huh?"

"Oh, yeah. She's great." He nodded.

"I know everyone was really impressed by how well you guys danced together. You know, when it was just the four of us out there."

Madison's gaze remained focused on her bag as she shoved in book after book.

Evan shrugged. "It was no big deal. It was mostly Lilly they were looking at. And you."

"No, I really think it was the two of you *together*," I said in my happiest tone. "So have you been to any more of her tennis matches?"

He cleared his throat awkwardly and stepped back.

" 'Cause Lilly said you stopped by yesterday's match to cheer her on. That was very cool of you. I couldn't make it because of ballet practice. But I'm sure Madison told you all about that."

Madison glanced at me sideways.

"Um, no. Why would I tell Evan that?"

"Oh, I don't know. I thought it would have come up when you were talking."

"Talking? When? In the two-second conversation we had before you walked over?" She shook her head, bewildered.

"I guess I was wrong. My bad." I looked at Evan. "By the way, thanks for the new gym bag. I haven't used it yet; my mom said I have to wait until I send out all my thank you cards. But I'm looking forward to it."

"Oh, Betsy picked it out," he said, before adjusting the strap of his messenger bag and walking away. "See you guys later."

"Yeah, bye!" I cheered.

I shot my head toward Madison, my eyes reduced to slits. "What was that?"

"What?" She slammed her locker shut and scanned the hallway for Emily, who was late for the second time this week.

"You and Evan."

"There is no 'me and Evan.' "

"It sure looked like there was."

"We danced at your party. I got to talk to him. He's not a bad guy."

"Well, I'm pretty sure Lilly likes him."

"Yeah, and I thought Emily liked Bobby," she snipped, just as Emily came into view.

"It's not like that."

"Me neither."

We both grabbed our bags and marched toward our friend.

* * *

"What do you mean you're not going?" Madison cried as we drove out of the school parking lot.

"I mean, I don't feel like practicing today. Can you just take me home?"

"But why?" Madison was shooting quick glances at Emily as she drove.

"Because I don't feel well," Emily continued.

"You're lying."

"How do you know? My stomach hurts."

"No, it doesn't."

"What do you want me to do? Puke in your car?"

I could see Emily's expression in the side-view mirror from my usual spot in the back. She didn't look sick. She looked sad. Her shoulders hunched forward and her eyelids drooped. She almost had that vulnerable look of someone who'd been crying.

"Em, look, I'm sorry you didn't get the part. It's just one performance. And you're doing really well in your role," I said, reaching for her shoulder.

"Mariana, it's not about that," she snapped, shooting me an icy stare starkly different from the sullen mood she had expressed moments ago. "God, does everything have to be about *you*?"

I cringed, a wrinkle forming between my brows.

"I didn't say that," I said softly.

"No, I know. I'm sorry," she mumbled. "I just don't feel well."

Madison flicked another brief look at her friend. "Is there something going on with you?"

"No, I just don't feel like going to ballet today. Since when is that a crime?"

"Fine. I'll drive you home."

"You're still going to Cornell this weekend, right?" I asked, half-afraid the sound of my voice would set her off more.

"Yes, definitely," she stated plainly.

We drove the rest of the way to her house in silence. When we dropped her off, there were no cars in the driveway. No one was home. She didn't look surprised. She probably wanted the solitude.

Chapter 33

It was a four-hour drive to Ithaca. We were halfway there and already through two of Madison's preselected playlists. The car was getting smaller.

"Seriously, how long is this drive?" Emily whined from the passenger seat, where her legroom was about double the space in the rear.

She was surprisingly on time this morning. And no one brought up the skipped ballet practice. She had never missed rehearsal before (aside from scheduled family vacations), so Madame Colbert didn't waste a second questioning her illness. Not like Madison and I did. We still hadn't managed to find out what was actually bothering her.

"Hey, you're not the one driving," Madison droned from behind the wheel. "Don't you think I'd rather be lounging around daydreaming to the music?"

"At least you have something to keep you occupied," Emily continued.

"What? Not getting us killed? Yeah, I guess that does pass the time."

"Can we please listen to something other than Justin Timberlake?" Lilly pleaded, tossing her head against the back of her seat.

"This is Nick Lachey," Madison argued.

"Is there a difference?"

"Uh, yeah."

"Well, then how 'bout this? Do we have anything other than this God awful pop music?"

"What would make you happy, Lil? Some Ricky Martin? A little Marc Anthony?" Madison mocked. "I'm sure I have your people on my iPod somewhere."

"All right, chill out," I piped up. "Lilly, this is Madison's car and she's driving, so she gets to control the radio."

"So, we all just have to suffer at her mercy?"

"Pretty much." Madison smiled wide into the rearview mirror.

The trees outside were already changing colors. The farther north we drove, the more colorful they got. Dozens of golden or red-leaved trees whizzed by on the hilly landscape. Within an hour, the scenery had gone from suburban to country, and the closer we got to Ithaca, the more rural the view.

But I still couldn't picture Vince's campus. My parents had described these "mini Grand Canyons" plopped in the middle of the university grounds with pedestrian bridges for students to cross. They even brought me back an "Ithaca is Gorges" T-shirt, thinking it was so clever. I had a hunch it was as unique as an "I heart New York" T-shirt in the middle of Times Square.

"So what exactly *is* the plan?" Madison asked as she swiftly changed lanes.

"Well, we lucked out because both of Vince's roommates are away this weekend. So we have beds to sleep in," I said, leaning forward to chat between the front seats.

"Two in a bed?" Emily groaned.

"Hey, it's better than the floor."

She shrugged.

"We'll probably just walk around for a bit. See the campus," I explained. "Then, we'll hang out at his fraternity. He got initiated last night, and he claims it's been 'nonstop partying' ever since."

"Vince could throw nonstop parties in the public library," Madison scoffed.

"This is true. But he said a lot of people come up for this. So we're not the only 'guests.' . . ."

My voice trailed off. I hadn't told them about Bobby yet. I thought if Emily heard that he was going to be there, she wouldn't come with us. And now that I'd kept quiet so long, I felt like I was lying. (Who created the whole 'lie by omission' term anyway?)

"Oh, cool. So there will be other high school kids?" Madison asked.

"Um, yeah," I mumbled, slumping back in my seat. "That's sorta the thing . . ."

"What?" Emily asked, twisting her neck toward me.

"Well, it's just, I mean, I was gonna tell you. . . ."

"What?" Madison asked, peering at me through her mirror. "Spit it out."

"It's just, well, Bobby's gonna be there," I said in a barely audible voice.

"What?" They all screamed in unison.

"Bobby McNabb?" Emily choked.

"*Our* Bobby. As in 'Locker Buddy Bobby.' He's going to be there?" Madison asked.

"Yeah. It has nothing to do with us," I said quickly. "His dad's an alum. He's taking Bobby up there to try to convince him to apply to Cornell."

"When did you find this out?" Emily glared at me.

"On Wednesday," I murmured.

"Three days ago! And you're just telling us *now*!" she shrieked.

"Why does it matter? He had plans to go long before he found out we were going. And he's our friend. . . ."

"So, then why didn't you tell us?" Madison asked.

Lilly was seated silently beside me with a slight grin on her face. She had been encouraging me to pursue something romantically with Bobby for weeks now, and I was certain she saw this weekend as our big opportunity. If it made Madison or Emily uncomfortable in the process, that was just a bonus.

I paused, my eyes shooting between Madison and Emily.

"You want the truth?" I asked.

They both nodded.

"Fine. I didn't tell you, because I thought you'd make a big deal out of it," I said, looking at Madison. Then I turned my gaze toward Emily. "And I thought *you* wouldn't come if you knew he'd be there."

"So, you intentionally wanted to put me in an awkward situation," Emily stated. "Gee, thanks."

"Why does it have to be awkward?"

"Because it is!"

"Because you two went out this summer?"

Emily opened her mouth to say something, then snapped it shut.

"What? Em, tell me. Because I don't understand. *Do* you like him?"

"I'm not having this conversation right now," she huffed.

"Well, why not? When *would* be a good time? Because I've been trying to get you to have this conversation for weeks now!"

Lilly's face glowed with joy as I spoke up to the two of them. She'd been going on relentlessly about my friends' dislike of her, probably with the secret hope that I would suddenly not like them too. And while that wasn't going to happen, I was certain that seeing us argue was boosting her hope that it would.

"Why do you want to talk about it? So you can feel better about yourself for dating him?" Emily asked.

"I am *not* dating him!"

"Whatever." She shook her head.

I paused, closed my eyes, and sucked in a long breath. Slowly, I unclenched my fists, relaxed my shoulders, and popped open my eyes.

"Em, I would never start anything with Bobby if I thought you liked him. But the thing is, I don't know if you do," I said calmly. "You don't talk to me anymore."

"Mariana, you were gone a long time," Madison butted in.

"I was gone for two months."

"And you changed." Madison glanced over her shoulder to-ward Lilly.

"Oh, so this is all *my* fault?" Lilly snipped. "Blame the Puerto Rican stowaway!"

I shot Lilly a look, thrusting my eyebrows, then turned back toward the front seats.

"Ya know, who cares if Bobby's gonna be there? This is our weekend," I said, hoping to lighten the mood. "Let's have fun."

A quiet stillness fell over the car, and we drove the next few miles in silence.

Chapter 34

I knew October was one of the best times to visit Cornell, but I didn't expect it to look so much like a cheesy collegiate brochure. It was the exact picture kids have in their heads when they imagine the word *college*.

Students in red and gray sweatshirts with frayed baseball caps walked through spacious quads that were dusted in burnt orange leaves. Rustling trees, full of autumn hues, lined every paved road and dirt path. Bikes were parked in front of stone buildings with quaint parapets and sweeping arches. Apples, from yellow to crimson, were sold in rustic roadside stands. And students lounged on faded grass, books spread open before them, enjoying the last few weeks before the harsh upstate New York winter roared in.

"Wow, I can't wait until that's me," Madison mumbled.

"Just the idea of being able to do what you want, when you want," said Emily.

"Studying outside when the weather's nice . . ." I added.

"Shopping in between classes . . ."

"Partying on the weekends . . ."

"Being away from our parents."

There was a palpable sense of longing in all of our voices. I had never been jealous of Vince before, not until this very moment. But he was right. This was so much better than Spring Mills.

We met Vince at his dorm. He helped us lug the immense quantity of belongings we had crammed into the trunk for our one-night visit. Each of us had our own 'weekend bag' (which in Madison's case was a piece of luggage large enough for a one-month excursion), plus we brought towels, sleeping bags, blankets, and pillows so we wouldn't be reliant upon his roommates' things. It took us three trips to unload the car.

"All right, so this is home!" Vince stood and swung his arms to showcase the room.

It was refreshingly spacious with three desks, towering windows, and painted white walls surprisingly not constructed of cinderblock. They each had their own closet and a five-shelf bookcase.

"Here's the kitchen." Vince chuckled, pointing toward an illegal coffeepot and hot plate resting on his bookshelf. "It took my going away to college for Mom and Dad to finally let me break the rules."

"And this is my room, Andre's room, and Paul's room." He pointed to each of their beds, all covered in different solid-colored comforters (in basic boy shades of red, blue, and green).

"Here's the living room." He gestured to a small thirteen-inch TV, illegally hooked up to cable, resting on a trunk with a black folding butterfly chair in front of it. "And the bathroom's down the hall. Don't worry, there are separate girls' and boys' bathrooms. You brought shower shoes, right?"

We nodded. Actually, we had made a separate trip after school to pick up cheap flip-flops worthy of a disgusting communal shower. We planned to throw them out before we headed home.

"You guys can just toss all your stuff on their beds. Then, we can head out."

"Where are we going?" I asked.

"I'm giving you the grand campus tour, which you should find very impressive given that I drank half a case of beer last night. I swear I have more alcohol than blood in my system right now."

"Aw, you should put that in a Hallmark card and send it to Mom and Dad," I teased.

"You try going through initiation sober. . . ."

"How was it?" My eyes lit up.

"Humiliating. They shoved us each into a tiny nook in the frat house and made us sit there for twenty-four hours. Thankfully, I was stuck in a shower stall, so at least I could take a piss. . . ."

"Ew, gross!" Madison squealed, cringing. "What about the other guys?"

"I don't want to know." He shook his head laughing. "Then, they brought us into this cigar-smoke-filled room where these old alumni asked the most ridiculous questions. The whole point was to laugh and tell us we were stupid."

"Gee, sounds like fun." I huffed.

"Well, you're missing the best part. They read our most retarded answers to the whole pledge class. It was hilarious. Some dude said he thought the Philippines were in the Caribbean— and he said it *to* a Philippino alumnus."

"And you like this?" I asked.

"Yeah, it was nuts. Then afterward, we got initiated." He shrugged.

"Well, how did they do it?" I asked.

"Was there a secret ceremony?" Madison added.

"If I told you, I'd have to kill you," he joked. "But seriously, I'm officially a brother now, and we're gonna have a slammin' party tonight to celebrate."

"Sounds good to me," Lilly said loudly, with a shiny grin. "I haven't had a beer since I left Utuado."

"Don't worry. I'll take care of that," Vince quipped. He snatched his messenger bag from his desk and headed to the door, foolishly thinking we were ready to leave.

"Vince, you realize I need to get ready, right?" Madison asked, staring at him cross-eyed.

"Ready for what?" he asked.

"I've been in a car for more than four hours! I'm not going out like this! There are, like, hundreds of college guys out there."

While Madison's expression was horrified, her outfit, hair, and makeup were absolutely perfect—though I didn't dare say it.

"You better sit down, Vince. This could be a while." I smirked.

We all plopped down onto the beds as Madison dove elbow-deep into her suitcase. I wasn't in a hurry. I liked seeing where Vince lived. His familiar movie posters on the wall, his family pictures on the shelf, his CDs lined up. Seeing all that well-worn stuff was oddly reassuring. It was like having him back.

An hour later we were finally strolling through campus. Vince led us on a tour of the gorges, which were as mystifying as my parents had described. Campus facilities sat around giant gaping holes in the earth that jutted out in sharp angles, dropping hundreds of feet toward bubbling creeks below.

We were currently standing about halfway across the steel suspension bridge above Fall Creek Gorge. Vince said it was the deepest gorge on campus, and by the looks of the massive abyss below, he was right. A rush of white water flowed over a mesh of brown rocks. I leaned onto the metal safety rail and could see a shallow waterfall off in the distance protruding from a wall of thick green and yellow trees.

"You know, kids kill themselves here all the time," Vince whispered ominously.

"Nuh uh," Madison scoffed, resting against the rail.

"Yeah, they do. At least one kid dives into the gorge each semester. But no one's jumped yet. . . ."

"Vince, you're lying."

Lilly and Emily stepped beside me. We all pushed against the rail, staring into the dramatic gorge.

"I'm serious. Cornell has the highest suicide rate in the country. Ask anyone. But, seriously, who knows if they're all *really* suicides. . . ."

"What are you talking about?" asked Lilly.

"Kids get drunk all the time. Can you imagine wobbling over this bridge wasted in the dark? I mean, accidents happen."

"You're saying kids just fall in?" Lilly asked.

"Don't believe him!" I warned.

"Fine, don't. But if you look all the way down, all the way to the bottom, you can see the wooden crosses students placed in honor of every student who's jumped," he whispered in a deep voice before taking a few steps back.

"No way," Emily muttered.

"Where?" Madison asked.

"All the way at the bottom. Off toward the right."

We craned our necks over the rail, peering into the dark. My hands gripped the metal spokes as I glimpsed a hint of something faint below. I strained my eyes, struggling to make it out, until suddenly the bridge rocked below my feet. My upper body flung back as I stumbled to catch my balance in the rapid ripple of quakes.

We yelped, our hands clenched to our chests, as we spun around to find Vince laughing hysterically. He was jumping up and down.

"That was awesome!" Vince yelled between cackles. "I can't believe you guys fell for that!"

He bent over with a spasm of giggles. I quickly darted toward him with my leather purse held high.

"You jerk!" I screamed, pounding him with my oversized bag.

Lilly, Madison, and Emily rushed over, their bags swinging.

"I can't believe you did that!"

"Jerk, jerk, jerk!"

"Stop it! Stop it! Can't you take a joke?" he hollered, his arms swatting wildly.

"That was rude!" I yelled with a massive thud.

"It was funny!" he said. "The bridge shakes."

He glanced up innocently, then quickly straightened his shoulders, perfected his posture, and calmed his expression.

"Um, hey! Good to see you," he said to a person standing behind us.

We all slowly placed our bags on our shoulders as discreetly as possible. A rash of heat sprinkled across my face. I didn't know why I cared that a stranger saw me assaulting my brother with an angry mob, but for some reason I did.

"Don't mind my sister," Vince muttered, clearing his throat. "Hey, wait. You're the alum from Spring Mills, right? My sister and her friends go there."

We all turned around, knowing in the pit of our stomachs exactly what was about to transpire, but still unprepared anyway. I landed face-to-face with Bobby and his dad, and the air sucked from my chest. My face burned from pink to fire-engine red.

"Bobby, aren't these your friends from the film screening?" Mr. McNabb asked, staring at us. We stayed mute.

"Um, yeah," Bobby muttered, nodding. "Uh, hi."

I forced an unnatural smile.

Chapter 35

We sat alone in Vince's room. He was at the frat house help-ing make dinner for his new brothers. Not that they needed help; the fraternity employed a full-time cook. But dur-ing initiation, they gave their greasy-omelet-maker the week off while pledges took over breakfast, lunch, and dinner duties. Vince was cooking spaghetti and meatballs while we dined on pizza and watched Madison apply her seventh layer of mascara.

"They're *college* guys," she insisted for the umpteenth time.

"They're college guys who were in high school just last year," Lilly pointed out as she stretched across Vince's bed.

"Not all of them. And regardless, they're still cooler than the bunch of losers we go to school with."

"Yeah, well when those 'losers' go to college will that instantly make them cool?"

Madison sighed and put down her mascara.

"Hey, I realize that Spring Mills is new to you, and the guys might seem '*fantastico*.' But we've been stuck with them for twelve years. We've seen them eat paste."

Lilly squinted her eyes as Madison casually yanked a lip-gloss palette out of her makeup bag.

"Whatever." Lilly sighed. "I really don't think you guys have much to complain about. The boys at your school are smart and nice and normal."

"What? Like Evan?"

My gaze shot toward Madison. She looked smug.

"Maybe. Why not?"

Madison pumped her shouders. "'Cause he's not that great."

"How would you know?"

"Because *everyone* knows."

"Look, we're at Cornell. Who cares about Evan Casey?" I said. "Seriously, there is a whole fraternity of guys over there who have never heard of Spring Mills. Let's enjoy that for the night."

"That's not true," Emily mumbled.

She was seated by the window with a slice of uneaten pizza resting on a paper plate beside her. Even as she spoke, she continued staring at the group of guys tossing a football in the quad.

"What? Because of Bobby?" Madison asked.

"Uh, yeah."

"Em, he's gonna be there with his dad," I stated. "It's not like he can have a rip-roaring good time. He'll probably leave before midnight."

She peered out the window, her mood hovering above a fault line between sullen and depressed.

I couldn't believe Bobby's father was an alum in Vince's fraternity. Of all the schools and all the frats, these two worlds had to collide at the exact wrong moment. Last year, a connection between Bobby and Vince would have been utterly insignificant. But now, with Emily pouting at the mention of his name and me sweating at the sight of him, things were getting complicated.

"So, how weird was it seeing Bobby on the bridge today?" Madison asked us through the mirror as she dusted her face with powder. "It was like that time I saw Dean Pruitt having dinner with his wife in a restaurant . . . like normal people."

"I know." I nodded. "Seeing teachers outside of school is bizarre. Like you expect them to exist only in that building."

I was hoping to shift the conversation and perk Emily up, but her sunken eyelids continued to hang heavily as she gazed out the window at nothing. I looked at Madison through the mirror and gestured toward Emily. She shrugged and shook her head, as if acknowledging the hopelessness of the situation.

"Hey, Em. You okay?" I asked.

No response.

"Um, Emily . . . Hello . . . Em!"

She shook her head and turned her dead eyes toward me.

"What? I'm sorry. Did you say something?"

"Is something wrong?" I asked softly.

"No, I was just thinking," she whispered.

"Dude, Em, you gotta lighten up," Madison griped. "We're visiting a college. On our own. Without our parents. And only Vince, 'he who has been arrested for underage drinking,' as a chaperone. What's there to mope about?"

"Nothing. I'm not moping. I just, I don't know." She ran her fingers through the short chocolate layers near her face. "We ready to go soon?"

"Yeah," I said.

"Well, that depends on how many more coats of makeup Madison cakes on," Lilly joked.

"Very funny." Madison tossed a makeup brush at her.

"Be careful! You don't want to waste any!" Lilly chuckled, batting the brush away.

We all giggled, even Emily.

About thirty minutes later, Vince swung by the dorm and walked us to his frat house. The place looked like Cinderella's castle. Thick gray stones soared three stories high with round, pointed towers flanking each end. A parking lot sat in the rear, covered in golden leaves shed from the grove of trees shading the property. In front was a stone patio that swept along the house to the rustic wooden door that led inside. If there were a moat, I was certain the door could serve as a drawbridge; that's how solid it was.

The party wouldn't start for another hour, so when we walked in, all of the brothers were setting up beer stations and entertaining alums who had strolled through hoping to see their old bedrooms. We sat down on the massive brown leather couches in the front atrium. The ceiling stood at least thirty feet above us, with a wooden railing encircling the balcony of the second floor. That's where the new brothers' bedrooms were, where Vince hoped to live next year. I was told that in the rear of the house was a staircase that led up to upperclassmen's rooms on the third floor (which had access to the castle towers) and down to the basement suites (which had their own outdoor patios and were only steps away from the twenty-four-hour kitchen).

The first floor atrium, where we were seated, was lined with sweeping archways that led to game rooms, TV rooms, dining rooms, and libraries. The party would be held entirely on this floor. Vince was currently setting up the speakers in one of the libraries; so Madison, Lilly, and I whispered to each other as we watched his brothers pass.

"Okay, he's hot," Madison said softly as she pointed to a blond guy with cropped hair, a goatee, and a crew team T-shirt.

"He's okay, but he's kinda short," said Lilly. "I like that guy."

She pointed to a dark-haired, dark-eyed twenty-something who looked like he had a mix of ethnicities running through his veins.

"You think he's Asian?" Madison asked.

"Probably half," I replied. "He kinda looks like Tiger Woods."

They nodded in agreement.

"Nice pick," I said.

"I still think the blond's hotter," Madison stated.

"That's because *you* are blond," said Lilly.

"So? What does that have to do with anything?"

"Blonds prefer other blonds. You guys are drawn to each other. Like every other color is inferior."

Madison grunted. "Not my fault you're a redhead."

"It's auburn," Lilly and I defended in unison.

"What-ev," Madison chuckled.

"I'd have you know that there are entire redhead fetishes out there," I stated.

"There are foot fetishes too. Is that really the company you want to keep?"

"Shut up," I huffed, shoving her shoulder.

"All right! I'm done!" Vince cheered as he entered the atrium. "Lemme take you guys on the grand tour. Introduce you to people."

We all stood and smoothed our carefully chosen skirts and jeans. Madison, of course, had chosen a black skirt and heels to highlight her perfect, petite butt. I, however, wore the same jeans I wore to the bonfire. Vince had warned me that the cuffs of my pants might have an inch of beer sludge on them by the night's end. Madison refused to take the advice, as expected. The day she chose practicality over fashion would be the day *Vogue* displayed "mom jeans" and sweater vests on its cover.

We followed Vince toward a wide sweeping staircase. His first order of business was to show us the restrooms we could use during the party. He had managed to gain us access to one of the brothers' private bathrooms so we wouldn't have to wait in line. Apparently, toilet privileges were a huge honor in the fraternity, and Vince was overjoyed at having pulled off such a major feat for his little sister. I couldn't wait to tell Mom and Dad. They'd be so proud.

Chapter 36

By ten o'clock the house was full of strangers. Girls with center-parted, straight hair and boot-cut jeans chatted with guys in gray T-shirts, baggy pants, and short haircuts. Red and blue keg cups were clutched in every hand. Top 40 tunes blared through the speakers, and the musty smell of beer filled the air.

My feet were sticking to the wood floor as I walked toward the bookcase my friends congregated before. I wasn't even drinking, and I was still the first to use the bathroom. I've always had the bladder of an infant. I had to pee right before every ballet performance, or I wouldn't be able to hold it the entire show. And after seeing the mildew-stained, urine-scented bathroom, which was considered "really nice" for Vince's fraternity, I guessed that my bladder would be getting quite a workout while I tried to hold it in for the next several hours.

"So how was it?" Madison asked as Lilly and I returned.

We peed in pairs, mostly so one could guard the door while the other was occupied. The lock, of course, was broken.

"Ya know those rest stops on I-95?" I asked, raising an eyebrow.

"That bad, huh?"

"Worse. Like hold-your-nose-to-try-not-to-gag gross."

"Well, that would explain why a group of guys just peed out the window."

"They did not!"

"Oh, yeah. They just opened the window over there and whipped it out." Madison pointed to a row of old windows nestled between two oak bookcases. "They didn't care who saw."

"One guy farted," Emily added.

"I can't believe these are Vince's friends."

I watched as Madison sipped her warm beer. She had been holding it so long it had lost its foam. She hated the taste. So did Emily and I. Lilly, on the other hand, had no problem sucking them down. She was already halfway through her second cup, which Vince proudly fetched for her.

Emily and I were empty-fisted. I debated getting a beer just to have something to hold. But people kept bumping into us, and I figured it wasn't worth the stains on my clothes.

"So, do we just keep standing here talking in a circle? Or do we go up to some of these guys?" Lilly asked as she scanned the room.

"You go first," I nodded at her with a crooked grin.

"I mean, isn't this why we came here? To meet guys? 'Cause we're never gonna do that standing here yappin' to each other."

"Yeah, but it's still early," Madison defended.

"And I'm sure Vince will introduce us to people. Just wait," I added.

Truthfully, the idea of walking up to a complete stranger and introducing myself made me want to throw up in my mouth a little. I wasn't shy, once I knew the person. But getting over that initial hump was another story. I preferred a solid, well-orchestrated introduction, and I was willing to wait for my brother to offer it.

"Hey, Em, I think that guy's checking you out," Madison stated, nudging our friend with her elbow.

I followed Madison's gaze to a very tall, very built, brown-haired guy with blue eyes so bright we could see them across the room. He was standing by the front door with a pack of equally gorgeous friends, who I could only suspect were basketball stars, because each one was taller than the next. The brunette slowly ran his hand across the back of his neck as his eyes smiled at Emily.

"Oh, my God. He is!" I cheered, batting her thigh with the back of my hand.

Emily shuffled her feet and slid her fingers through her glossy brown hair. "No he's not."

"He definitely is," Lilly agreed, craning her neck to see him.

"Okay, we're staring at him like rejects," Madison warned, turning her head back around. "We're gonna freak him out."

"Why don't you go over there and talk to him?" Lilly suggested.

"No way." Emily shook her head.

"Why not?"

"Well, first off, we're jail bait," Emily pointed out plainly.

"What are you talking about?" Lilly asked.

"You know it's illegal for any of these guys to actually hook up with us, right?" I thought it was an obvious detail.

"Shut up! Seriously?"

"Lil, you're fifteen! These guys could be in their twenties."

"Oh, good point."

Just then, the massive front door opened and in walked a pack of older men ranging from their thirties to their fifties. They were all decked out in dark suits with crimson and cobalt ties. Most were on the pudgy side, and more than half looked like well-worn fathers. It was clear they were the men who donated to the house we were standing in; who provided scholarships to the students currently attending; and who paid the bills for their cook, their furniture, and their flat screen TVs. Near the edge of the crowd, I spotted Mr. McNabb, and right behind him was a pool of teenagers, Bobby among them.

I turned toward Emily, who drew in a quick breath.

"Ya know what?" Emily said suddenly. "I want a drink. Lilly, will you show me where you got that?"

She raised her chin at my cousin's plastic cup.

"Um, well, Vince got it for me. But I think the keg's in the back."

Emily spun around and charged toward the game room. Lilly was right behind her.

Bobby made a beeline straight for us. His dad and his peers were engulfed by the brothers, and their teenage sons looked happy for a much-needed reprieve.

"Do you have any idea what it's like listening to a forty-eight-hour sales pitch from your father?" Bobby asked as he sauntered over.

"My dad's the head of marketing for a Fortune 500 company," Madison remarked, staring at her phone. "I get sales pitches on whether to order chicken or fish."

"But is your dad insisting that you go to his alma mater?"

"Actually he is." She smiled. "But I'm fine with it. I'd love to go to Duke. Practically, my whole family went there."

"Yeah, well, great for you. But I want to go to NYU in Manhattan. Not some pretentious school in the middle of nowhere."

"I don't think it's pretentious," Madison stated as her manicured fingers flew over the keys of her cell.

Bobby narrowed his eyes at her and pulled his lips tight. He was about to pop.

"Did you tell your dad how you feel?" I asked.

"Uh, yeah. Of course. And you'd think since the man teaches at Penn, he'd be a little more open-minded regarding the quality of academic institutions other than the one on his diploma. *But noooooo.*"

I stifled a laugh and shot my palm to my mouth. "Sorry, it's not funny."

"Errr!" he grunted. "You know what? I need a beer. You want a beer?" He looked at me.

"No, I don't drink beer."

"So? When in Rome . . ." He shook his head.

"No, thanks. Won't your dad see you?"

"You know, I hope he does. Then, at least it would give him something else to lecture me about. Maybe I could play it off as his precious fraternity being a bad influence."

Bobby took off in search of the keg, leaving Madison and I behind.

"That kid needs to chill out," Madison said as her phone beeped, signaling another text.

I tried to catch a glimpse of her screen, but she tilted it away. Before I could try again, Emily and Lilly wobbled over.

"I just did my first keg stand!" Emily shouted as she tripped slightly. She grabbed the bookcase to steady herself.

My eyes flicked toward Lilly, who simply shrugged.

"You did what?"

"A keg stand! Vince and this kid Joe held my legs up as I chugged beer from the keg tap. I rocked!" she cheered.

"Seventeen seconds." Lilly nodded. "Incredibly impressive for a first-timer."

My mouth dropped toward the beer sludge below. Emily wouldn't even drink out of my sport bottle during ballet. She thought water fountains were germ farms. She wouldn't eat hotdogs from venders because of sanitation concerns. And she just put her lips on a dirty keg tap shared by God only knows how many frat guys before her.

I stared at her full cup of brew. "*Is that her first one?*" I mouthed to Lilly.

She shook her head "no."

"Em, don't you think you might want to take it easy? You've never gotten drunk before."

"I've drank . . . drunk? drunken? before." She giggled as she questioned her ability to conjugate English verbs. "Remember, at my cousin's wedding."

"Yeah, you had three glasses of champagne and threw up," I said.

"So? I still drank!" Her pearly teeth showed as she smiled wide.

Madison's fingers again floated over her cell phone, catching Lilly's eye.

"Who you texting?"

"No one." Madison shrugged.

"Clearly, it's someone. Or you wouldn't be texting."

"It's nothing," she said, before pressing send and flipping her phone closed. She looked at Emily, then at her watch. "Wow, you've been gone for thirty minutes, and you're already stumbling!"

Emily's hand slid off the bookshelf supporting her, tossing her off balance. Lilly quickly grabbed her arm.

"Did I forget to mention the Jell-O shots?" Lilly asked, her shoulders raised as she clenched her teeth.

"Mariana!" Vince yelled as he pushed his way over. "Did you hear about Emily! Dude, she kicks ass!"

Three frat buddies were tailing him. Two of them had giant wet stains down the fronts of their shirts, which I prayed were from beer.

Emily beamed prettily and stretched her arms over her head like a ref signaling a touchdown. "Whoo hoo!" she shouted.

"Emily's a champ. You should have seen her!"

"Yeah, I heard all about it." I nodded at him, my brown eyes wide.

"Oh, don't be like *Mom*," he droned. "Ricky over here just shotgunned a beer in five seconds. Five!" Vince patted his red-headed friend on the back.

Ricky was staring at me like a child molester. I scrunched my nose as he stepped close. The rank smell of alcohol hung on his breath.

"Hey, baby. I have red hair, you have red hair. Why don't we . . . get together?"

I swallowed the bile in my throat.

"Back off, buddy. She's my sister!" Vince yelled, shoving him away.

"Hey! Did you guys hear they filled up the pool with gold-fish!" another brother shouted as he darted toward Vince.

"No way! Where?"

"Outside the TV room! There's, like, a thousand fish in it! Chuck already ate, like, three of them!"

We all groaned and clutched our stomachs. Just the thought of having a live fish, I didn't care how small, swimming inside me sent a pulse of nausea waving through my belly. Emily gripped her hand over her mouth and for a second I thought she might puke, but she slowly regained her composure.

"Ah man! We had this killer beach party last week," Vince explained. "Some kid brought an inflatable pool and filled it with tadpoles. . . ."

"I really don't need to know anymore." I cut him off quickly just as a black-haired, heavy-set guy halted in front of Lilly.

He didn't even attempt to mask the fact that he was staring down her V-necked blouse. "Dude, bombs!" he yelled, drool on his chin.

"Those real?" another guy asked.

"She's fifteen!" Vince hollered.

All the guys flinched, groaning loudly. "Why the heck is she here?"

"That's not fair!"

"God wouldn't make 'em if he didn't want us to see 'em. . . ."

"Back off! All of you!" Vince shoved them toward the exit of the room.

"Don't mind them," he said. "But I'm gonna check out the goldfish pool. Wanna come?"

"No, we're fine. Thanks," I answered.

Then he patted my shoulder and took off toward the back room with his boys.

"How is eating live fish appealing?" I asked.

"To Vince, lots of strange things are appealing," Lilly stated.

"What? Like you know Vince so well?" Madison asked, glaring at her.

"He *did* live with me this summer."

"Yeah, well, I've practically *lived* at the Ruízs' for the past sixteen years."

"So this is some sort of competition?"

"I hope not. For your sake." Madison cocked her head.

"Oh, please! My brother is a spaz. Let's not fight over him," I huffed.

Emily swung her head back as she chugged the last bit of liquid from her cup.

"I need another," she moaned, peering at Lilly.

I tried to catch Lilly's eye, but it was too late. Emily clutched her arm and yanked her toward the keg.

Chapter 37

There had to be hundreds of people in the house. Though it was enormous and spacious, everyone was crammed together with sweat dripping down their necks. Cornell's fraternity houses, like its dormitories, were not air-conditioned. Of course it was October in Ithaca, and the outdoor temperature certainly didn't need any cooling, but the massive body heat indoors was getting unbearable.

"I'm melting," I whined, as I unpeeled my shirt from my chest and used it to fan myself.

"I know. Who would've thought New York could be so hot," Madison stated, as she pushed up the sleeves of her deep purple sweater. It seemed an appropriate choice when we were in the dorms, but now it looked as though Madison was greatly regretting the light wool.

"Maybe we should go outside and cool off," she said before quickly glancing at the screen of her cell phone.

"Waiting for a call?" I asked.

"No. I'm just wondering where Emily is."

"She's with Lilly somewhere. Relax, they're fine."

Madison and I scanned the room full of guys. So far, the only boys Vince had introduced us to were either grossly intoxicated or wearing a half-case of beer on their clothes. The cute jocks by the door never made it over to say hello to Emily or anyone else. And I was starting to think that Lilly was right. If we were going to meet anyone, we'd have to do it ourselves.

"Hey, check that guy out," Madison said, discreetly pointing to a dirty-blond surfer-looking guy near the opposite wall.

"Very cute," I whispered. "Do you think that's his girlfriend he's with?"

"No, I already saw her holding some other dude's hand. He left a second ago."

"Nice catch."

"Yeah, I've been watching him."

"Ew, stalker."

"Hey, he's been looking back. He smiled at me once."

"Really?" I said, perking up.

"Wait. He's looking over," she said quickly, turning away.

I swiftly craned my neck.

"No! Don't look!"

Too late.

"Oops, he saw me. You should go over and talk to him."

"I can't. It's too weird. I'm waiting for him to come to me."

I nodded.

Just then, Bobby and Lilly squeezed their way toward us holding plastic cups brimming with foam.

"Wow, you look hot," Bobby commented, staring at the beads of sweat trailing toward my nonexistent cleavage.

"Why, thank you." I smirked, straightening the neckline of my red V-necked shirt.

"I meant temperature. Not that I don't think, I mean . . ."

"I get it. I get it." I giggled.

"So, why don't you drink?" Bobby asked.

I shrugged, tossing my hands up.

"*Chica*, you thought you didn't like piña coladas until you gulped three down this summer," Lilly noted.

"That was different. Those tasted good."

"You'll get used to the taste of beer," Lilly said.

"You sound like my mother, only you substitute 'beer' for 'broccoli.' "

"It's not *that* bad," Madison added, taking a tiny sip from her cup.

"*Et tu*, Madison?"

She smiled, then her eyes quickly filled with concern. "Where's Emily?"

"Oh, we left her with Vince," Lilly stated. "He's already eaten two goldfish by the way."

"I don't want to know." I shook my head.

"Did she do any more keg stands?" Madison asked.

"No, but she is pounding beers with the skill of an alcoholic," Lilly joked.

"Oh, great. I hope you plan to be the one sitting up with her all night while she pukes," I scoffed.

"She'll be fine."

"Does she always drink this much?" Bobby asked, his forehead wrinkled.

"No, she never drinks," I defended. "Hence the problem."

"I don't know. She's been in a pissy mood all day," Madison stated.

Bobby nodded as if he understood.

I wiped at the sweat that was spreading across my brow. I hadn't been this hot since I'd danced at Lilly's *Quinceañera*.

"Hey, you wanna go find my dad? Maybe he can get us some sodas?" Bobby suggested, staring at me as if he were worried I might pass out from heat exhaustion.

I looked at Lilly and Madison. "You okay here?"

They nodded. So I followed Bobby into the crowd.

I tried to make my way to Vince at the goldfish pond (which was an inflatable kiddie pool filled with water and tiny orange fish). But there was currently a quest to find a Slip 'N Slide, and Vince was on the search committee.

His friend Joe, who was shirtless and painting his hairless

chest with ketchup and mustard, informed us that there were sodas in the house kitchen. Only his directions to the back stairs led us to a library where we interrupted a half-naked couple who unlocked lips just long enough to tell us to "Get the hell out!"

So, now we were semi-lost, wandering from room to room, hoping to find either Bobby's father or a refrigerator with nonalcoholic beverages.

"If that door wasn't the back stairway, then it has to be on the other end of the house," Bobby stated.

We pushed through a dense crowd of drunken students—my shoulders slamming into theirs as we thrust forward. I was so overheated and the air so limited that my heart pounded in my ears. I closed my eyes, inhaled deeply, and tightened my grip on Bobby's hand. Before I knew it, a strange guy twice my weight crashed into me, flinging me into a complete stranger. Another girl shoved me in the opposite direction, apparently for having splashed someone's beer onto her arm. My lungs clamped down as the room spun.

Bobby clutched my arm and tugged me toward the main staircase. As soon as we hit the steps, the crowd thinned. Guests weren't invited to the second floor unless accompanied by a brother, but given my relationship with Vince and his prearranged bathroom privileges, the frat guys let us through. As soon as we stepped onto the balcony, the air cooled. My lungs filled and my heart returned to its normal rhythm.

"Sorry. It was just so crazy down there," I whispered, catching my breath.

"Yeah, you looked a little freaked out."

"Crowds like that, I don't know, they make me feel out of control or something. Like I'm being attacked," I mumbled, as I breathed slowly and looked down at the party below.

"You kinda were," he joked. "Anyway, I'm surprised the brothers let us up here."

"Vince worked out a deal to let us use some guy's bathroom."

"Seriously?" Bobby asked with excitement. " 'Cause I *so* have to pee."

"Yeah, it's like two doors down on the left." I pointed.

"Which one?" Bobby stared down the dark hallway.

"I'll go with you. The door doesn't lock, so I'll have to hold it for you."

We walked down the dimly lit hall, the sounds of music blaring from downstairs. I stopped in front of the bathroom, and Bobby walked in. No one was in sight. It was almost peaceful compared to the chaos below (if you could find peace amidst the smell of sweat socks and boy).

I heard the toilet flush, and Bobby opened the door, wiping his hands on his jeans. "Don't worry. I washed them. There's just no paper towels."

"Yeah, sure. That's your excuse."

"Please, that bathroom's so disgusting, even if you didn't use it, you should wash your hands before leaving."

"It's like the funk just jumps right on you."

"Please, don't tell me I smell like that." He smiled.

"No, you smell nice."

A silence fell over our conversation. Bobby looked directly into my eyes, grinning. A gush of goosebumps flushed over me. Slowly, he leaned in, lowering his head until our lips touched. He felt soft and warm, and I reached my hand to his neck as he pushed his chest against mine and clutched my waist. My shoulders relaxed as I sunk my fingernails into his curly hair.

"You have *got* to be kidding me!" screeched a voice from behind us.

I held my breath, and slowly rotated. I knew it was Emily.

She glared at us, openmouthed.

"Well, this is just *perfect!*" she barked, waving her hands as she stumbled drunkenly.

"Em, come on, wait. It's not what you think," I said rapidly.

"Uh, yeah. It's kinda hard to misinterpret!" she snapped, swaying slightly. "I can't believe this."

Just then footsteps resounded from the stairway, and Emily spun around. It was Bobby's dad.

"Are you guys all right? I saw you two come upstairs, and you didn't look good." He pointed to me. "Are you sick? You okay?"

I flicked my eyes toward Bobby, who immediately sighed and gripped his hair with his fists. "This is not a good time, Dad," he moaned.

Mr. McNabb's eyes swept toward Emily. He took a sudden step backward, as if deciding it best to walk away.

"Oh, no, wait! Don't go!" Emily shouted, her drunken head bobbing on her neck. "This is the *perfect* time!"

"Emily, don't. Okay?" I interrupted.

"No, see, you don't understand." She looked at Bobby's dad, whose brow was clenched so tight I thought he might pop a blood vessel. "Go on, tell 'em Mr. Mc*Naaaab*. It's about time, dontcha think?"

She looked toward me and Bobby, her palms down as she gestured in circles to all of us. "You see, this here is just a big ole twisted family reunion."

I watched Emily's eyes fill with tears. Bobby's dad stumbled back a step. He looked as though she were pointing a rifle at him.

"Don't be shy now. I'm mean, come on, Mr. *McNaaaabb*. Be a man! You are *sleeping with my mother*!" She spat on him as she yelled the words.

My heart stopped as I gasped loudly. I spun toward Bobby whose face had begun to collapse.

"Emily, I, uh, I don't know what you're talking about. Uh, clearly, you, uh, have me mistaken," Mr. McNabb stuttered.

"Oh, so you're *not* the man who's having an affair with my mom? And you're *not* the man *I saw* leave my house this summer?"

His pupils swelled to the size of walnuts as his lower lip quivered.

Time froze in that moment. I couldn't move or say anything to stop her. Bobby's jaw continued to collect dust, Mr. McNabb blinked with shock, and Emily kept right on screaming.

"Do you know how disgusting this all is?" she ranted. "You're having *an affair with my mother,* and then *your son* goes and asks *me* on a date! Oh, my God! You should have seen my mom's face when I told her who was taking me out. I thought she was having an actual heart attack. But I'm sure you know all about this, don't you? I'm sure you sat around *in my parents' bed* talking about what to do to keep your silly little kids from ruining *your sex life*."

Mr. McNabb's face contorted painfully. He said nothing as he slowly tried to back away from my best friend, who had rapidly turned into someone I had never seen before. I couldn't believe all this was going on and she never said anything, that this was what the past couple months of brooding had been about. How could I have been so wrong . . . about everything?

"Don't you walk away from me!" she hissed, her finger pointed. "You're *screwing* my mother. I think that gives me the right to be heard."

Mr. McNabb stopped in his tracks and his eyes darted to Bobby, whose lower lip was trembling. I could tell he was trying so hard to bottle his emotions that I almost wanted to cry for him.

"Emily, look . . ." he started.

"Don't you say my name like you care about *me*! You've ruined my life! You've destroyed my family. My *best friend* is making out with *your son*! My God, why don't you just shoot my dog while you're at it?"

"Your dog died two years ago," I muttered.

"Don't try to be funny." Emily pointed at me.

I quickly shut my mouth.

"Dad . . ." Bobby squeaked, shaking his head at his father.

Mr. McNabb's green eyes welled as he absorbed the crushed expression on his son's face. I reached toward Bobby, but he swatted my hand and darted toward the staircase, brushing past his dad on the way. Mr. McNabb ran after him.

Emily said nothing. She didn't stop them.

Chapter 38

Emily erupted into spurty sobs as soon as Bobby and his dad stormed away. I wrapped my arms around her as her tears stained my shirt.

"Em, Em, I'm so sorry. I am," I whispered as she wept. "You should have told me. I would have never. I mean, you know I would never. I'm so sorry."

Shards of agony rippled off her as I stroked her dark hair. I didn't know what else to say. Nothing like this had ever happened to any of us. Our parents had all been married for more than twenty years. They were friends. They sat next to each other at ballet recitals; they attended each other's holiday parties; they took each other's kids on vacations. The thought of Mrs. Montgomery having an affair, and with *Bobby's dad*! A mix of anger and betrayal surged through me.

This was why Emily had been so distracted, so upset by Bobby's presence, yet so insistent that she had no feelings for him. This was why Bobby's dad reacted so strangely when he first met Emily at the film screening, and why Emily's mom was so abrupt with Bobby at my birthday party. I felt like such a fool. I thought Emily was acting immature.

"Em, I'm so sorry," I said softly, shaking my head.

"No, you didn't know. It's my fault," she choked between cries as she lifted her head from my chest.

"None of this is *your* fault."

Her eyes were swollen red, and her nose was starting to run. She brushed at a tear swimming down her blotchy cheek.

"It's been going on for at least a year," she mumbled. "At first, I thought my mom really *was* working late. But then, I don't know, I just *knew.*"

She plucked the elastic from her wrist and tied her short brown hair into a high ponytail. Her breathing was growing more stable. She sniffed back the tears that wanted to flow.

"I didn't know who he was though. Not until this summer. Not until I went out with Bobby. The way she reacted, it was like my mother wasn't my mother. I didn't know what was wrong. At first I got mad; I thought she was being a witch for trying to convince me not to see Bobby. I mean, she didn't even know him!" She grunted in disgust. "But I guess she did."

Not a single person passed us in the hallway, which I considered amazing given the amount of partygoers downstairs and the amount of brothers that lived on the floor. It was as if sheer will was keeping them away.

"And then, one night, I came home unexpectedly from Madison's. I was supposed to sleep over her house. My dad was away on business, *again.* I had forgotten my overnight bag. Mr. Fox ran me home to get it and as we pulled down the street, I saw a man getting into a strange car in my driveway. And my stomach dropped. I don't know why. I just knew it was him. . . . He looked right at me as he pulled away. *Right at me.*"

She gazed into the distance as she spoke, as if seeing the entire scene playing in her mind. The pain I saw in her eyes was like nothing I had ever seen there before, and it broke me that she felt she had to keep this to herself for so long.

"When I walked into the house, I called for my mom. I heard her racing around her bedroom, but when I walked in, she was in the master bath with the shower running. She acted like she had just suddenly decided to take a shower. And then I saw the bed; it was a mess. The sheets were all rumpled and tossed around. I knew the maid had been there that afternoon. I knew the bed should have been made."

She paused and took a deep breath, then turned to face me. "I didn't know for sure that it was Bobby's dad until school started. Until I saw him drop Bobby off one morning. And then, you guys started talking and it just . . ."

"If I had known . . ."

"I know," she said.

"But you should have told me."

"When you got back, you were so different. Everything was weird. I just, I don't know. . . ."

"I'm so sorry. But this thing, this whatever, with me and Bobby . . . it's over. Right now," I said with determination.

"No." She shook her head. "This isn't *your* problem."

"Yes, it is."

I left Emily seated on the stone wall of the outside porch while I went to fetch Madison and Lilly. I didn't know how I was going to explain everything. Frankly, I was kind of surprised the entire party didn't hear the argument. But everyone was drinking and dancing, completely oblivious to the life that had unraveled upstairs.

Before I could maneuver my way back to where they were, I saw Madison charging straight for me. I figured she must have discovered what had happened. I stopped in my tracks.

"I'm sick of this. I'm so *sick* of this!" she shouted as we stopped in front of the doorway.

"What? Huh?"

"Your cousin. Your *freakin'* cousin!" She pointed toward Lilly, who was giggling with the tan, blond surfer-guy Madison had been eyeing before I left.

"Oh," I mumbled.

"He comes over to talk to me, to *me*!" Madison yelled. "And

Lilly just barges in. She literally cut me out of the conversation with her stupid little accent. 'Oh, you lived in Spain last semester? *Hablas español?*' Blah, blah, blah!"

I pressed my fingers to my temples and rubbed. "Madison, we have bigger issues right now."

"No, I don't care. You've been forcing us to hang out with her for months now. And you know what? I don't like her!" she screamed.

Heads turned all around us. I seared a hole into the side of Lilly's giggling face, hoping she'd turn around. She didn't.

"Mariana, I've been your best friend since birth. And ever since you've come back, you've been acting like this random *chica*—who you've known for, like, a few months—is more important just because she's some distant relative! Well, I don't care! I don't want her in my life!" She pointed her blood red, polished finger at me. "You brought her here. Now get rid of her!"

My head jerked back. I really didn't need another confrontation right now. I had left Emily distraught and alone on the front porch.

"Madison, she's my cousin. I know that pisses you off, but you're gonna have to deal with it. She's not going anywhere," I snapped. "Maybe if you took some time to actually get to know her, like I did, then you would like her. But you've been acting like a baby ever since you met her!"

"That's because I didn't *want* to meet her! But I could have dealt with it, I could have dealt with her, if she wasn't such a conceited snot. She thinks she's *so* great. That everyone just *loooooves* her!"

Finally, our argument had gotten loud enough for Lilly to hear. She swung her head and spotted me.

"Madison, look, I'd love to continue this but—" I started.

"No!" she interrupted. "I don't want to hear about your little drama! I want you to tell me what you're going to do about your cousin!"

"*Do* about me? What the hell are you talking about?" Lilly asked, as she marched over, her eyes wide.

Madison flung her hand in my cousin's face. "I don't even want to look at you."

"Why? Because Brad found me more interesting than you? Not my fault." Lilly smirked.

"Oh, what? You think all guys find *you* more interesting?"

"Than you? Yes."

"Yeah, I wouldn't be so sure." Madison pulled her phone from her purse and waved it in the air. "Your pretty boy, Evan, he's been texting *me* all night. Actually, he's been calling me, e-mailing me, IMing me, all week! Ever since Mariana's party. Seems he found my dancing a little more interesting than your skanky salsa."

"You bitch!" Lilly shouted, lunging for the phone.

"Stop it! Stop it!" I screamed, jumping in between the two of them before any frat guys got excited at the prospect of a girl-fight. "I don't give a crap who's texting who, or who's talking to who! Emily is on the porch right now in hysterics. And I don't have time to deal with you two!"

Madison's face immediately changed. She swung her head at me, shock in her eyes. "What?"

"We've gotta go. Now."

Chapter 39

When we got to Emily, she had already vomited three times on the porch. Tears poured down her cheeks as we stumbled back to Vince's dorm, stopping at every bush so she could dry heave. Thankfully, he had given us one of his roommate's spare keys. We let ourselves in, and she passed out as soon as she hit the pillow. We left an empty trash can by her bed just in case she couldn't make it to the bathroom the next time the vomit ensued. Then we sat in the hall, and I relayed the entire story. I think Madison and Lilly would have been less shocked if I told them I was pregnant with a kangaroo's baby.

At around one in the morning, Vince finally realized he had invited his sister and her teenage friends to a frat party and then ditched them to slide down a ramp into a pool of goldfish. He came barreling up the stairs, his white shirt and jeans soaked and his sopping hair slicked back.

"Oh, my God! You're not dead!" he cheered, as he darted over to hug me.

"No, I'm not. No thanks to you."

"You have no idea. I spent the last half hour racing around the house thinking some guy was doing . . . I don't even want to talk about it." He sighed.

"You *left us* at that party, Vince!"

"I know. I'm sorry."

"I couldn't find you anywhere. We had to walk ourselves home!"

"I know. I went on a fish run. Chuck and Larry ate half of them, and the rest got lost in the yard when the pool broke. . . ."

"Vince, seriously, you have no idea what tonight has been like," I said.

Vince glimpsed our sullen faces. "Wait, why are you all sitting in the hallway? One of my brothers, they didn't—"

"No, no," I interrupted.

Then I told him the whole story.

We didn't speak the entire drive home. There wasn't much to say. Lilly, Madison, Vince, and I had stayed up until the sun peaked through talking about Emily's mom and Bobby's dad. We examined it from every possible angle. Even Vince was supportive. Normally his advice consisted of, "dude, whatever, that sucks." But he actually listened to the entire saga without judgment.

I think the fact that it was Emily's mom, someone we knew so well, someone we trusted, freaked us out more. It could easily have been any one of our parents. I had already seen what an affair had done to my father. Given my grandfather's history, and the chaos his extramarital love life created across multiple generations, I was the last one to say that Emily would be okay. It had been thirty-five years since my family left Puerto Rico, and my uncles were still reeling from the aftermath.

Emily stared out the window the entire drive, dizzy and nauseated from a hangover mixed with devastation. She would have to confront her mother when she got home. If she didn't, Mr. McNabb would certainly tell her (if he hadn't already). I could see the dread mounting in her eyes the closer we got. And when we finally pulled into her driveway, Madison turned off the engine.

"Do you want us to go in with you?" she asked.

Emily shook her head. "There's nothing you can do."

"We can wait out here," I offered.

"We can make sure you're okay. Stay in case you wanna run out?" Madison added.

"No. I have to deal with this." Emily gripped the door handle and took a deep breath.

As she walked toward the front door, it suddenly opened. Her mother stepped out. Her hair was mashed on top of her head in a frizzy nest, her glasses sat on her cheeks, a robe covered flannel pajamas in the middle of the day. I looked around and noticed there was only one car in the driveway.

"Hey, guys. Where's the SUV?" I asked.

"He's not here," Madison stated plainly, referencing Emily's father. "What if he already knows?"

Emily paused a few feet from her mother. Neither said anything. When I saw Emily's shoulders shake with sobs, I clutched the door handle, prepared to go comfort her.

"No, don't!" Lilly said, holding me back.

I watched as Emily's mom rushed off the porch toward her daughter. She hugged her, and they both cried. Then her mom looked over and waved us off.

"Should we go?" Madison asked, twisting her neck to look at me.

"I think we have to."

Madison started the car and pulled away. We left Emily weeping with her mom on the front lawn.

Chapter 40

After a few days, the world returned to a more normal state of calm. Emily and Bobby came back to school, ballet practices were in full swing, and Lilly and Madison had even stopped attacking each other. It was amazing how a crisis could solve almost as many problems as it created.

"So have you talked to your dad?" I asked, as we sat on my back porch sipping sodas and munching on fat-free chips.

"He's taking me out to dinner on Friday night," Emily said as she pulled her knees up and hugged them close to her chest. "He wants to prevent any 'confusion.' Whatever that means."

"He still at the hotel?" Madison asked.

"Yup."

"At least he's making an effort," I stated.

"I know. It's not his fault. *He* didn't have the affair. But he's also never home. . . ." Emily fiddled with the lid of her soda.

"Look, your parents are fighting with each other. Not you," Lilly offered.

"That's very insightful, Lil," I stated.

"Thank you. I try."

"What about Bobby?" Madison asked. "Have you seen him?"

"I'm avoiding him like the plague. It's just too weird." She looked at me.

"Hey, he hasn't spoken to me either. Today was his first day back in school, and he stared at his notebook all through chemistry."

"I can't believe you kissed him," said Madison.

"Gee, thanks for bringing *that* up." I rolled my eyes and stared at the trees in the rear of my yard.

"Don't. He's a nice guy," Emily offered. "If you like him . . ."

"No, no way." I tossed my hands in the air.

"My mom said she broke it off with his dad. . . ."

"Still, could you imagine if we actually dated? How could I ever look his father in the face?"

"Well, it wouldn't be his father that you'd be dating," Lilly stated simply.

A lull fell over us as we stared at the leaves dripping from the trees.

"So, Madison, you still hate me?" Lilly blurted out, breaking the silence.

I nearly choked on my sip of soda. She was blunt.

"What? We're all sitting here acting like everything is normal. I thought I might as well bring it up." Lilly shrugged.

Madison stared vacantly at her. "I don't know what you want me to say to that."

"The truth."

"I don't know you very well," Madison stated.

"And whose fault is that?"

"Maybe it's the swarm of jocks you've surrounded yourself with since you got here. Or all the guys you've been chasing after simultaneously. Or the best friend you stole out from under me."

"Mad," I whined, staring at her with concern.

"I didn't steal Mariana. Not like you stole Evan," Lilly stated, an eyebrow raised.

"Like I'm gonna apologize for *him* calling *me.*"

Lilly rolled her eyes. "You knew I liked him. But, whatever, I'm not gonna make a big deal out of it."

"Well, good. You shouldn't," I said.

Lilly's eyes snapped toward me.

"What? You don't remember what you did with Alex this summer? You deliberately kept us apart 'cause you were jealous."

"I *was not* jealous!"

I cocked my head. "Yeah, you were."

"Was not. And anyway, these are completely different circumstances."

"Not really. You felt overshadowed by 'the new person,' " I said, wiggling my fingers for effect.

"That's because all my guy friends were falling all over you."

"The way the Spring Mills guys are falling over *you!*" I pointed out.

"You had guys falling over you?" Madison asked, peering at me. "You never told us that."

"That's because you never asked," I said with a shrug. "Anyway, Lil, you of all people should understand where Madison's coming from. And Madison, Lilly's not my best friend. She's my cousin."

Madison grunted.

"I know you feel like she doesn't count because she hasn't been around my whole life, but look at the family who has! My uncles practically ruined my birthday party, my cousins are spoiled brats, and my aunts are nit-picking snobs. I mean, can you blame me for wanting to cling to the few family members I actually *do* like?"

Madison and Lilly eyeballed each other.

"I'm still gonna talk to Evan," Madison stated.

"And I'm still gonna talk to Mariana," Lilly added.

Just then my father slid open the glass doors to the porch and stepped outside. His work shirt was unbuttoned on top and his tie was loosened. He looked toward Emily.

"You girls all right?"

We nodded. "We're fine, Dad."

"You sure? You don't need anything?" His gaze stayed locked on Emily.

"Mr. Ruíz, you don't have to pretend you don't know," Emily said. "The entire town of Spring Mills knows. 'Swarthmore professor has affair with UPenn professor, news at 11.' "

My dad offered a sad smile. "I'm sorry you have to go through this."

She thrust her shoulders. "At least it's out in the open now."

He nodded, knowingly.

"Well, if you need anything . . ."

"Thanks," she said.

My dad stepped back inside and closed the glass door.

"Well, at least, your family probably won't move out of PA as a result of this," I joked.

"And there probably aren't any bastard children you don't know about," Madison added with a grin.

"See, it could be worse," Lilly stated.

We all chuckled. It was all we could do.

Chapter 41

Thursday night, my parents had Teresa over for dinner. With everything that had happened with Emily's mom, they felt compelled to try at least one more time to fix things with my family. They invited my uncles, but only Teresa showed. She didn't even bring Carlos.

"Thank you for a lovely meal," Teresa said as she dabbed at her mouth with her napkin, her plate clean.

"No, thank you for coming," my mom stated politely.

The conversation hadn't exactly flowed all night. True to form, my parents acted like the entire scene at my party never happened. No one brought it up. With each passing second, things felt more awkward, and I was rapidly losing my patience.

"The weather's supposed to be nice tomorrow," my mom said with a benign grin.

I had officially had enough.

"You know my friend just found out her mom's having an affair," I blurted.

Teresa's head jerked back.

"Mariana!" my father warned.

I ignored him and kept going. "The man she had an affair with, his son goes to school with us. He's a friend of ours."

Teresa stared at me, her forehead creased.

"Her father moved out. Her mom cries all day. And Emily's wrecked."

I shrugged, pumping my eyebrows.

"Mariana, I really don't think this is appropriate," my mother said.

"No, it is." I snapped my eyes at Teresa, then at my dad. "I get it now. I get why Uncle Diego is so angry. If he feels even half of what Emily's feeling, then I get it."

"Mariana!" my father yelled.

"What, Dad? It's true. Grandpop should have dealt with this a long time ago. It's the lies that made the situation worse. Emily said that the minute she confronted her mom, the minute she got it out in the open, she felt better. Well, you know what? No one had the chance to confront Grandpop. And *that's* who everyone's mad at."

Teresa smiled a bit, nodding. "You're right." She turned to my father. "I didn't know our father. I was raised by a woman your family hates. The woman who did *all this* to you." She tapped her shoulders. "But that woman is my *mamá*."

My dad ran his hand along the back of his neck, saying nothing.

"There's something else."

She glanced at me and then my parents.

"Carlos and I are getting married. I wasn't sure if I should tell you, or invite you, but I guess, I hope you can be happy for us."

"You're engaged!" I cheered. "Do you have a ring?"

My eyes flicked toward her barren finger.

"Not yet. We're gonna pick one out this weekend. The wedding's going to be in a couple of months. And . . . I'd like you all to be there."

My parents exchanged a look.

"Of course, we'll be there," my mother said.

"You realize my *mamá* will be there as well," Teresa stated, cautiously.

My parents locked eyes again just before the phone rang.

Lilly, who had excused herself from dinner early to finish her history homework, picked up the receiver from upstairs.

"Uncle Lorenzo!" she called. "It's for you! It's Uncle Diego!"

No one said anything as my father slowly got up and walked to the phone.

Chapter 42

I waited for Bobby at his locker Friday morning. I knew he'd been getting to school late. So had Emily. She said it was hard getting out of bed lately. Clearly, Bobby felt the same. So I camped out by our lockers, refusing to leave until he arrived. When the bell rang to launch first period, I was officially late for the first time in my life.

Finally, Bobby turned the corner. When he saw me waiting, he halted immediately. I almost thought he would turn and run the other way, but he trudged forward.

"Hey," I said, as he blew past me.

He spun the dial on his locker.

"How are you?" I asked.

He grunted, then opened his locker.

"Look, I'm sorry about what happened. At Cornell. Are you okay?"

He looked at me, and I could tell he was livid. I wasn't even the messenger, and I was pretty sure I was still going to be shot for this one.

"Of course everything's not okay. My dad's sleeping in the spare bedroom, my mom cries half the night, and the entire school knows what a pathetic mess it all is."

"You know, Emily's upset too."

"I'm sure she is."

"It's not her fault."

"I know," he said, running his hand through his blond curls. "I knew something was wrong . . . with my parents. I'm just, I'm so *stupid.*"

"No, you're not." I shook my head. "And you don't have to avoid me either. We still have the film festival coming up at Thanksgiving. And I want to help."

"Oh, God, I forgot. I should just cancel it."

"No, don't."

"No one's gonna show up."

"I will." I smiled. "An audience of one. That's better than nothing."

He grinned back.

That night, Lilly and I sat in front of the TV. She had my laptop resting on her thighs as she researched the French Revolution on the Internet.

"You know, maybe things can still work out for you two?" Lilly suggested as she scanned Web pages.

"Bobby and I will be lucky to be friends after this." I slumped farther into the couch, resting my head on a pillow.

"But, Mariana, I know you like him. If this whole thing didn't happen . . ."

"But it did happen."

"And you're still helping him with the film festival."

"As friends."

"Sure," she mocked, nodding her head. "We'll see."

She flicked through Web sites as I flicked through TV stations.

Suddenly, she reached out and grabbed the remote from my hand.

"Hey!" I squealed, fighting to snatch it.

"Mariana."

"Give it back!"

"*¡Caray!* Mariana!" she said, glaring at her computer screen. "*Mira, chica.* Check your e-mail."

She handed me the laptop, and I quickly navigated to my inbox.

There was only one person I could think of who would e-mail Lilly and me at the same time.

Hola chicas!
Greetings from Utuado. Mariana, I'm glad your birthday was amazing and that you liked my present. I knew you would. Lilly, I hope you're enjoying the States and not driving Mariana too crazy.

I wanted to see if you guys would be around next month. I'm planning to visit the University of Pennsylvania the week before Thanksgiving. A campus recruiter contacted me and arranged the trip. Mariana, if it's not too much trouble, I'd like to stay with your family a few nights and maybe check out Villanova. Would that be okay?

I hope you're as happy to see me as I will be to see you. I knew this summer wasn't good-bye forever.

Hasta luego,
Alex

It looked like I was about to get another visitor.

Here's a sneak peek at the third book in the series,
ADIOS TO ALL THE DRAMA,
coming in January 2009 . . .

He was arriving in less than a week. When I left Alex standing on the side of the road in Utuado, waving at my car as it pulled away from my Aunt Carmen and Uncle Miguel's home, I truly thought I would never see him again. Sure we made plans to keep in touch via e-mail, but there's a huge difference between a few electronic submissions and a half-semester face-to-face visit. Especially when his accommodations were two doors down on the left, next to the hall bath alongside Vince's room.

"So, does this mean you're gonna start wearing makeup to breakfast?" Lilly asked as she helped me clear out the drawers in what would soon be Alex's room.

"I barely wear makeup to school. I doubt I'll start caking it on to eat Cheerios." I tossed a bunch of my mom's old sweaters into a plastic storage bin bound for the attic.

"But what if Alex is pouring the milk in your Cheerios?" Lilly raised an eyebrow.

"Well, I may have to brush my teeth . . ."

I grabbed my mom's old cardigan and placed it neatly in a bin. Most of the extra closets in our house held my mom's "overflow" wardrobe. She didn't throw much away out of a belief that it would eventually come back into style—it was a holdover from her childhood growing up in the projects. When you go from

K-Mart to Chanel in less than thirty years, it's hard to part with those Chanels even when they're dated.

"I still can't believe he's up and moving here to be with you," Lilly stated plainly.

"This has nothing to do with me. He's visiting colleges."

"Yeah, if you believe that . . ."

"I do!"

"He's staying in a room down the hall from yours. Is that standard procedure for every kid who wants to tour universities in the greater Philadelphia area? Because if so, your parents need to up their rates . . ."

"I wouldn't talk, Miss Freeloader."

"Hey, my parents send money!" She tossed a lavender-scented sachet at me.

"I'm just saying if you didn't move here from Puerto Rico, maybe Alex wouldn't be so inspired to do the same. It could be *you* he misses." I narrowed my eyes.

"Nice try, but I don't think so."

Lilly carefully lifted one of my mom's formal handbags. Each elegant clutch, leather satchel, or logo-patterned purse was to be individually placed in the fabric dust bag it came in, then nestled into a cardboard box and labeled, then stacked into a plastic bin. Sometimes I thought my mom cared more about those purses than she did her own life.

"So are you guys gonna just pick up where you left off? Have a big smooch fest at the airport?" Lilly blew kisses at me.

"I don't know," I mumbled. "I don't want to act like I expect anything or like I think this trip has more to do with me than it does school . . ."

"But it does."

"No, it doesn't," I said firmly as I locked the lid on the transparent bin.

"You realize your family is single-handedly boosting the Latino population at your school district at an alarming rate," she joked.

"Not exactly. Vince is away at school."

"Ah, but holiday break is just around the corner. The numbers are swinging in our favor."

She was right. My parents' home was quickly becoming a halfway house for Puerto Rican teens looking to migrate from Utuado.

Alex was visiting as part of a mini-exchange program. Somehow his tiny mountaintop private school had arranged to send him to the States for two months to tour American universities. He would keep up with his classes in Utuado online, utilizing Spring Mills High School's computer labs, libraries, and all other facilities. He'd also be passing me in the halls, eating with me in the cafeteria, and bumming rides from my friends.

I glanced around the yellow-and-green guest room. My grandmother, my mom's mom, used to stay here when she visited. It was decorated specifically for her with the thick plush carpet she preferred, the colors she favored, and an ivy-stenciled border that mimicked her bedroom in Camden. She stayed in the room a lot after my grandfather died. Aside from our maid, hardly anyone stepped foot in it since she passed away two years ago.

Now it would be Alex's room. Only I couldn't picture him in it. I couldn't picture him here.

Catch up with Diana Rodriguez Wallach's first book,
AMOR AND SUMMER SECRETS,
available now from Kensington.

As soon as I opened the heavy red door to our house, I was struck with an eerie vibe. There were no strange noises or items out of place—the knickknacks were where they were supposed to be, the furniture was dusted and fluffed—but something felt off, like that moment right before the guest of honor realizes there's a houseful of people waiting to yell "surprise!"

"Mom? Dad!" I shouted as I walked into the marble foyer.

I wiped my sandals on the doormat, walked towards the spiral staircase and yelled up. "Vince, you here?"

No one responded.

I walked through the living room and glimpsed the spotless kitchen ahead. There were no dishes in the sink or seasoning scents in the air. It didn't make sense. It was six o'clock, my mom should be cooking dinner. She cooked every night at this time. She loved to cook.

I continued towards the back porch and gazed into our freshly landscaped yard. There sat my brother, my mother and my father on the wrought iron patio furniture drinking iced tea like a cheesy commercial. I tilted my head as I slid the glass door open.

"What's going on?" I asked, as their heads swiveled to face me.

"Mariana, sit down," my dad said, patting the navy blue cushion on the chair beside him.

My brother was smiling—not a happy smile, more like a sneaky "I know something you don't know" grin.

"Okay, what's up?" I asked, my eyes darting from side to side.

"Iced tea?" my mom asked, grabbing the crystal pitcher and a tall glass from the bamboo tray beside her.

"Um, okay. Uh, will someone please tell me what the heck is going on?"

"Dad and I came to an arrangement," Vince said as he stared at his designer sneakers.

"You're going to Europe!" I squeaked, my hand shooting towards my mouth.

"Not exactly. But *I am* traveling."

"Okay, then what? Where are you going?"

I grabbed the glass of iced tea from my mother.

"Lemon? Sugar?" she asked in her sweetest voice.

"Sure."

My mom was smiling so wide, it almost looked robotic, like her face was programmed to stay in that position. It wasn't a good sign.

"All right, why are you all being so weird?"

"We're not being weird," my mom said in a flat, peaceful tone. She was bracing herself for an argument. I could tell. She was setting a mood.

"Look, Mariana. Your brother and I talked," my dad started. "I knew he was serious about wanting to travel. But I didn't think it was safe for him to be so far away unchaperoned. So I came up with a compromise."

"I'm spending the summer in Puerto Rico," Vince interjected, glowing.

"That's awesome! Good for you!"

My mom and dad exchanged a look.

"I still have family there," my dad added slowly. "And an aunt and uncle of mine have agreed to be hosts for Vince . . . and you."

"And *me*! What do you mean, *and me*?" I coughed as I choked on a gulp of sweetened tea.

"I thought it would be a good learning experience for both of you," he stated as he stared at the recently manicured bushes rather than my horrified eyes.

"What? What are you talking about? I don't want to go anywhere."

"Mariana . . ." my father continued sternly.

"Don't '*Mariana*' me. Didn't it occur to you to ask me first? This is ridiculous. *Mom*!"

"Honey, look, it'll be fun," she offered. "You'll get to go to the beach. You'll meet your relatives, be in a different country."

"But I have friends *here*! I have Madison's party! I can't miss that. I *won't* miss that!"

"Your friends will still be here when you get back," my dad added gruffly.

"Dad, are you nuts? I can't do this to Madison. She's counting on me!"

"She has an entire staff to count on," he huffed.

"That's not what I meant and you know it! It's her sixteenth birthday! That's a once in a lifetime thing. I have to be there for her, she's my best friend!"

"Mariana, I realize you're upset now," my mother cooed. "But once you get to Puerto Rico, you'll forget all about this and have fun. Really, you will."

"You honestly think I want to *forget* all about my best friend? Are you mental? Have you ever had a friend in your life?"

"Oh, come on, Mariana! You're missing some stuck-up, superficial party for a spoiled little rich girl. Who cares? You're better off." Vince pumped his eyebrows.

"I don't care what you think of her. Like you have room to talk. Trust me, I could say a lot worse about *your* friends," I snipped, my eyes frozen. "Madison's a good person. And she's my best friend. This party is the most important thing in her life. I'm not going to miss it. Why the heck am I even being dragged into *your* mess?"

I jumped up from my chair and swung around to face my parents.

"I am *not* going."

"Mariana, you have plenty of summers and birthdays to spend with your friends. It's not the end of the world," my dad said, unsympathetically.

For the first time, I understood just how Vince felt when he fought with our father; Dad didn't hear a word we said, nor did he care what we thought. His mind was made up before our mouths even opened. We were in two totally different realities.

"You really think this is just a birthday? No big deal? God, you really have no idea what goes on in my life! What type of parents are you? I've done nothing wrong!"

My dad blew a puff of air from his cheeks and glared at my mother, the vein pulsing on his forehead. She immediately stood up and rested her hand gently on my shoulder—a move I've seen her do a thousand times.

"Mari, it'll be fun. Trust me. A tropical island. Your parents nowhere in sight. You can hang out with Vince. You'll do all kinds of stuff, *together* . . ."

A spotlight suddenly lit up in my brain. I finally understood what was happening here. I *had* to go with Vince, but not as his traveling buddy. I was his fifteen-year-old watchdog.

"Oh, this is great! You act like an irresponsible idiot and now I have to go babysit you from across the ocean! Thanks for ruining my life, Vince!" I screamed.

"You are *not* babysitting me!" Vince jumped to his feet.

"Like hell I'm not!"

"Mariana, listen to me!" my father shouted, slamming his hand on the iron armrest as he stood. "You are going to Puerto Rico with your brother. It'll be safer if the two of you are there together. Plus, your Spanish is better."

"Says who? I got a 'B' in Spanish last quarter." Tears filled my eyes. "And you never even talk about Puerto Rico. You don't speak to anyone from there. Since when do you care about any of those people? I care about my friends *here*."

My father looked into my teary eyes. He paused for several seconds, and I actually didn't think he was going to respond until he added, "You have a lot of family there you should meet. I probably should've gone back, with all of you, a long time ago. I think this'll be good for all of us. At the end of the summer, your mom and I will come visit. We'll all travel back together. Mariana, it's done. It's settled."

I swallowed a knotted lump in my throat. He already had the plans made. He probably had them made before he even told Vince. Anything I said at this point would be futile. My father had no intention of taking my feelings into account. He didn't care about my friends or Madison's party or what I wanted. I had no choice. He was sending me off to slaughter (or Puerto Rico) whether I wanted to go or not.